W9-CQN-878

POLICEMAN'S LOT

POLICEMAN'S LOT

by

Elizabeth Linington

1817 HARPER & ROW, PUBLISHERS
New York and Evanston

A JOAN KAHN–HARPER NOVEL OF SUSPENSE

FIRST EDITION

LIBRARY OF CONGRESS CATALOG CARD NUMBER: 68-28232

H-S

The more one analyzes people, the more all reason for analysis disappears. Sooner or later one comes to that dreadful universal thing called human nature.

—OSCAR WILDE

POLICEMAN'S LOT

one

          Maddox got back to the office after lunch at a few minutes after two. He passed the desk in silence without a glance at its occupant or D'Arcy lounging beside it.

The man at the desk winked at D'Arcy. "Could it be the man's just opposed to changes, period, I wonder."

"I suppose," said D'Arcy.

"It couldn't be anything to do with me, could it?"

"What, for instance?" asked D'Arcy. Maddox's footsteps faded away down the hall upstairs, and Johnny O'Neill sat back in his chair and laughed.

"I never knew a Welshman yet that wasn't born two drinks under par. They need jiggering up."

"Well, you do your best, Johnny." D'Arcy grinned.

Changes had hit the Wilcox Street precinct station, but only in the normal course of events. They hadn't had a replacement for O'Brien and probably wouldn't now; the force was as usual shorthanded. That promising young man Mark Chandos, who had just made Detective last year, had been transferred away to the Harbor division. And when Ed Carter had retired in April, they'd got to replace him, transferred up from Central downtown, Johnny O'Neill. Redheaded Johnny O'Neill, Maddox's own age, with his disarming slanted grin, had managed to annoy Sergeant Maddox almost at once.

"Jiggering up," he repeated now. "But it's the hell of an uphill job, D'Arcy, and be damned if I know why I take the trouble."

D'Arcy started to say he'd been wondering about that too, when O'Neill sat up, his eyes over D'Arcy's shoulder, and said politely, "Yes, ma'am, can we help you?" D'Arcy turned.

The woman hesitating just inside the door came in farther and said, "Yes. Yes. I—it's about my son. I just can't imagine *what's* happened, and I'm worried to death. I've called everybody—everybody I can think of—and nobody knows a thing and I just can't imagine— It's not like Harry, he's always considerate, and besides where would he go? At that time of night? He—"

"Just take it easy, ma'am," said O'Neill. "Mrs.—"

"Arthur. Mrs. Floyd Arthur's my name, my husband's dead but I— Ruby Arthur."

"And what seems to be your trouble, Mrs. Arthur?"

"I told you," she said impatiently. She was an ordinary-looking woman in her forties, with short dark hair starting to turn gray; her one claim to looks her large dark eyes under arched brows. She was neatly and drably dressed in a sleeveless cotton print dress. "It's Harry. My son. I don't know where he is. It's not *like* him. And I've—"

"You want to make an official report that he's missing?" asked D'Arcy.

She turned to him. "Yes. Yes, I guess I'd better, if that's the way to start you looking for him. Because I just can't imagine—"

"Then you come upstairs to the office with me and we'll get all the information down," said D'Arcy. Something new. If it didn't sound like much. He shepherded her up the wooden stairs and down to the detectives' office, and introduced her to Maddox, who was looking through some photo-

2

stated record sheets. Maddox was not looking very jiggered up, D'Arcy reflected, as yet: their thin dark pessimistic little Welshman. "Mrs. Arthur wants to make an official missing report." D'Arcy gave her a chair and sat down at his desk, and Maddox put down the photostats and picked up a pen.

"Who's missing, Mrs. Arthur?"

"Harry. My son. Really, going all round Robin Hood's barn like this. I just can't understand it. It's not *like* him. Harry—you can set your watch by him. He's exactly like his father—always was. And where he can have got to, because I've called everybody we know, and—"

"What's the address?" asked Maddox.

She gave it to him absently. "Leland Way . . . Yes, we live together. My daughter Leila's married, they live in Highland Park, but of course Harry and Ruth aren't figuring on getting married until next year, saving up for a down payment on a house. Harry makes good money—just like Floyd, all he ever has on his mind is work and save—not that he's a tightwad, I don't mean, he always buys me nice presents, my birthday and Christmas, and—but, home and work, and that's all. He—"

"How old is he?"

"Twenty-one. Started out with a newspaper route when he was eight and he's held some kind of job ever since, school and all. He's *reliable,* Harry, and—"

"When and where did you see him last, Mrs. Arthur?"

She gave a long sigh and sat back in the straight chair. "I've never known him *do* such a thing," she said thinly. "Never. I know a lot his age are wild, running around and all, but Harry—just like his dad, steady as a rock. I guess you'd have to know him to really see how funny it is. He never came home last night at all. And he's never done such a thing."

3

Maddox laid down his pen. "Well, it's a little early to report him missing, Mrs. Arthur. Less than twenty-four hours? A young man—with money on him, I suppose—"

"Mr. Bell said you'd likely say that," she said resignedly. "He agreed with me, but then he knows Harry, of course. He said he'd be glad to talk to you, you want. He said anybody didn't know Harry wouldn't think it was awfully funny. And I don't know how I can explain to you. Harry doesn't run around any. Work and home. He works two jobs —his regular one at building, he's on a contractor's crew, a new tract up in La Crescenta, and then he works nights at Mr. Bell's gas station on Melrose. And aside from work, well, he'll be over to see Ruth—I told you they're engaged—his free night, but like as not they won't even go to a movie, just sometimes. Harry isn't much for going out, and neither is Ruthie—such a nice girl and just right for Harry."

"Yes," said Maddox. "When and where did you see him last, Mrs. Arthur?"

"Why, yesterday at supper, of course. He came home at the regular time, a few minutes after six, and I had supper all ready. It was hamburger and carrots and peas and mashed potatoes and chocolate pudding. I get off at five, I work at Stella's dress shop, it's just a few blocks up on Sunset so I can walk. I got home about five thirty, like usual. And I fixed supper and Harry came home and we ate and he helped me with the dishes, and then he took a shower and shaved again and went to the station. He's on eight to eleven there every night but Sunday. And he never came home at all. I never knew till this morning, I went to bed around ten thirty and it wasn't till I got up this morning I found he'd never come home. His car not there or anything. So I was scared and first thing I called Mr. Bell and he was scared there'd been a holdup or something—only likely we'd have heard—but he went right over to the station and

4

everything was all right, the register all closed out proper and the place locked up. Only no sign of Harry except his car."

"His car?" said Maddox. "That is a little offbeat. It was left at the station?"

"That's right. Just sitting there, Mr. Bell said. But all the money put away in the safe—he trusts Harry and lets him use it, see, and nothing wrong at all. Just like Harry'd closed up as usual at eleven. Only why didn't he come home? I've called everybody I can think of, all his friends, and nobody knows a *thing*. And Ruthie—" Suddenly she looked ready to cry.

"Well, now," said Maddox slowly, "I think it is a little early to begin to think there's anything wrong, Mrs. Arthur. It could be that somebody he knows dropped by and asked him to a party after the station was closed—something like that. It was Saturday night, after all. Maybe a friend of his you don't know. And—"

"You don't know how Harry *is*," she said. "He'd have let me know—and a party wouldn't go on this long. I—I'm awfully afraid something's happened—but what?"

"Well, if you want to file an official report, we will." Maddox took down the statistics. Harry Arthur, twenty-one, five-eight, a hundred and fifty, dark hair and eyes, no marks. Wearing tan twill trousers and shirt, brown moccasins. "But I think you're worrying with no reason, Mrs. Arthur. Young men—"

"Not," she said definitely, "Harry. You'd have to know him to see how funny it is." She got up. "What are you going to do, look at the hospitals and—"

"We'll look around," said Maddox. He stood up with her politely. "And you keep in touch. Call and let us know if he comes home tonight."

"I certainly will—but I'm awfully afraid—it's just not *like*

5

him." She looked at them uncertainly for a moment, added, "Thanks anyway," and went out.

"It could be something, Ivor," said D'Arcy. "I know—twenty-one—but people do come all sorts, and she ought to know him. The steady, hard-working kid like that—the two jobs—"

"There's also the saying, All work and no play," said Maddox. "So all right—steady. Conceivably he could have given somebody a message for her, I'm staying over with Bill and going on a picnic tomorrow, and it never got delivered. We can check the hospitals and so on, but I think it'll fizzle out. . . . I wonder if César's found any of those hoods."

"I said I'd take half the list. I ought to be doing some work," said D'Arcy lazily. They sat silent a moment, both thinking of the probable long hot summer ahead. The first little heat wave this week, in late June, had brought a slight rise in the crime rate already; it would get worse as the summer wore on.

School was out, and the kids at loose ends—Satan finding work for idle hands, and they had a little wave of vandalism going, as well as the ordinary shoplifting and the occasional brawls between the juvenile gangs. And a good deal more of the dope problem than last year, with all the attendant petty and not so petty crimes growing out of that.

On Friday night the newish hillside home of Mr. and Mrs. George Vedder had been broken into by at least two men—Mr. Vedder, aged sixty-eight, at home alone, had seen only two. They had, after beating Mr. Vedder severely, ransacked the place and got away with an estimated five grand in jewelry, a mink coat, all Mrs. Vedder's clothes, the color TV, a new Smith and Wesson .38 revolver, and a transistor radio. Mr. Vedder, from his hospital bed, had given rather vague descriptions of the two men, and the men at Wilcox Street were now looking at pedigrees for anybody who was given to that kind of caper.

There had been a burglary on Thursday night at a jewelry store on Sunset; they hadn't any lead at all on that. If the burglar was so foolish as to try to pawn the stuff, they'd probably get him and the loot; a very vigilant eye was kept on the hockshops in L.A. County; but it had looked like a professional job, and the burglar probably had his own private fence.

Sergeant Ellis and Lieutenant Eden were helping the Feds track down a lavish amount of counterfeit twenty-dollar bills that were getting spread around town. So far the passers remained one step ahead, and the outraged cries of the merchants getting stuck were growing in volume.

Yesterday morning a corpse had been found in the street on Fernwood Avenue, probably victim of a hit-and-run. Fernwood was a narrow old residential street below Sunset, dark as a pocket at night; there wouldn't be much traffic along it then. But there was no I.D. on the corpse—a man about fifty. They were waiting for the autopsy report and any speculation from Dr. Bergner, about that.

On the whole this had been a quiet week, but with the heat wave getting started things could get less quiet any day.

Maddox stood up, yawning. "I've got a few more names from Central's records. Hoods who've used that m.o. If you can say there is much m.o. about the break-in and beating the householder. Do I have a premonition they'll do it to somebody else before we catch up?"

"Borrowing trouble," said D'Arcy; and Sergeant Daisy Hoffman put her blond head in the door and asked if they'd seen Sue.

"Carstairs? No idea where she is," said D'Arcy. "Sorry."

"Oh," said Sergeant Daisy. "Oh, maybe she's downstairs."
Maddox scowled. "Being made up to by that damned
Irishman. It's not—it's not dignified. It's—"

They both looked at him with covert interest. "I expect
she's somewhere around," said Sergeant Daisy vaguely.
"These damn runaways—we've just picked up another one.
As soon as school's out, I swear, they get the yen for Hollywood. I'll ask Johnny if he's—" Her head vanished.

"That damned Irishman," said Maddox.

Rodriguez came in towing a sullen-looking big man behind him. "Sit down, Carl. Relax. Just a few questions."

"Goddamn fuzz—I ain't done a thing, not a thing, just on
account I take a fall once, you damn guys—"

They had all heard that broken record so often, it scarcely
penetrated. Joe Feinman came in and joined Rodriguez.
They started asking questions. "Friday night? I gotta think.
I ran into this guy I know at a bar somewheres, that was
maybe about five o'clock, I guess—"

The inside phone rang on Maddox' desk. "Don't tell me,"
said D'Arcy, "something new."

"Maddox."

"You have a new homicide, Sergeant Maddox," said
O'Neill's cheerful voice in his ear. "Never a dull moment is
our motto. Over on Rosewood Avenue."

"Damn," said Maddox. "What is it?"

"I tell thee all, I can no more. The female citizen only told
me, 'You better send an ambulance, there's a dead lady here.'
The ambulance I have dispatched. You can go find out the
details for yourself. And if Aunt Daisy's still looking for Sue,
she's on her way up now. Have fun with the corpse."

Maddox put the phone down with unnecessary violence.
He said to D'Arcy, "Come on. We'll have to look at it."

In the hall outside, they met Policewoman Carstairs just

8

hurrying up toward Sergeant Hoffman's office across the hall. "Oh, hi," she said casually.

"You joined the force," said Maddox, "presumably to act like an upstanding peace officer, not to—to stand around flirting with the desk sergeant. You—"

"Well, for heaven's sake," said Sue crossly, "if I can't take forty minutes for lunch on a Sunday—and a three-minute chat with Johnny is *not* what I'd call—"

"Go, go. Your sergeant's looking for you," said Maddox. Sue marched past looking annoyed. "Demoralizing the whole damn— That girl used to be a good officer. Why the hell we had to get that damned Irishman— Aunt Daisy, I ask you. Talk about insubordination."

D'Arcy followed him down the stairs and on the way to the door exchanged a glance with O'Neill, who winked at him. O'Neill was leaning back in his chair humming "The Rose of Tralee" in his soft tenor. It occurred to D'Arcy, not for the first time, that Johnny O'Neill was a good-looking fellow.

He hoped the new one wouldn't turn out to be much of anything. He had a date with Sheila Fitzpatrick tonight.

Rosewood Avenue had been a middling good residential section once, thirty years back. Today it was a depressed-looking street of 1925-vintage stucco houses, with the Hollywood freeway roaring past its four-block length.

They identified the place they wanted by the ambulance in front. One intern was leaning on it, smoking. He eyed the racy-looking blue Maserati with admiration as Maddox pulled up behind the ambulance. "That's a hot-looking heap. Import?"

"Yes. So what's the word?" asked Maddox impatiently. "Stroke, heart attack?"

The intern grinned. "More like a bullet. We know how fussy you boys are about messing up the scene, we just left it. Little mystery for you. Two women live together—one walks in and finds the other dead. She says. But you needn't worry, Sergeant—she'll probably look in her crystal ball and find all the answers for you. They're fortunetellers or something."

"Fortunetelling is illegal within city limits," said Maddox.

"Not when you call it a religion," said the intern.

There were curious neighbors standing around in little groups, staring at the ambulance, at the house. It was an old place, somewhat larger than most along here, and it needed a coat of paint; the front lawn had been neglected and was brown and patchy. Maddox and D'Arcy went up to the small square cement porch, eyes on them. The front door was open; a neatly lettered, professional-looking sign hung on a small bracket above the mailbox. THE COMMUNITY CIRCLE OF LIGHT, it announced, MEETINGS WEEKLY 8 P.M. WEDNESDAYS, SITTINGS BY APPOINTMENT.

In the front room, which was dark and smelled musty, they found the other intern with a big, gaunt, dark woman who was talking steadily in a high-pitched voice. She sat on an old couch upholstered in faded green velvet, clutching her outsized black leather handbag on her lap, and talked compulsively.

"But nearly twenty years together—and never a cross word. Sylvia and I understood each other through and through, such an advanced soul, dear Sylvia, we complemented each other so well— But I simply could not believe it, because for one thing dear Mr. Clemens came through so very clearly at the sitting last night and he's been so helpful and kind, I would have expected he would have warned us, because surely he would have known if Sylvia was in any danger of passing over suddenly—and he never said a word, it was all about what a lovely time he was having with all his old friends—and I'd surely have expected— And when I left, dear Sylvia was just sitting there quietly reading—she hadn't an appointment until four—she'd only taken half a glass of milk for lunch, preparing for the sitting with Mrs. Nestor, of course—and she reminded me about the chops, for after a really successful sitting she would be quite famished—the power coming through, you know. And really when I came in and found her—found her—I'm afraid I quite lost my head for a moment. Sylvia— But it was most kind of Mrs. Miller to call the authorities for me—seeing as she has been quite unsympathetic in the past, and some unkind words passed—but I must remember, as our friends beyond are always urging us, I must harbor no base thoughts, but only dwell on Love and Good. But one would surely think that *some one* of the friendly souls beyond would have warned Sylvia—not that death is anything to fear, but some preparation for the transition— Such a shock, just coming in to find her like that—"

The intern gestured silently, and Maddox and D'Arcy went through the shabby living room to a cross-hall, uncarpeted, with a glimpse into a large square kitchen at one end and, at this end, three doors. Two square ordinary bedrooms, reasonably tidy, an old-fashioned bathroom with black and white tile, and another room at the very end of the hall, a third bedroom, larger, but not furnished as a bedroom.

There was a square, plain wooden table in the middle of the room, with four rattan chairs around it; three were upright, the fourth overturned on its side. An old, worn wall-to-wall carpet, beige. In one corner was an inexpensive portable phonograph on a little coffee table, and a record rack beside it. The album at the head of the rack was *Inspirational Hymns*. The curtains at the one window were of blue velvet, looking dusty. A religious picture hung on one wall, an old steel engraving of "The Return from the Tomb." And sprawled on the other side of the table, as if she had fallen from the overturned chair, was the body of a woman.

They looked at her in silence for a moment. She lay on her back, legs twisted sideways, and there were two small black holes in her forehead. She hadn't bled much. She had been, perhaps, in her fifties: a stout woman, but not flabbily fat, with a round, fair-skinned face and blue eyes and a good deal of sandy-reddish hair which had come unpinned from its big bun on her neck and spread loosely about her face. Her eyes were wide, fixed, shocked in death. She had been wearing a full flowing cotton house robe of light blue, and the long skirt had fallen about her quite gracefully. One plump little bare foot showed beneath the skirt, the blue velvet slipper fallen off.

After a moment D'Arcy said sadly, "Small bore. Looks like. Reason nobody heard the shots—if nobody did."

"Or took them for backfires," said Maddox. "We can ask."

"All that— Sittings?" said D'Arcy.

"Séances. Old-fashioned word, I understand. We'd better call the lab boys, get the routine started." Maddox looked at the crystal ball on the table. What a setup, he thought. What a— She'd been looking in the crystal ball for a client and the client didn't like what Sylvia saw?

He sighed and went out to find the phone, handling it gingerly—you never knew where a lead would turn up. After summoning the lab boys, he went back to the living room and found D'Arcy there starting in on the other woman.

"We're sorry to bother you at a time like this, Mrs.—Miss? But we have to ask—"

"That's quite all right," she said overemphatically. "Quite. I do understand. And I am feeling much better now. Really.

12

This kind young man here—not that in the ordinary way we believe in any medication—rest and prayer and meditation—And I cannot really feel any *grief*, except for myself left alone—death only a transition to a much more desirable state, as certainly all our learning has most abundantly made clear—"

"I gave her a shot," muttered the intern. "Poor old dear's heart was jumping around like hell. She'd had a shock all right, she wasn't acting."

Which was useful to know. And when they asked specific questions, she was surprisingly lucid, if garrulous. She was, it seemed, Madame Cecilia. Well, Cecilia Taylor, but professionally known as— The deceased was Madame Sylvia. Well, Brown. She had had an appointment for a sitting with Mrs. Westfall at one o'clock, Madame Cecilia said, and so she had left at about twelve thirty—the bus, so tedious, they were not at all regular—and Sylvia was just as usual then, reminding her to pick up the chops. Sylvia's appointment at four o'clock was with Mrs. Nestor, so far as they knew nobody else was expected at all, but Mrs. Nestor would never have dreamed of harming Sylvia—and besides, it wasn't four o'clock yet, of course. Nobody would want to harm Sylvia. Everybody, on the contrary, was very grateful to dear Sylvia. A burglar, said Madame Cecilia. It must have been a burglar.

They asked her to look around for anything missing. The lab men were there by then, starting the routine in the room with the body. She looked, and said doubtfully there didn't seem to be anything gone—Sylvia's moonstone necklace safe, and her mother's engagement ring. "Of course I was wearing my scarabs, well, I still am, of course, so lucky and helpful to bring the power, and I did so want to get something to please Mrs. Westfall. And I believe Sylvia was wearing her bloodstone ring, she generally did, they didn't take that, did they? I can't see that there's anything gone, but—"

Enemies? Threats? Why, nobody like that—nobody would have had any reason to hurt Sylvia. "She devoted her life to helping others—we both did, Officer—and everyone so pitifully grateful! We were able to put them in touch with loved ones—and—"

"A little mystery, the man said," said D'Arcy. They stood on the little porch; the neighbors were still standing around out there. "On top of everything else."

"So we start doing the routine on it," said Maddox. "Something may show. The neighbors may give us something. These are narrow lots, houses close, somebody may have seen someone go in. My God, a medium."

"Fake? The con game?"

Maddox shrugged. "Pay your money, take your choice. Could be."

"So we start the routine. Probably the con game all right. And some sucker getting annoyed."

"I don't know about that," said Maddox soberly. "It could also not be. That other woman sounds typical—honest enough, just maybe deluding herself. I've read enough of the evidence—and evidence a cop has to know something about—to be convinced we've got proof of *that*, D'Arcy. That a man doesn't stop existing, bang, as a conscious entity, just because he's what we call dead." Maddox was a voracious reader, of course. "But as to whether any and every discarnate spirit may be available to any sentimental true believer who starts the hymn singing and invites 'em to drop in for a chat—that's something else again."

"And aren't you right," said D'Arcy gloomily. "So the routine. Ask the neighbors. Sure, the Cecilia woman pretty genuinely shocked."

"But we'll do some prodding there too."

14

Dabney came out and said, Not many liftable prints. They'd be finished in a while, he said, and the ambulance could take the body. They'd recovered both slugs, not much damaged; they'd gone right through. Shot at close range, but not contact: no powder burns. He went on to the lab truck at the curb.

"So we may get a make on the gun," said D'Arcy. "You really believe that? About proof? That Dr. Rhine—well, I haven't read much of it—"

"Quite adequate evidence," said Maddox absently. "Which doesn't say that every Madame Sylvia is in genuine contact with the Great Beyond. . . . And that's another thing, damn it. Carstairs going to church regular."

"What?" said D'Arcy. "Church?"

"And that damned Irishman going to the same one. She says. Transferring from one downtown. What the hell is anybody named O'Neill doing in the Episcopal Church?"

"I couldn't say," said D'Arcy. "Hadn't we better start to question the neighbors? Get on with the routine bit?"

"Oh hell, I suppose," said Maddox.

two

What they got from the neighbors was just a little less than nothing. Mrs. Miller next door had seen a man going up the walk of the next house at about one thirty, she thought. She couldn't describe him or even say what size he was. The time coincided roughly with the interns' estimate of the shooting.

"I didn't take much notice of what went on there," said Mrs. Miller virtuously. "When they first come, we all thought there'd be Goings On, but there wasn't—no loud parties or like that—the phonograph on sometimes pretty loud but just hymns. But we got used to it, didn't pay notice. Not that I hold with all that, I don't figure dead people can come back and talk to you. Do you think they can?"

Maddox said diplomatically there were different opinions. "You couldn't say whether you'd ever seen this man before?"

She shook her head. "Just some man going up the front walk. I didn't pay notice." And nobody had been at home in any of the other houses nearby, and more distant neighbors hadn't seen or heard a thing.

They talked to Cecilia again and got this and that, odds and ends. Background. It seemed that Sylvia had been married once, years ago, but he'd been, said Cecilia, a very earthy person and after Sylvia had got interested in occult matters and begun to develop her own mediumship, she had divorced him. It was years since Cecilia had even thought about him. She didn't even recall his name. She was quite open about the Community Circle: a dear good membership of the faithful, and they donated as much as they could at meetings, not rich people. Of course both she and Sylvia charged for private sittings too, not that it was all for money, of course, but they had to live, and it was only sensible. And the advertisements running in the occult magazines, to answer questions by mail. Psychically.

They brought her back to Wilcox Street to take a formal statement, and sent her home in a squad car. "If she's got anything to do with the homicide," said Maddox, "I'll eat my badge. And the lab has been over the place."

"Those two had a nice little thing going," said D'Arcy. "There's one born every minute, all right. Twenty dollars the private séance, my God. For watching Madame Sylvia pretend to go into trance and relay messages from Uncle Bill. People—"

"A little less and a little more," said Maddox thoughtfully. "I think. Judging by Madame Cecilia, D'Arcy. I don't think either of them was consciously fraudulent. May even have a little ESP—it's latent in a lot of people. But you'd be surprised how many sentimental, eager-to-believe people can dredge up this and that from the unconscious and really sincerely believe it is Uncle Bill. And how many are all too anxious to believe along with 'em. In a way, the Sylvias and Cecilias are suckers too."

"I don't believe it. They knew what they were doing. Taking the marks—twenty bucks for—"

Maddox didn't pursue it. He knew a little more about that angle than D'Arcy, and while there were a lot of conscious fakes around on that lay, who knew exactly what they were doing, taking the marks and faking the spirit voices, they weren't the same type as Cecilia and Sylvia. And did that have any bearing on the homicide? Probably not.

"I suppose we'll have to talk to everybody in the dear little regular group who attended the meetings. And come up with nothing—unless one of them had a fight with Madame Sylvia over something."

"Unlikely," said Maddox. A little job, yes. They had kept a register for guests to sign, so there was a list of names and addresses. But the kind of people who were attracted to such places as the Community Circle of Light were seldom given to violence: silly, gentle, timid, or thrill-seeking people with time on their hands and quite often sincere if vague religious impulses in their hearts.

Rodriguez and Feinman came in. Rodriguez was looking hot and annoyed. "A waste of time, but completely," he said, flopping down in his desk chair, pulling his tie loose, and lighting a cigarette. "The hoods! Any of 'em we've looked at could be the ones pulled the Vedder job, except two who've got alibis. We prodded some more at Vedder—he's better, they'll let him out of the hospital tomorrow, tough old boy—but he couldn't do any better on descriptions. I hear we've got a new homicide."

"A *medium*," said D'Arcy. "Two mediums. The Community Circle of Light, my God. And not a lead on it."

"*Vaya,* a little something exotic for a change," said Rodriguez. "Black Masses and orgies?"

Maddox laughed shortly. "Anything but. When you come to think of it, two drab little middle-aged women eking out a fairly modest living solely on their own delusions and the eager dreams of other people."

"I thought you said you halfway went for this—"

"There's evidence. Good evidence. But a really good trance medium, D'Arcy, is not very apt to be living in a back street holding weekly séances and passing the hat for love donations. And offering to answer three questions by mail for five bucks, via the crystal ball or cards. And just

18

why the hell Sylvia got herself murdered I can't imagine. It's an offbeat one." He drummed restlessly on the desk. It was getting on toward five thirty.

Ellis and Lieutenant Eden came up the hall with the Fed, Brandon. They were all talking and they all sounded annoyed and frustrated. They went into Eden's office and the door banged. And Dr. Bergner wandered into the detective office, chewing a cigar, and said, "Wasting the taxpayers' money sitting round gabbing. Here's the report on your hit-run. Nothing much. Probably not much loss. I see you've got another one for me. I'll see to it tomorrow—I'm taking my wife out to dinner," and he drifted out.

"You mind if I take off a little early?" asked D'Arcy. "I've got a date too." He yawned. The first real heat was always enervating.

Maddox glanced over the autopsy report. Detailed description of the corpse: by all indications the habitual drunk, and he'd been drunk when he was hit. The lab had his clothes. Maddox shoved the report over to D'Arcy. "Get O'Neill to phone the description in to Missing Persons, and you can take off. No loss, as the good doctor says, but we have to go through the motions."

"If they pull another one," said Rodriguez thoughtfully, "the hoods, we might get a better description."

"That is not a constructive attitude, César," said Feinman, "but you're right, of course, we might. My feet hurt. I think I'll take off early too."

D'Arcy went home, to the old house above Silver Lake he'd kept on out of inertia after his parents died, shaved and showered, and went to pick up Sheila Fitzpatrick. He took her to The Nine Muses and they talked photography exclusively over drinks and dinner, winding up back in D'Arcy's darkroom.

Maddox went home, put a TV dinner in the oven, and

perused his shelves of books for something on parapsychology. He ate the dinner absently, concentrated on *Between Two Worlds*.

Oh, the evidence. But not from the ones like Madame Sylvia . . .

When he got to the station at ten to eight on Monday morning he found Dick Brougham hanging around waiting to brief the first man in. "Funny little thing came up," said Brougham. "Looks funnier the more you think about it. I left a report, but I thought you'd better be filled in."

"Oh Lord, what now?"

"Well, it *is* funny. The hospital called about three thirty and I went up there—called up a squad car too. Hollywood Receiving." Which was only about six blocks up Wilcox, of course: the emergency hospital for this area, also an ordinary big hospital. "They lost a doctor. Right off the floor."

"What?"

"It looks offbeat, Ivor. A Dr. Charles Grantby—supervisor of the emergency room nights. Been there for years—everybody knows him. He's on duty from midnight to eight, I gather overseeing all the emergencies as they come in, prescribing treatment. Man in his fifties, resident there. So, O.K., he's on duty as usual last night—they were fairly busy —and all of a sudden he's not there. Everybody thinks he's just somewhere else for a while, but finally they realize he isn't, if you get me, and they look for him, and finally call us. And we looked, and he's just gone. Wherever. His car's in the hospital lot, his room there looks ordinary, clothes still there, so where is he? Everybody says, very reliable man. It's funny."

"Funny peculiar," said Maddox. "Very. I'll be damned."

"And a Mrs. Arthur called in—her son hasn't come home yet. Another one missing?"

"That's just what. Hell," said Maddox. "Funny you can say."

"I told the hospital one of the day men'd be over to follow up."

"I suppose we'd better." Another one. Damnation, thought Maddox. And Sylvia— Well, ballistics should give them something on the gun sometime today.

Harry Arthur. Possibly another funny something. Call his description around—the mother said he'd have had identification on him, but it was possible he'd been mugged and his wallet lifted; he could be lying in a hospital somewhere unidentified. Maddox swore, went downstairs again, and gave Johnny O'Neill the description of Harry Arthur. "Spread it around, hospitals and jails. See if anybody's noticed him."

"Speedy service guaranteed," said O'Neill cheerfully. "Will do. *Good* morning, Aunt Daisy, and very bright and beautiful you're looking." He picked up the phone.

"Blarney," said Sergeant Hoffman indulgently, and passed on up the stairs, adding, "And *don't* detain Sue—we've got this and that to do."

"I will be bold, brave, and resolute, and speed her on her— Good morning. Wilcox Street precinct, Sergeant O'Neill speaking. We'd like to know—"

Maddox went out. Why they had to be saddled with—

"It doesn't make sense," said Steve Kane earnestly. "It just doesn't. Dr. Grantby." He looked at Maddox, a big beefy young man, one of the orderlies on night duty at Hollywood Receiving. "We can't figure it."

"We've pieced together this and that. Told most of it to the detective who came last night." Dr. Gurley yawned. " 'Scuse me. Get us up at this hour." Gurley was one of the interns on duty last night. "It's damn queer all right. Grantby of all people."

"So what have you pieced together?" Maddox looked round at them. They had turned out for him four of the night staff; none of them had been in bed more than an hour and they all looked sleepy and tired. Two orderlies and two interns.

"It was a kind of busy night," said Kane. "Sunday. Not as bad as Saturday, and not as bad as downtown at Georgia Street, but busy enough. Accidents, and an attempted suicide, and a knife fight, and so on. And the twins that got born right in the ambulance entrance—but that was early, about one A.M. Dr. Grantby was right there like always."

Gurley lit a cigarette, yawning again. "I'd better outline it for you—you say sergeant?—why it could happen, whatever the hell did happen and why. Dr. Grantby's the emergency supervisor. That is, he's all over Emergency—surgery, admittals, treatment, anywhere. See? It's his job to meet the ambulances, see what each case is, say what's to be done, if you get me. He isn't actually operating or in most cases helping out—stitching up the patients himself—oh, he'll give a hand if we're really rushed, of course—but usually he just has a first look at each one comes in and says, Take him to surgery, or Pump out the stomach, or A shot of morphine, or whatever. And the orderlies bring 'em on to us."

"I see," said Maddox. "So last night he was there on the job to start with?"

"All kosher. We came on at midnight together," said the other intern, Reeves, a big sandy young man. "Everybody likes Dr. Grantby, Sergeant. He's a very reliable man, and a nice fellow. A good doctor. We just can't— Well, we were busy, as Steve says. I've known a lot worse nights, but—busy. And Dr. Grantby'd be going out to meet each ambulance, looking over the patients in the admittal room, and pretty often he'd come into surgery, or treatment, with the patient —just a minute or so, to explain what he wanted done, to Gurley or me or somebody else. And back to the admittal room. You see?"

Maddox nodded. "When did you miss him?"

"That's hard to say," said Gurley. "You aren't exactly clock-watching, Sergeant, you're stitching up the knife cuts and so on. I know I definitely saw him at two fifteen, we'd just finished that couple in the head-on collision, the transfusions, and sent 'em up to intensive care. Dr. Grantby came back down the hall and I remember he said, Nothing new in, we can take a breather, and offered me a cigarette. I looked at the clock then. That's the last *I* saw him. Now you tell the man what you remember, Steve."

Kane's brow wrinkled. "It was after we got busy again, like I told you. There was an ambulance came in with four people in it—another accident—and I and Bill and a couple other fellows went out when it pulled up at the door—and just as I got to the back of it, there was this guy there. He says, I want to see Dr. Grantby, you tell him come out here. Something like that, I wouldn't swear to the words. I was in a hurry. And I thought then—I mean, if I thought about it at all—it was maybe one of the guys off the ambulance. I didn't pay notice to his face. But when we'd got the stretchers in and Dr. Grantby'd seen the people—he did go with one of them, into surgery I think—when he came back, I told him somebody was asking for him at the ambulance entrance. And about then Dr. Gurley put in a call—a stretcher to go upstairs—so I went, and I didn't see the doctor go out but—"

"Put that at what? Two thirty?" asked Maddox.

"Around there, or a little later," said Kane.

"But I think I saw Grantby after that," said Reeves, "so that mightn't mean anything. Might have been one of the ambulance attendants, some little thing."

"You're not sure you saw him later?"

"Well—I thought it was. After that accident case. We had another little breathing space then and I stood in the hall and had a cigarette and a cup of coffee with Gurley. I thought I saw Dr. Grantby come out of surgery and go into the rest room across the hall, but I couldn't swear—"

"But you finally realized he was missing."

"When the next ambulance came in. It was a thing—Steve came rushing to me, man with his leg nearly off and bleeding, and where was Dr. Grantby? I was too busy to ask for a while. Then when we had that one off our minds, we got to wondering—looked around—and he wasn't anywhere in Emergency. Which seemed impossible," said Gurley wearily. "I mean, a lot of people all around, but nobody'd seen him."

"When we had a little time," pursued Reeves, "we sent Steve to look in his room—he's resident here, you know— thought maybe he'd suddenly felt ill, or— But he'd have said so to somebody! Wouldn't he? Anyway, no sign of him at all. Then we looked around and found his car still in the lot. His reserved space. And then we thought maybe we'd better call the cops, because it looked funny. Because Grantby of all people wouldn't just walk off the job."

"The front office is in a tizzy about it," said Gurley. "Understandably."

"I gathered," said Maddox. "I'd like to hear something about Dr. Grantby. Personally."

"Well, he's a very good man," said Reeves. "Capable. Reliable. He's been emergency supervisor here for about five years. He was in general practice, but he left it when his wife died and came here. We'd heard all about it—he—well, he's a—a talkative little man. I guess he and his wife were pretty close. He said he just couldn't seem to settle down after she died, and there were plenty of doctors to listen to the neurotic female patients and their squalling kids, and so he took this job. Sold his house and all. His daughter was married before he lost his wife, she lives in Denver, he's got two grandchildren. He's about fifty-seven, fifty-eight. But what could that have to—"

"Well, you never know," said Maddox. "Description?"

"Descrip—— Well, he's not a big man. About five four, would you say, Gurley?—a hundred and forty—going bald, what hair he's got is gray—he only wears glasses for reading —er—blue eyes or maybe gray."

"But what the *hell* can have happened to him?" asked Kane. "Right out from under all our noses—people around—"

It was indeed very funny-peculiar. The respectable reliable doctor. Maddox said he'd like to see Dr. Grantby's room.

"I'll take you up," said Gurley. "If you can figure it out you're smarter than we are, Sergeant. And I hope nothing drastic has happened to him."

"—Some criminal," said Mrs. Myra Peebles, "wanting to rob her. It must have been, Officer. A dreadful, dreadful thing. Madame Sylvia. Such a *spiritual* woman she was—not that Madame Cecilia isn't—but somehow Madame Sylvia imbued one with such faith, such— And she was a very, very wonderful medium, we all received such great comfort from all the wonderful messages from our dear ones beyond. And I—"

D'Arcy contemplated his long legs stretched out before him and felt depressed. This was the fourth regular member of the Community Circle of Light he'd talked to, and they were having that effect on him. All alike as peas in a pod,

25

and he got what Maddox had meant. Just not the type to go in for the violence. The list of names from the guest register were mostly women's names—about a dozen men, and the one of those he'd seen was male in name only, a spinsterish, fussy little man who kept parakeets and was writing a book on dreams.

"—had introduced several friends to the Circle, and while a few of them came to scoff, I was able to bring them to the realization of this great reality. Mabel especially was entirely enlightened and I do wish you could have seen her *joy* when Madame Sylvia brought her such beautiful messages from her little daughter who Passed Over when she was only nine. It was really quite thrilling. Mabel came regularly after that and I believe she had some private sittings too. But I forgot what it was you asked me, Officer? Goodness, it just doesn't seem possible. Madame Sylvia. Some dreadful criminal, because who could have wanted to harm her at all? When she just lived to help others, to bring this wonderful truth to— What? Oh no, I hadn't been there since the meeting last week, I couldn't afford private sittings—but we had some most wonderful experiences at the regular meetings, you know, why, just lately Mr. Mark Twain—that wasn't his real name, was it, I forget—came and spoke to us, so inspiring. Oh dear, it doesn't seem possible that Madame Sylvia should be— Of course she always told us we shouldn't say *dead*, but *translated*—really what it—"

D'Arcy stood up. If all of them were like this— The guff, he thought. Swallowing it whole. The silly stupid citizens. Not an ounce of harm in the woman, and not much sense either. Mrs. Peebles, a widow on the pension. Dropping the fifty cents into the collection plate at the Community Circle of Light. Pleased as all get-out to have the message from the Great Beyond: all is love and happiness, having wonderful time.

How indeed and why indeed had Madame Sylvia got herself knocked off? Reluctantly he had to agree with Maddox: whether the two mediums were conscious fakes or not, they were small-time: no criminal associations.

It was five of twelve. D'Arcy thanked Mrs. Peebles for her help and knocked off himself, to go back to the Grotto on Santa Monica Boulevard for lunch.

"I can't figure it," said William Bell. "I just can't. Harry Arthur. As steady a young fellow— I tell you, I hired young guys before, spell me nights, usually you can't rely on 'em. But Harry! I'd've trusted him with anything I got. Straight as a die, and a good worker—had to be busy, not a lazy bone in his body. And—"

"It looked as if he'd closed up the usual way, Saturday night?" Maddox reflected that one of the nuisances of this job was that you were forever chopping and changing around, from one case to another. Well—these two cases. If they turned into cases. Mysterious disappearances. Two very different people. Harry Arthur and Dr. Charles Grantby. Nothing said that Harry hadn't taken off voluntarily. Only if so, why hadn't he taken his car?

"Sure. Same as usual." Mr. Bell gestured at the station office; they were standing beside Maddox's Maserati, his nice little girl, outside the pumps. "All shipshape. No, there wasn't a note. Just his car there." An old but well-preserved Ford two-door, white. Nothing significant in it at all; Maddox had looked. "I just can't figure it. Anybody knows Harry could tell you, reliable as—as—" Groping for a word, Bell paused and looked past Maddox. "Well, here's a guy could tell you." He went past Maddox. "Morning, Mr. Bolton. You want a fill-up? We was just talking—this is a detective, Sergeant what did you say?—about Harry. Young Harry Arthur. He's took off somewhere, and nobody can figure—"

The car was a two-door Buick, maroon. Maddox strolled up: somebody who knew Harry? The driver was a middle-aged man, balding, rather portly. "Harry?" he said. Bell poured out information, adjusting the gas pump.

"He'd done some work for you—you know Harry, Mr. Bolton."

"Oh yes. A very good workman too. He built me some bookshelves." Bolton had a pleasant, light, resonant voice. He had his left arm out the window, and Maddox noted idly that the tip of the little finger was missing. "Well, really, that is very odd. He always seemed very—steady. But young men—" He blinked behind very thick glasses. "No, I hadn't seen him for a while—it isn't often I come by evenings. It is odd."

"Anybody knows Harry'd say the same," said Bell when Bolton had paid him and driven off. "Mr. Bolton, he's one of my regular customers—stockbroker downtown. Like he said, Harry'd done some outside work for him. I can't figure what's up with Harry. You want to talk to Jake? The mechanic? He knows Harry too, he could say—"

"Was he here on Saturday night?"

"Acourse not, he's off at six."

"Then I don't suppose he'd know anything," said Maddox. "But I'd better talk to him. Just in case."

Jake, however, could throw no light on what had happened to Harry Arthur.

Maddox went back to the Grotto on Santa Monica to have lunch. There he ran into D'Arcy at the door, and as they took a table he spotted, across the room, a gay foursome just being served—Sue Carstairs, Daisy Hoffman, Rodriguez, and Johnny O'Neill.

"What the hell are we doing here at this thankless job?" he asked D'Arcy. "I'll have a Scotch and water and the steak sandwich."

"Yes, Sergeant. Well-done."

"Same for me. Medium," said D'Arcy. "Those damn-fool females falling for Madame Sylvia's racket—a handful of nothing, like César says."

The little group across the room exploded into laughter as, apparently, O'Neill finished a story. Maddox lit a cigarette. "Talk about offbeat. That doctor. And—well, I told you. The type that go for the Madame Sylvias— I wonder if the husband could come into it? I know, evidently she hadn't seen him in years, but it could be he— And on the other hand—"

"There are about forty names on that list. Who came to meetings regularly. I'll bet, all the same type. Giving us nothing."

"We have to work it."

"I know, I know."

The waitress came back with their drinks and they both took long grateful swallows. It was hotter today.

Maddox went back to the station after lunch to check with Missing Persons downtown and see what the inquiries to the hospitals had turned up, if anything; he found Mrs. Arthur waiting for him with a girl about twenty.

"This is Ruthie. Ruth Snyder. We thought—maybe you'd like a picture of Harry. Because now it—all this time—"

"And I don't care *what* you say!" burst out Ruthie. "Harry never went away like this just on his own! He wouldn't! You don't know how Harry is, it's— Something's *happened* to him!" She looked frightened and stubborn. She was a middling pretty small girl with ash-brown hair in a plain loose cut; she was as neatly and drably dressed as Harry's mother. "You've just got to find out—"

Maddox looked at the snapshot of young Arthur. It was a good clear snapshot, of a stocky young man in slacks and sports shirt, standing in front of a stucco-and-wood ranch house.

"Leila took it last month when we had dinner with them," said Mrs. Arthur. "It's good of Harry—we thought—"

"Because *where is he?*" wailed Ruth Snyder. "You've just got to find out what—"

Harry Arthur was a solid, square-jawed, strong-looking young man, facing the camera straightly. You could see he was young, but it was a good face, a face to trust, thought Maddox: a reliable man. Just as everybody said. Mr. Bell— the regular customer there—and, doubtless, the contractor Harry worked for on his regular job.

"Thanks very much," he said. "We'll use this." Spread it around: ask press cooperation?

"You'll let us know, what—?"

"We'll let you know," said Maddox. There could still be a plausible explanation; likeliest that he'd got mugged and his I.D. taken.

As for Dr. Grantby—well, the routine. See those ambulance attendants. Have the Denver police contact his daughter? You really never did know what might turn up, people being people. Even the ordinarily reliable, upright, respectable citizens. You had to check every angle. Just in case.

He went upstairs to the office. It was empty: Rodriguez and Feinman out looking at the hoods. He called Denver and asked for cooperation; he had the daughter's name from the hospital records. Denver was obliging and would get right on it.

Not that there'd be anything there. How could the daughter know anything?

And it wasn't often they got the real little mysteries. As, come to think, all these new cases posed—Madame Sylvia, and—

The inside phone rang on the desk. "Oh, hell," said Maddox, picked it up, and said his name.

"You're the only brain in," said O'Neill. "We have now a

shooting in a bar, Sergeant *agrah*. Over on Beverly. I can't tell you whether it amounts to homicide—the citizen was excited. Just, a shooting. I've sent an ambulance. The routine gets tiresome, doesn't it? You want to go look at it?"

"Have I got any choice?" asked Maddox. "What's the address, damn it?" He took it down. He went downstairs and past the desk.

O'Neill was leaning back in his chair, whistling "Killarney" softly between his teeth. He gave Maddox his charming grin, and Maddox hunched a shoulder at him ungraciously.

three

At Scotty's Tavern on Beverly, Maddox found two squad cars, an ambulance double-parked, and an excited crowd of citizens. He slid the Maserati into a red-painted zone and got out. One of the uniformed men was directing traffic around the ambulance, and shouldered a path through the crowd for Maddox. Inside, the interns were just lifting a stretcher; the blonde woman on it was unconscious.

"Bad?" asked Maddox tersely.

"Serious—she's lost some blood," said the first intern. "The bartender's got her purse for you." They went out with the stretcher.

The bartender, a big burly man bald as an egg, with a bulldog jaw and a rasping bass voice, had more than the victim's purse. He and the other uniformed man, and two civilians probably customers at the bar, were standing vigilantly over another big man, dark-haired, about thirty, who sat head down in one of the booths, silent. "He's the one did it, mister," said the bartender as Maddox came up. "He—"

"Sergeant," murmured the man in uniform.

"Sergeant—whatever—took five years off my life. They'd been arguing, but not loud—I had an eye on 'em. Neither of 'em high, but I could tell they were having a fight. But when this guy pulls out the gun and starts waving it around, I think I want 'em out right now—only before I can get over to the booth, he does it. Shoots her. And she screams, and everybody in the place starts to mill around and ask questions and all I can think of is get the gun away from him— I told Mr. Davies here to call you guys, and—"

"You know them? Regular customers?"

"Not so regular. They been in before. I heard 'em call each other Bob and Marian."

"Her name's Marian Dickerson," said the man in the booth unwillingly, sullenly.

"And you?" asked Maddox.

After a dragging minute the man said, "Bob Thorsen. I didn't mean to shoot her. I—it went off."

"Mister, it sure did," said the bartender. "It sure did. The gun's on the bar, Sergeant. Al's looking after it. And the dame's bag."

"O.K.," said Maddox. "You'll be asked to make a statement—and if these two gentlemen witnessed the shooting, so will they. All right with you?"

"Any time," said the bartender, and the two customers agreed. Maddox took down names and addresses and beckoned to the other uniformed man.

"Bring him up to the station, will you? I'll meet you there." He picked up the gun and handbag.

He had just slid the Maserati into a slot in the lot across from the precinct station when the squad car followed him in, and the man guarding Thorsen got out and handed him over. Maddox marched him in and O'Neill raised his brows.

"Quick work, Sherlock."

"There for the picking up," said Maddox. He trusted somebody else was in upstairs.

In the office, he found Rodriguez and Feinman in, still looking frustrated. "Something?" asked Rodriguez, eyeing Thorsen.

"Something." Maddox sat Thorsen down, drew Rodriguez

33

and Feinman up the room, and told the tale briefly. "So," and he stepped back to Thorsen, "I'm supposed to tell you all about your rights as a citizen," and he went through that rigmarole. "Do you want to call a lawyer?"

"So what for? I never meant to shoot her, it went off. I wouldn't want to hurt Marian, God's sake, I just sort of lost my hair, she was bein' so damn stubborn." Thorsen looked sullen. He was a heavy-shouldered young man, not bad-looking if he'd been shaved and cleaned up. "We're gonna get *married*, I wouldn't hurt Marian on purpose. It just—"

"Went off," said Maddox. It might have at that; it was an old Colt automatic, and if the safety catch had been off, hair-trigger. "What were you arguing about?"

"Well, see," said Thorsen, anxious to explain now, "I've been out of a job awhile. The last one I had, well, hell, I hadda couple drinks too many once and the boss—well, he wouldn't give me no recommend like they say and I couldn't— And Marian and I, we're gonna get hitched as soon as her divorce is final, see, and so I wanted—I been pickin' up odd jobs but it's a drag. And my brother-in-law he offers me a good job drivin' a truck for him, but it's back in K.C., see. He's got a little truckin' business there—so this is fine with me, only when I tell Marian she don't want to move from L.A. We been arguin' about it ever since. Off and on."

"I see," said Maddox. "And you were arguing about it some more in the bar just now."

"Well, she was so damn stubborn. Offer of a good job, it wasn't *sensible* not take it," said Thorsen. "Not *sensible*. But I couldn't make her see— She likes L.A., nice climate, and she gets good tips the place she works— She's a cocktail waitress, fancy place out on Wilshire—and it snows in Kansas in winter and all like that. Well, that's a woman for you. They ain't got any logic to them. And sure, I got mad. I got good and mad, because Marian's a swell girl and I don't want to go back East without her, see, and what I pulled the gun for, I tell you, I thought maybe if I made her think I meant it for real, she'd back down. That was all. You know how women are. And then that damn bartender let a yell out of him and it like to startle the daylights out o' me, and—and it went off. I never meant to—"

Maddox looked at Rodriguez, who sighed. The citizens forever coming all sorts. Thorsen talking about logic.

"Is she going to be all right?" he asked Maddox anxiously. "I never meant to hurt Marian. Is she?"

"I don't know," said Maddox. "Will you sign a formal statement—what you've just told us?"

"I guess that's all right. If I have to. Are you—"

"You don't have to," said Maddox wearily.

"Oh. Then I guess not. But will Marian—can I go see Marian? Is she in the hospital?"

"No and yes. You're going to jail," said Maddox.

"But I never meant—"

"But you did, Mr. Thorsen. Shoot Marian. Whether you meant to or not. You like to take him in while I type the report, César?"

"Anything to oblige." Rodriguez got up, smoothing his neat mustache. "Come on, Mr. Thorsen." Thorsen still protesting, he led him out.

Maddox called the desk and asked O'Neill to start the machinery on the warrant; Thorsen would be booked as material witness until that came through. And now there was the report to be typed up in triplicate.

"People, people," said Feinman. "And we wonder why the world is in such a mess. Progress we've made since the days we were dodging the sabre-toothed tigers?"

"Not much, I sometimes think," agreed Maddox. "But of course, Joe, we do see more of the seamy side than most people."

"You mean we're in a position to know just how much of the seamy side there is. Other people can shut their eyes to it."

"Maybe," said Maddox dispiritedly. "Maybe that's so."

"If you ask me," said Feinman, "and I might add that the rabbi agrees with me—we were talking about it just last week—we've just got to what Daniel was talking about. Seventh chapter of same. Satan more active than he's been ever before."

"It sometimes looks that way," said Maddox. The thermometer on the wall across from him read ninety-eight. The first real heat wave building up all right, a degree or so every day. And with this little incident cleared up—except for typing the report on it—he should get back to work on something else. What had he been thinking about when the call came in? Dr. Grantby—and Madame Sylvia. See the Cecilia woman again?

"The rabbi said to me—"

The inside phone rang on Maddox' desk. He swore automatically and picked it up.

"—Prophecy sometimes symbolical and sometimes literal. But in the seventh book of Daniel—"

"Maddox. What the hell now?"

"Visitors for you, you lucky lucky people," crooned O'Neill. "Two squad cars just fetched them in. Some of our enterprising younger generation, just spotted rifling parked cars in the lot at Robinson's. One of the so-called males had some reefers on him. They're on the way up."

"Oh, thanks so much."

"What now?" said Feinman.

"Some more of Satan's handiwork. A—" All hell broke loose in the corridor outside and they both jumped up and made for the door. In the split second as he crossed the room, the thought slid into Maddox's mind that that was

36

really the one criterion for a cop: when trouble erupted, the born and trained cop was the one who jumped toward it instead of in the other direction.

In the hall, two middle-sized men in uniform were wrestling with an enormous and very hefty kid who was screaming and slavering, yelling incoherencies, obviously berserk. A little crowd of kids scrambled away up the hall. The berserk one was kicking and flailing out, arms and legs, and knocked one of the uniformed men off his feet against the wall, the other one swearing steadily as he tried to grapple with him. Maddox and Feinman came up in a hurry. Feinman got the kid by the shoulders and tried to yank him round, and the kid made a sudden lunge and toppled him over backward. The uniformed man was nursing a bloody bitten hand. Maddox fell on top of the writhing mass and chopped the kid across the neck, ungently, with the side of his hand. The noise stopped; the kid jerked and lay still.

Feinman crawled out from under him. "For the love of God," said one of the squad-car men, breathing heavily, "I don't know what hit him! He came along quiet until we got right upstairs and then all of a sudden he—"

"You *hit* him," said one of the other kids. Maddox turned to look at them. Four of them: two boys and two girls. You had to look twice to see which was which. The boys maybe seventeen, eighteen; the girls younger. The boys in identical skin-tight dark pants, colored sports shirts none too clean, both with nape-long hair also unclean, and one with attempted sideburns. One of the girls was dark, a little too fat, sleazily dressed in dirty white shorts, a halter top, and thong sandals. The other one was mousy-fair, thin, in pink capris and a sleeveless blouse. "You *hit* him," said Sideburns. "Police brutality. Ritchie ain't eighteen yet. You can't—"

"But I did," said Maddox mildly. Ritchie, stretched out peacefully on the floor, probably outweighed both the uniformed men by twenty pounds, damn what age he was. "Don't tell me what I can do, punk. Get in that office. You all right?" he added to the squad-car men.

The first one was getting up. "God, what hit him? He exploded just like a time bomb. Yeah, I'm O.K. He caught me a crack on the head—"

"All right. You go down and tell the desk man to call an ambulance for him. And you can watch over him until the interns take him."

The second man said it would be a pleasure.

The dark girl said dispassionately, "Big tough cops. You prob'ly killed the poor bastard. He's been on a trip like. It sort of caught up with him like it does. You leave him alone, don't bother him, he gets over it, but the tough cops, they got to show what big guys they are."

"That's right," said Feinman, feeling his nose. "Just let him wreck the station house and beat up the cops, and he'll feel better. So he's on the acid, is he?"

The mousy girl began to cry noisily.

Probably a minute and a half had gone by since it started, and by now the door of Sergeant Hoffman's office was open and Daisy and Sue coming out. Taking in the situation at a glance, Sergeant Daisy advanced to the mousy girl and put an arm around her.

"I want *my mother!*" wailed the girl. "I want to *go home!*"

"All right, dear, you just come in here with me."

The dark girl looked at Sue Carstairs coolly. "Lady cops. I'll be damned. You gonna give me a sweet-talk lecture, I'll likely get sick."

Sue looked back at her as coolly. "That's just too bad. You get in there with your pal." The girl swaggered after Daisy, and Sue looked curiously at the stertorously-breathing Ritchie. "So what's this all about?"

"I haven't heard any details," said Maddox.

"They were going through cars in Robinson's lot," said the uniformed man. "The girls standing lookout for them. We've got a car full of stuff they'd picked up, clothes, and a transistor radio, new merchandise left the way people do— all sorts of stuff. And he," he nodded at Sideburns, "had a dozen reefers on him."

"So you go hear the female side of the story," said Maddox to Sue. And this, of course, was another facet of the thankless job: something new was always coming along. He herded the two punks into the office, and Sue went back across the hall.

The uniformed man prodded Ritchie with one foot and felt his bitten hand.

"—And I didn't know how it'd *be*," sobbed the mousy one on Sergeant Daisy's shoulder. "Nagging me all the time about school and too much make-up and that teacher had a real grudge on me but nobody—and I just couldn't stand it and I'm sixteen nearly and that's old enough—and what's school, anyway, and I got so tired of all the bit about be a lady—and I—and I had nearly sixty dollars saved up from baby-sitting and my allowance and I thought—be on my own, do like I want, and that was lots more than the bus fare and I thought I could get a job easy—"

"Yes, yes," soothed Daisy, providing her with a Kleenex. "What's your name, dear?"

"B-Brenda Ann Schultz. Only I didn't, everybody asked how old I was and said no, and even that woman where there was a room to rent and I went and—*she* asked a lot of questions and I was scared—and all *week*, and what with the room and all, there wasn't much left. And then I met J-Jill and she said—she made me— I hadn't but five dollars left and I didn't know—and she knew those b-boys and I was scared but—"

39

"I shoulda known better than take up with her," said the other girl. "Real dismal deal. But Barney thought she was kinda cute."

"All right, Brenda," said Daisy. "Where's your home?"

"K-K-Kernville," hiccuped Brenda. "I didn't know how it'd *be*. I didn't know there were people like—those awful boys, things they *said*, and J-Jill was just as bad—"

"Did they hurt you?" Statutory rape maybe; the added charge.

The dark girl laughed. "Barney was real hot for her, but he hadn't got no chance at her yet—beats me why, but I got a thing going with Buddy. Only he got kicked out of his pad on account he owed the landlady, and we were figuring to rent another pad with what we got for—" She shrugged. "I guess we get free rooms downtown now. Overnight." She grinned at Sue; she could, Sue thought, be a pretty girl. If. There was too much make-up, make-up slapped on over the unwashed face, and she was already some way over- weight. "Not that you keep us long. I'm only seventeen."

Seventeen. "And next year you'll be eighteen," said Sue, "and we can keep you longer, Jill. Did you ever stop to think of that?"

"What's your father's name, Brenda? Can you tell us your phone number at home in Kernville? Would you like us to call your parents and have them come, or send money for you to come home?"

"Oh, *yes!* Please. I want to go home— Daddy'll be just *wild,* but he'd—" Brenda, of course, they couldn't keep. Not sixteen: a first offense: and Brenda probably (not certainly) having learned a lesson. Sue took down the phone number as she gasped it out, and went out to find a private phone.

Maddox came out just as Sue emerged from the office

across the hall. "I do get so tired of the punks," he said. "The younger generation."

"Don't we all. One of them came apart. A little innocent. Another runaway getting picked up by the punks," said Sue.

"Oh?"

"We can't keep her. Maybe she's learned something. I'm just about to call Daddy to come fetch her home. The other one—" Sue grimaced—"is past reclaiming. Permanently."

"Like that. And sidetracking us, wasting time, when there are all these other things." D'Arcy came up the stairs. "What've you got?"

"Nothing," said D'Arcy. "Nothing but a case of misanthropy, if that's the word I want. Listening to all the damn-fool idiots who went to those séances."

"I don't think it's quite the word," said Sue. "Misogynism?"

"Well, whatever, I've got it," said D'Arcy.

Maddox grinned at him. "Do you feel up to helping me question Cecilia again? After I've typed up this damn report?"

"For God's sake, take César."

"He's busy. And it's your day off tomorrow, you can relax."

"I'd rather," said D'Arcy, "be on that Vedder thing. Or even the counterfeiters. Damn you."

"And I don't know what to do about the funeral," said Madame Cecilia helplessly. "Money—I'm not sure what Sylvia had in the bank, not much, and— The rent and all, I don't suppose I can go on living here, it's a hundred dollars a month. Sylvia usually earned a little more than I did, the private sittings—always so good and kind to me—" She looked at Maddox and D'Arcy opposite her there, her mouth slightly open, breathing hard. "You don't know what a *worry*—" The dark living room with its old-fashioned furniture smelled of dust and stale food, and it was airless, very hot. D'Arcy pulled at his collar. Madame Cecilia, looking even more gaunt and somehow pitiful, made vague gestures. "One is primarily interested in helping people, but it's—it's not a very *easy* way to— One must admit. And Sylvia always managed everything. I really don't know what I will do. What was it you asked me?"

Maddox repeated his question.

"Her *husband?* Well, really, I don't suppose she'd thought of him for years. He might be dead for all we knew. I don't know why you'd be interested. What?"

"It looked," said Maddox, "as if she'd been—er—looking at the crystal. When you came in yesterday. The crystal ball on the table. Do you think she would have—um—accepted a client who came without an appointment, and been—"

"Scrying," said Madame Cecilia vaguely. "You can do it all sorts of ways, with a saucer of water or a mirror or— They say you can *develop* your psychic powers, through prayer and meditation. I had tried, so very hard, but the power doesn't come through as strong as dear Sylvia's—I'm afraid I disappointed Mrs. Westfall—but really it is quite difficult to meditate properly when one is so worried about money, I know it shouldn't intrude—so materialistic—but— What? The crystal— Oh, Sylvia frequently used it to meditate, before a sitting. To—to reinforce the power. I suppose she might—if someone had come and asked for a sitting, her appointment wasn't until four—and the money, you know— she might have done that. One of the regular attendants— Mrs. Meeker had had some private sittings, and Mr. Koenig, as well as some of the older—er—clients, and I suppose—"

"Miss Taylor, did you ever employ anyone here? As a gardener, or for odd jobs, or—"

"Oh no, of course not, we couldn't afford— A labor of love, it *should* be, to help— But I really don't know what I'll do now. We don't even own the furniture here—" She gazed around the musty room. "We've been here six years, it was nice to feel settled. Much nicer than that awful old place down at the beach, when Sylvia had the booth on the pier. I really don't know—" She looked lost.

And outside Maddox said, switching on the engine, "You believe me now? Deluding themselves, the innocent frauds. Eking out the very modest living. That one the weaker vessel. You can feel sorry for her."

"All right, all right. But where are we on it? No criminal associations, no enemies, no personal motive on Sylvia. So where do we look?"

"It's offbeat, you can say. . . . Like that doctor. That is one very funny thing, D'Arcy. I turned the lab loose on his room and car. Nothing shows. He's just gone. No history of instability, just the opposite. Upright, respectable, and busy man—reliable. Bang, vanished. Out of a crowd of people all around."

"He was translated," said D'Arcy sleepily. "Too good for this world. The angels wafted him away."

"Whoever did, angels couldn't have done it neater," said Maddox gloomily. And it was then—what with the interruption of the younger generation—getting on for five o'clock, and most of the day wasted.

They found Rodriguez back from the red tape at the county jail, contemplating an early edition of the *Herald*. "The hospital is not averse to publicity," he said, and showed them the front page. Their newest mystery had got a minor headline, DOCTOR VANISHES FROM DUTY. There was a cut— "Dr. Charles Grantby, 58, who disappeared under mysterious circumstances from the hospital," and Maddox looked at it interestedly. Dr. Grantby was a nice-looking man, by the cut, with a humorous wide mouth, intelligent eyes, a firm jaw. An eminently sane-looking man.

"The publicity may help," said D'Arcy. "By what you told me, that's a funny one all right, Ivor. But this—"

The inside phone rang. "While you were out," said O'Neill, "a Grand Panjandrum called you. A, not the. I would guess. One Dr. W. Hadley Prince, supervisor of Hollywood Receiving. He desires that you should call him before six to give him the police theory of the case. *The* case, you note. We haven't any other cases to work, Dr. Prince implies."

"I haven't any theory, damn it," said Maddox. "I only heard about it this morning, for God's sake. What can I tell him? I haven't come back and I haven't got the message."

"Which I will tell him if he condescends to call back. Thank *you*, Sergeant."

"Why the hell we had to get that clown—" Maddox slammed the phone down and got out a cigarette. "Did anybody remember to send that drunk's prints to Central and Washington?"

"I did," said Rodriguez, looking at the open *Saint Mystery Magazine* on his desk. It was so much more interesting between book covers. "After all, if he's got any family to pay the funeral expenses we'd like to know. Enough of the taxpayers' money gets wasted as it is."

"Say it twice," said D'Arcy.

The inside phone rang and Maddox picked it up. "For the love of *God*, what now?"

"I have a Lieutenant Trask of the Denver Police Department, asking for you and nobody else. Are you in to a fellow cop?"

"Put him on, put him on," said Maddox resignedly.

There was a series of clicks, and the long-distance call came through clearly. The Denver boys had seen Mrs. Diana Pierce, daughter of Dr. Charles Grantby, said Lieutenant Trask. Mrs. Pierce was much alarmed at the news that her father had disappeared from his job. She knew nothing about it. She had had a letter from him just yesterday, and he had said nothing about leaving his job—an ordinary cheerful letter it had been. He enjoyed his work, so far as she knew his health was excellent, he was contented in his life. He had mentioned the possibility of visiting her during his vacation in September. And Mrs. Pierce would come to L.A. at once if she could help in any way.

"Well, another handful of nothing," said Maddox, after thanking the Denver police and adding that there was no reason for Mrs. Pierce to come, what could she do? "And what the hell is there for us to do on it? There's nowhere to look, damn it. Spread his picture and description around, and wait. Just a damn mystery. Vanishing away from the busy hospital—"

"And I don't see anywhere to look on Sylvia," said D'Arcy. "Those damn-fool people going for the guff—messages from Uncle—but not the kind to know which end of a gun was which."

The inside phone rang. It was five thirty, and the thermometer now read ninety-nine. As the days (what with the daylight saving) got inexorably longer, the temperature went inexorably up. Inevitably. This time Maddox didn't swear. He just picked up the phone.

"And I wouldn't blame you if you leave it for the night shift, Sergeant *avic*," said O'Neill, "but you have a new corpse. Up in Griffith Park. Of all places. One of the grounds keepers just called in."

"Griffith Park—"

"Up in the picnic grounds off Western Canyon Road. Do you want to leave it to the night shift?"

"For God's sake," said Maddox. "Technically it's still a working day. I'll go look at it."

four

The lab photographer was busy else-
where so they gave D'Arcy the loaded camera. Rodriguez
said he'd come along for the ride through the park. They
took D'Arcy's old Dodge. It might be a little cooler in the
park.

Griffith Park was a place unique to L.A.: that great tract
of acreage, all surrounded by Big Town, lying straddled
across the Hollywood foothills separating Hollywood from
the San Fernando Valley. There had been golf courses laid
out in the park, there was the big observatory and plane-
tarium atop Mount Hollywood, and the big new zoo; and
throughout the park picnic areas and bridle trails; but largely
it had been left as Nature made it, a wild tract of land
covered with brush and trees, and much of it was vertical.

Roads wound through the park, narrow roads; the scenic
route from Hollywood to the valley was over the top of the
park. Western Canyon Road entered the park from Los
Feliz and wound up past the picnic grounds at Fern Dell,
doubled on itself to pass the Nature Museum, and then
curved up further into the park, eventually to merge with
Mount Hollywood Drive. D'Arcy took the curves at sedate
speed; just after they had passed a park sign, with an arrow
pointing left, bearing the legend CHILDREN'S PLAYGROUND
AND AZALEA GARDENS, there came into sight ahead a black
and white squad car nosed into the shoulder. D'Arcy parked

behind it. A man in uniform was waiting for them, smoking; he bent and tidily and safely buried his cigarette stub.

"You'll need a guide," he said. "It could have stayed there years without being found. Lucky for us—or maybe not at that—the park people've started some new ground cover after the fire here last year, and were checking on it. It's this way." He led them into high grass to the left of the road. There was a wide cleared space at the roadside just ahead, for parking, and another sign, PICNIC AREA. Past the usual tables, stoves set in cement blocks, drinking fountains, they went into dense shade of tall trees, and then the ground began to slope and they came out to a brush-covered hillside. "Actually, if we'd known," said the patrolman, "we could've reached it easier—that's still Western Canyon Road," and he gestured.

The narrow road, doubling back again, wound around the picnic grounds and back; it passed the steeply sloping hillside about ten feet below them here. "So why didn't you tell us?" asked Maddox. "Where is this body, anyway?"

"Sorry, sir, I didn't think, the man who called in wasn't—and I just left the car—this way." They slithered down to the road; another steep drop fell away on the other side of it, brush-covered to at least three feet high.

"Hold it," said D'Arcy. "Better get some general scenes. Which way is the body?" The patrolman pointed straight ahead; down there they could see another man waiting for them, standing silently. "Now what damn fool set this thing for—" D'Arcy adjusted the stop and lens of the Speed Graphic and took three shots. They went on down from the road, and the man waiting lifted a hand to them.

The body was about thirty feet down from the road. The parks keeper, a middle-aged man in slate-blue work uniform, nodded at introductions and said, "Never've seen it if I

48

hadn't come down this way just by chance, on foot, see how the new growth's coming. I figure he was just rolled out of a car up on the road. You look close, you can see places he tore up little plants and smashed others, rolling down here."

They looked, and agreed. The body was lying face down, arms spread out, legs sprawled: the body of a man. And looking at it, a nasty little notion grew in Maddox's mind. "So get on with it, D'Arcy," he said sharply. "He hasn't been touched?"

"No, sir," said the parks man. "I read enough mystery stories to know that much. I went back to the office and called in, and come right back here to meet the squad car. Lucky most people are gone by five or so, this early in summer."

D'Arcy took five shots of the body *in situ,* and put the camera down safely ten feet away, and Maddox and Rodriguez bent and turned the body over.

"Hell and damnation!" said Maddox softly. "I half suspected it from the clothes. So this is where Harry Arthur got to."

"That's him?"

"That's him." The face wasn't much damaged. There was a blackened, extensive bruise on the forehead, and very probably a skull fracture under it. His nose had bled, judging by his lower face and the front of his shirt, which also bore black grease stains, as did his trousers. The tops of his moccasins were scarred with deep scrapes, the leather partly shredded. Harry Arthur, twenty-one and by all accounts one of the upright people, working two jobs and saving up to get married.

Harry Arthur not the kind who usually came in for anything like this. "Damnation," said Maddox again. "And what the hell did happen to him, how'd he end up here?" He knelt and began to feel in the pockets. "Why would the casual mugger—" His voice died. "Look at this."

"¡Como!" said Rodriguez, peering over his shoulder. "That's very funny, Ivor."

It was. Harry Arthur still had his wallet, in his right-hand hip pocket, and its contents looked intact. In silence Maddox went through it. All the little slots for the I.D., driver's license, Social Security card, National Automobile Club card, bank-account card, and snapshots—his mother, Ruth Snyder, another couple, himself and a man his own age grinning widely into the camera. In the billfold were three twenties, two tens, and thirteen single dollar bills.

"I'll be damned," said D'Arcy.

Maddox dug further. The right-hand trouser pocket yielded a dollar and forty-four cents in coins. A handkerchief. A Bulova wrist watch, stopped at ten to seven. A bank book issued by the Security-First National Bank, in Arthur's name: a checking account book. The balance was $2,397.57.

Maddox stood up with the spoils balanced carefully on his own handkerchief. "What could be the answer on this one, boys? Talk about funny."

"He's been dead awhile," said the parks man. "You can tell." They could. In this weather—

"There's the ambulance," said D'Arcy. The ambulance had come the long way round, and was just stopping on the road above.

"So, Saturday night, do we say?" said Maddox. "When he didn't come home? Was prevented from coming home? How? His car at the station—it still is. When it could have been a voluntary take-off, nothing to say it wasn't—no reason to make a big thing of it. I did think of the mugger. Harry was young and strong, but no more than medium-sized, and if he was taken from behind— But now we find him like this, with his billfold untouched and nearly a hundred bucks on him—what makes sense?"

The interns were thrashing down toward them with a stretcher.

"It wasn't a mugger," said Rodriguez. "The billfold intact, and also no mugger would go to so much trouble, lugging the body up here, for God's sake. Saturday night? You said he'd closed up the station. At eleven? Then he can't have been dropped here the same night."

"No. Yes," said Maddox, correcting himself. "Time does go by, César. It's late June. Ordinarily the park gates shut at eight P.M., but now the Greek Theatre's open, no. Open to when?" He looked at the parks man, who shrugged.

"You don't want people shut up here overnight. Some of the shows run overtime. We figure to give it forty-five minutes after the curtain's down, shut the gates down on Los Feliz, but a real popular show that draws a big crowd, it'll take 'em an hour before they're all out. With the parking areas jammed and the road down so narrow. The one running this week, the curtain comes down about eleven twenty."

"So. There was time all right, on Saturday night. But what happened?"

"Things that could," said D'Arcy. "Your first idea, some pal asked him to a party after he shut the station. Maybe came up just as he was shutting it, and took him on somewhere. And he got into a fight at the party, or—"

"The personal motive," said Maddox. "At least the personal, outside thing. Yes, but according to everything we heard about Harry, he wasn't that type." He looked at the interns. "Estimate any time?"

"Thirty-six hours anyway," said one. "Of course in this heat—maybe not that long. But that'd be my guess."

"Saturday night," said Maddox. "Well, of course a man's mother and fiancée are maybe not the best objective judges of him. I suppose it could be that he wasn't quite the paragon he sounded. But—" he shook his head. "Offbeat. We don't usually get such offbeat ones. And now I think, *three* offbeat ones coming along at once. Damnation."

"Can we take him?" asked the intern.

D'Arcy had taken several shots of the body face up. "Take him," said Maddox. "And so now we have to go break the news. Damn. Females weeping all over me—"

"Why did it have to be Harry?" wailed Mrs. Arthur. "The best son anybody ever had—never in trouble any kind, always so good and ambitious and steady—"

"We know, Mrs. Arthur. Please don't make it so hard for everyone else." Sue Carstairs patted her shoulder gently, sitting beside her on the old overstuffed couch in the apartment on Leland Way. Maddox had cravenly called for help in confronting the newly bereaved, from the junior division.

Ruth Snyder sat at Mrs. Arthur's other side and wept silently; the pretty young woman introduced as Harry's sister Leila sat grave and red-eyed with the big young man who was her husband, Bill Pollock, keeping a protective arm round her. And in the straight chair facing Maddox sat an aggressive young man named Rex Slaney, who was the young man with Harry in the snapshot in the billfold: Harry's closest friend. Mrs. Arthur had called Slaney first after Maddox had, dinnerless, interrupted her meal to break the news. It had been Slaney who had come down to make the formal identification of the body. And he now faced Maddox, at nine thirty, hot-eyed and belligerent.

"What the hell you mean, he had any fights with anybody? Harry! You trying to say—"

"Not implying anything, Mr. Slaney," said Maddox. "But we'd like to find out who's responsible, and one of the first

52

things to ask is, had he any quarrel with anybody lately?"

"Well, he hadn't. Harry was a very quiet guy," said Slaney. "Easygoing. He didn't— I don't mean he didn't have a temper. Principles. You know. But he hadn't had any trouble with anybody. Lately or as far back as I can think. That's straight."

"All right," said Maddox. "You'd know?"

"I'd know," said Slaney stubbornly. He had sandy hair and a pugnacious jaw. "We were both busy, working, but we usually saw each other once a week or so—Sundays."

Maddox rubbed his jaw. He wasn't going to get anything out of the women, he saw: naturally. Sue was being her usual efficient self at soothing them. Good-looking female, Carstairs, he thought absently: her neat dark cap of hair and fine white skin. "Er—" he said (see Slaney alone later), "Miss Snyder—was there maybe another fellow who—"

"Oh, for God's sake!" said Slaney. "No. No. They started going together when Ruth was in the last year at high. No trouble ever. They just got engaged and that was that. There wasn't any reason for anybody to want to kill Harry. It's crazy. Any personal thing, my God."

"My Harry—why did it have to be—minding his own business—I was always scared the station'd get held up and he'd get shot—"

"Now, Mother—" Leila came to Sue's aid, but she looked at Maddox gravely. "That's so, what Rex says, Sergeant. There just couldn't be any—any personal reason. With Harry. There couldn't. We all know everybody he knew, and—and he didn't have fights. Of any kind. He was—easygoing. Like Rex says."

The husband sighed and shifted in his chair. "Yeah, that's right. A steady young fellow, quiet."

Maddox sighed. He would talk to Slaney alone, later.

53

There must have been other girls before Ruth Snyder; there must have been differences of opinion, and— But anything immediate?

"I'll tell you the only possible thing I can think of," said Slaney angrily, angry at blind fate that reached for Harry. "That occurs to *me*. That could have happened. And it's wild, but it's all I can think of. Because it seems—well, what I thought was, it just could have been that he had a ruction with some customer at the station that night. He'd told me about some of the funny ones came in. Just now and then. The drunks sometimes and— Anyway, I thought, suppose. Some nut, or somebody trying to cheat him. And there was an argument, and after Harry'd shut up the station and was ready to go home, this nut laid for him. Who knows what kind of nut? It's all I could—"

"That's a little far out, Mr. Slaney."

"Why? It's the only possible thing I could—"

Pollock nodded seriously. "You might have something there, Rex. I can sort of see that happening. Anybody runs a public business can tell you about the people." Pollock was a butcher, his own concession at a big market. "The funny people. Most people O.K., but you do get the queer ones. Nuts, some way."

"I know it sounds far out," said Slaney. "But it could have happened like that. And with Harry, I can't see any other—"

Maddox thought about it. Quite suddenly (he should have thought of that before) he remembered that Harry's keys hadn't been on him. Nor anywhere around. He'd have had keys. . . . And of course what Slaney outlined was *possible*. Just. You did find the hotheaded, hair-trigger nuts. Who for some very small reason or no reason at all would lash out. Even the nuts who planned a little ahead. Not much.

But that was definitely not the kind who would go to the bother of hiding the resultant body. Not nohow, thought Maddox. It had been a little bother to get Harry up there— But could he have been killed up there? Say around that picnic area? Could he? The shadow of another possible tale took shape in Maddox's mind. Somebody Harry knew casually, inviting him on a joyride after work. It had been Saturday night, after all; he wouldn't have had to get up early. If Harry wasn't quite the paragon they all made him out to be— Maybe the casual pal with a couple of girls and a bottle? And Griffith Park, with the gates open late now, such a nice private place—

Like the grave Harry would now occupy.

Maddox rather liked that idea. It was plausible. It fitted. And a fight could easily have developed, especially given the bottle—the girls. The autopsy would tell them if he'd been drinking. Have a good look around that area up there, for any blood.

It was not an idea he could pursue here and now, of course. "Well, we'll keep that in mind," he said diplomatically, and stood up. "We're very sorry to bother you right now with all this, but we want to get on it."

"And you better get on it, and find out who!" said Slaney. "My God, Harry! When you see all these beatniks and the damn hippies, and the guys burning draft cards—what damn loss to anybody, one of them? But one like Harry— He tried to enlist when he got out of school, you know, they turned him down account of that punctured eardrum he got swimming."

"But why did it have to be *Harry?*" moaned Mrs. Arthur.

"Sorry to let you in for all that," said Maddox, switching on the engine.

55

"Part of the job," said Sue. "Those poor people. He does seem to have been one of the younger generation to point to with pride."

"Seems," said Maddox. "I've got a little idea on that."

"Cops have to cultivate suspicious minds," said Sue with distaste. "It's a funny one, if he was all they say, isn't it, Ivor?"

"We'll see. . . . Did I tell you we made that Ritchie? The berserk one today. He's got quite a little pedigree downtown—all unofficial, of course, he's still a minor. Known back to age thirteen. He's graduated from reefers to H to the acid bit now. They found some on him—the LSD."

"And so I suppose he gets the slap on the wrist this time too."

"What else? Released on probation to the family. Which is his father, a pro burglar now out on P.A. He'll be eighteen in December," said Maddox, "and after that—but we're really not supposed to lean very hard on any of 'em, you know. Minor or major."

"Oh, I know, I know. And that doctor—that's another funny one. By what was in the paper."

"Every once in a while the funny ones come along." There was also Madame Sylvia.

They were silent until he pulled up in front of the court on Janiel Terrace where she lived with her mother. "Thanks," he said again.

"Don't mention it. We aim to please. Don't bother to get out."

"All right. You're looking very fetching these days, Carstairs," said Maddox. "I like the new haircut."

"Why—thanks so much." Sue got out and shut the door. "Night."

"See you." The Maserati took off.

Sue stared after it. That Maddox. Anything female chasing him hot and heavy—he didn't have to lift a hand. Whatever it *was* about him. Which Sue Carstairs had better sense than to do. And in all the fourteen months he'd been at Wilcox Street, with Policewoman Carstairs very ostentatiously not chasing him, he'd never once even looked at her as if he realized she was female. Reliable old Carstairs, the fellow peace officer.

Sue shook her head, not quite believing he had said those casual words. After all this time, he couldn't really—

On Tuesday morning, Maddox found the ballistics report on slugs from Madame Sylvia on his desk. It was enlightening just so far. The gun was either a Hi-Standard .22 regular model, the special model, or the little snub-nosed Colt .22. Not a new gun.

It was something, not much. However, he was shelving Madame Sylvia for the time being.

D'Arcy's day off. Overnight, another home broken into up in the hillside area above Franklin, and Rodriguez and Feinman were out on that.

Maddox went down to the lab and asked for an observer. Not really much use giving Mr. Bell's gas station the full treatment; the station had been open for a full day at least since Harry Arthur had vanished from it. They gave him Joe Rowan, who had transferred to the lab a few months ago, and he briefed Joe as they drove to the station on Melrose.

Harry's car was still there. Would it be any use to tow it in and go over it with the vacuum cleaners?

Mr. Bell had a good deal to say; he had heard the news about Harry on the news last night. He was shocked and grieved, and Maddox had to listen for a while. How Harry'd been the best young fellow Bell ever knew, steady, ambitious to get on. "He meant to go into contracting for himself, when he had the money." Kind to his mother, head screwed on the right way and all. "Like he had the sense to see, college no use to him, he hadn't that kind of mind, smart as a whip Harry was but not that way, he was working part-time for this same outfit before he got out of school." The paragon. Maybe and maybe not, thought Maddox. And, apparently the family also thinking he was, if they turned up anything to the contrary, all the more upsetting to the family, which would be a pity, but if possible they would like to find out what had happened to Harry, and why.

Rowan went prowling around the station, and about twenty minutes after they got there he called to Maddox. "Here's something with a vengeance."

Maddox went and looked, pursued by Mr. Bell. Rowan was stooped over, looking at the big metal trash can against the wall of the garage. This was an old independent station: there was the usual little glass-fronted, one-room office just beside the pumps, and a work area behind it with a lift, and behind that a small garage. Harry's car was parked at the very rear of the work area against the garage. The big trash can stood on the other side of the door to the garage.

"What?" said Maddox. "What about the can?"

"Behind it. Nearly."

"What— Oh. Oh, for—" Maddox bent. On the cement there, nearly hidden by the can, a bunch of keys. As if carelessly dropped.

"You can both witness the position," said Rowan, and hooked his ballpoint pen through the key ring and lifted it. "Well, well." He dangled the keys in the air.

"Those are Harry's keys!" said Bell excitedly. "I'll be damned! What are they doing here? I haven't been near the trash can since—they pick it up on Thursdays. I looked around some, see if there was anything at all could say where he'd gone to, but I never spotted—"

"Harry's keys all right," said Rowan. "You said he was a smart young fellow? Not so very."

"What?" Bell was indignant. "Why—"

"The luggage tag."

Maddox had noticed it. On the ring with the keys, car keys, keys to the apartment, the miscellaneous keys everybody carried: the little tag with the name and address stamped on it.

"That's how you can see they're Harry's. He had that made up special, he was careful but anybody can lose—"

"Yeah," said Rowan. "Yeah. You ever stop to think, Mr. Bell, that if you lose a set of keys with your name and address attached, you could be giving some pro hood your front door key and telling him just where that front door is? If you ever lose a set of keys, Mr. Bell, with or without an address along with 'em, you get your locks changed pronto."

"Oh," said Bell. "Oh, I never thought of that. But what are Harry's keys—"

Rowan went on prowling. He asked if Harry's car had been moved. "No, that's where he left it, he came on Saturday night. Nobody had the keys, acourse." Rowan nosed back and forth along the cement, out from the garage door, and presently squatted down and beckoned Maddox. "What do you think?"

Maddox came and looked. In this old station, the cement was stained and discolored in places: old oil had seeped into it, and where cars had stood and work been done before the automatic lift had been added, old grease and new had lain. About in the middle of the cement here, between the station office and the garage, was new grease, in patches: oddly irregular patches. But Rowan was pointing somewhere else. Up from the grease was a dark splotch not the same color: a crusty dark brown splotch, dry, which at casual glance was just more stained cement you might find in an old gas station.

"That's just about the right color for blood about that old," said Rowan. "We'll just see." He took a plastic envelope from his pocket and began carefully to scrape at the splotch.

"Blood?" said Bell. "Blood? Here? I never— But how could it be—"

Maddox watched Rowan work, and he thought, that clinches it. They wouldn't have to make like bloodhounds up there in Griffith Park. Here. Right here, Saturday night. It must have been. And that said, it had to be some personal motive.

Didn't it? Had to be somebody with the motive on Harry Arthur, not just the attendant at the station. Because the nut Slaney had talked about—some customer who'd got to arguing with Harry over anything, and worked up a temper to the point where he could kill— Well, the sudden thing like that, the nut would just have left him here, not gone to all the bother of carting him up to Griffith Park.

"Listen," said Bell. "Listen. You mean you think that's Harry's blood? He got it right here? Murdered? But he'd closed up just like usual. Put the money away. Locked up. Turned out the lights. He'd—"

Maddox was working it out. "If that is blood, that's what it says all right. That he was first attacked here, anyway. And —after he'd closed up the station. Yes. You can see that. He was—he must have been—on the way to his car, keys in his hand, ready—when he was attacked from behind. There was that grease on his shirt and pants. I thought that was a little funny, he wouldn't have been servicing cars while he was here. Yes. Read it. He was knocked down face forward on the cement there, and very possibly that's where he got that dent in his forehead—Bergner'll tell us more—and his nose began to bleed. And he flung his arms out as he fell, and threw the keys away—and just by chance they landed— I'll be damned."

"There's quite a patch here to look at," said Rowan.

"Look," said Bell. "Look, you think it was *here*."

"It seems to shape up that way, now," said Maddox.

"Look," said Bell. His mind moved slowly; he wasn't used to quick imaginative reasoning. "Somebody going after him here? Even with the station lights out, all the street lights out there, neon signs, along here—a lot of 'em on all night—who would? I mean, and why? There wasn't a holdup. First thing I think about, when Mrs. Arthur called me—money in the safe, about an average take for Saturday night —show you what I thought of Harry, let him use the safe— only one but me knew the combination. Anybody going after him, there has to be a reason—like wanting the cash. I don't see—"

"There could have been reasons," said Maddox absently, thinking of some. "Whoever, whatever, he wasn't robbed either. Nearly a hundred bucks on him."

"Yeah, I'd paid him two weeks' wages in cash," said Bell. "Fifty-two bucks. But listen, you mean like somebody he knew, that had some reason want to kill him? Harry? If that is blood—you think, if I get it straight, somebody he knew was here, just as he was shutting up the station—and either already had a reason to kill him, or they had a fight or something right then, and whoever it was—"

"It could be something along that line," said Maddox.

"No, it couldn't," said Bell. "You're way off there, Sergeant. In the first place, it wouldn't've been. Anybody could say, on Harry. He didn't fool around with females, he had a nice girl of his own he was goin' to marry. He didn't drink—oh, a beer now and then, that's all—didn't gamble or run around.

But one thing I do know, Sergeant, there wouldn't've been nobody here when he was closing up the station."

"Why?"

"Because," said Bell simply, "he was conscientious, Harry was. And he'd never in this world have let anybody—even his best friend it might be—see him working that safe. To let anybody know he knew the combination. My safe, that I trusted him with. That, I know."

Maddox looked at him. A small point. Conscientious Harry.

Somebody lying in wait? How melodramatic could you get?

But it did look clear now that Harry had been attacked right here, at the station. After he'd closed up, and as he was walking toward his car.

By somebody not interested in money. Either Harry's or Mr. Bell's. By somebody who had gone to some trouble to cart Harry's body (dead or only dying?) up to Griffith Park.

He swung and looked across the street. Any good to ask questions around, if anything had been noticed last Saturday night by anybody there? Immediately opposite the station was a small coffee shop. Not the sort of place to have a liquor license, and very likely it had been closed and dark before eleven. Next to it, in a medium-sized building, a gymnasium with a sign in the front window advertising a special reducing course. Next to the station on this side of the street, a stationers'. N.G. there.

The only thing that came clear in his mind was that it had to be the personal thing on Harry.

Because Griffith Park—a good six miles up there—

"Damnation," he said. The offbeat one.

He looked at his watch. It was five minutes to ten. Rowan had collected his scrapings. Maddox thanked Bell absently. "You mark what I say," said Bell. "I knew Harry. Steady, honest, reliable fellow. He appreciated it, that I trusted him with the safe. He wouldn't—"

Back at the office, Maddox stared at the ballistics report on those slugs and ruminated. The other thing. He had an appointment at eleven, at Hollywood Receiving, to talk to those ambulance men. On Dr. Charles Grantby. The damnedest thing—

The inside phone rang. "The Great Panjandrum," said O'Neill. "Dr. J. Hadley Prince in person desires to confer with you, Sergeant."

"Oh hell," said Maddox. "Put him on."

five

Dr. J. Hadley Prince, however, sounded quite human and worried at first. Maddox gave him a little doubletalk, and the doctor lost his temper. "What are you people *doing* about it, is all I want to know! As far as I can make out you're not doing one damn— One of my oldest friends, Grantby, and talk about a nine days' wonder—just walks out—and after all the police—"

"Are only human, Doctor," said Maddox. "We've got other things going on right now too. I'm coming over this morning to look some more. It struck us just as funny as it did you. Yes, sir, I've talked to people who know Dr. Grantby. Yes, I know there's no history of instability or—"

Prince snorted. "Sanest man I know. Solid. What the hell can have happened? Well. You'll let us know—or if there's anything the hospital can do to help."

"Thanks very much, Doctor. We'll be in touch." Maddox put the phone down and immediately it rang. "Well?"

"This is an interesting precinct, my boyo," said O'Neill. "I'm glad I got transferred. Thought it might be a little boring after downtown, but what with your glamorous female division and all the offbeat cases— We've got another funny little thing now. Just thought you'd be interested. Squad car just came in—Carmichael—and gave us a present. Seems he was on tour over on Loma Linda a while ago when a citizen hails him. One Rodney Teagarden, retired barber.

64

Teagarden says he got up early to do some gardening, and found this gun under a bush in his front yard. Wasn't there yesterday. He doesn't know what to do with it, doesn't especially like guns, and was thinking of calling the cops when the squad car came by. He gave it to Carmichael, who just gave it to me."

"What is it?" And that was a queer one indeed, thought Maddox.

"It's a Hi-Standard twenty-two revolver. Not new, but looks in pretty good shape. It hasn't been lying around outside long."

"And I suppose Teagarden, Carmichael, and now you have had your paws all over the thing. Not that it probably makes much difference. You'd better send it to the lab."

"I had figured that."

"So, do." Maddox wondered. A Hi-Standard .22. A lot of them floating around, every model: the brand sold by Sears Roebuck. But funny. Funnier if it should turn out to be the gun responsible for Madame Sylvia. Which was a very, very long chance. But at least a gun—could you say?— somebody wanted to be rid of. Maybe thrown into Mr. Teagarden's front yard last night?

D'Arcy was off. Maddox got up, and in the hall outside ran into Sue, fumbling for her car keys. "The little darlings," she said. "We got Brenda started home with Daddy. The rest of that bunch is down in Juvenile Hall, and we've just located a family for that girl Jill Shafter. East L.A. I'm going to see what the setup is. If I'd known the L.A.P.D. expected me to be a social worker—"

"You taking any bet Juvenile will keep them, whatever the families look like?"

"Well, it's not always their fault, Ivor—all the laws and restrictions. But maddening all the same." They came past the desk downstairs and O'Neill lifted a hand at Sue. "I'm in a hurry, Johnny—" but she went over to the desk. Maddox stopped in the door to get out a cigarette, but all he heard was O'Neill's laugh and lowered intimate tone. That O'Neill.

And now switch his mind to Dr. Charles Grantby. The other offbeat thing. Perhaps the most offbeat of any of them. What *had* happened to Dr. Grantby?

"That is the billy-be-damnedest thing I ever heard," said the ambulance driver, shaking his head. "We been hearing about it from the doctors and orderlies. Boom, he's gone. Right out from a crowd of people. Like the devil carried him off." He and his partner had been on night duty last Sunday night, and they were the only ambulance attendants here not yet interviewed; the night men at the precinct had seen or talked to the others, and come up with nothing.

"Well, in case some human agency was concerned instead," said Maddox, "we have to ask the questions."

"I see that, but what can we tell you?" The driver spread hamlike hands. "We're busy. I've known busier nights than last Sunday—an ordinary Sunday night—but busy enough. We brought in, how many, maybe fourteen, fifteen loads, midnight to six, and we're not the only ambulance in town. Mostly traffic accidents. It was along about three o'clock, I guess, we came in with this guy, a drunk rammed his new T-bird into a building and he was bleeding like hell, one leg nearly off, and anyway we come in and the orderlies come out and take him, and we hadn't a new call so I took a minute to work on the valve on the oxygen tank, there was something wrong with it, and it's about then one of the interns comes out and says have we seen Dr. Grantby."

"Did you know him? By sight? By name?"

"Sure." The other man spoke up. "He was night supervisor here for a long time. A nice little guy. Quick sort of

66

way with him, even if he was old. Talk with you just like he was anybody. Some of the interns kind of uppity, but he wasn't. And then they started asking us about the last trip in—because there was something about some guy asking to see Dr. Grantby then, only—"

"Oh, you were the men on that ambulance too. When was that?"

The men looked at each other, consulting. "Maybe forty minutes before? Call it two twenty A.M. In between we had that heart attack, where we gave the guy oxygen, but his doctor got there and he came back O.K., we didn't bring him in. The two-twenty one was another accident, multiple, a bad one out on the Hollywood freeway, and we were busy unloading them. At the entrance there. *I* don't remember anybody asking for Doc Grantby, but this orderly did."

"Did either of you ask to see him?"

"Why the hell for? No. We were busy. In fact, we'd hardly got that bunch unloaded than we get another call and off we go."

Maddox looked round the bare room. This was the first room of the Emergency Ward, giving on the ambulance entrance. The first place emergencies were brought. There were three tables, several big oxygen tanks in a corner, a sink, cabinets, sterilizers. The outside door gave directly on the ramp, where the ambulances could be backed right up to the door. He went to the door and looked out.

Fountain Avenue, a quarter block away, was hardly a main drag; it would be fairly dark at night. Wilcox Street was the wider, brighter street, but still not a main drag. The driveway in from Wilcox was fairly narrow; the hospital parking lot was round at the other side of the building. "How is it out there at night?" he asked. Difficult to guess in daylight.

They came and looked out with him. There were big arc lights, fluorescent lights, on the building, and that was all. "Well, it's not as light as day," said the driver. "No. But light *enough*. To see what you're doing. To get them out. And there's light coming out from in here."

The arc lights were up pretty high. "I shouldn't think," said Maddox, "you'd get much light at all except just in the one spot there at the back of the ambulance when you back it in."

"Well, that's where you want it," said the driver.

"Yes. Thanks so much."

"Sorry we can't tell you more, but that's it. Beats me," said the other man. "Him just vanishing like that. And a nice little guy too."

Maddox watched them out. He opened the other door opposite the ambulance entrance, and looked into a hall. Rooms both sides of it, and people coming and going— interns, nurses, orderlies. This wasn't the busiest time of day for this ward, but emergencies could happen at any time. He had been allowed to look around here. Eight, ten rooms —treatment rooms—besides the emergency surgery: a dispensary; a linen room. And beyond the surgery, the elevators up to the main floor of the hospital, also a staircase—and at the opposite end of this hall, an outside exit to the parking lot.

Dr. Grantby could have gone in any of three directions. Up to the main floor. Out to the lot. Out the ambulance entrance. Choosing his time, he could have slipped out without being noticed. Voluntarily slipped out.

But. The very stable reliable man. (Like Harry Arthur.) The sanest man Dr. Prince knew. And he hadn't taken his car, or any clothes. Maddox leaned on the wall and lit a cigarette, remembering Dr. Grantby's room here, upstairs.

A very neat room, everything arranged comfortably, probably his own upholstered armchair by the window, generous ashtrays. Hairbrush on the dresser, one of those trays for overnight deposit of keys and change: the drawers all very tidy, good quality underwear and shirts and handkerchiefs. In the closet, five suits, one new, all good quality, and six pairs of shoes on trees. A shelf of books, the queer mixture that said Grantby was a reader: *Don Quixote,* Shakespeare, Balzac, Mark Twain, Robert Burns, Ogden Nash, a row of medical textbooks, some old Christies in paperback, modern short stories, O. Henry, and—Maddox's eyebrows had risen—Nandor Fodor's *Between Two Worlds.* The doctor open-minded.

All right. Say he hadn't gone voluntarily. How had it been done? Obviously he couldn't have been taken away forcibly down the corridor. Any of a crowd of people apt to pop out of any room any minute to see. But the ambulance entrance —once out of the little pool of light right outside the door, it would be damn dark out there. And access from there, down a path round the building, to the regular parking lot.

But why? (Same like Harry Arthur.) What possible reason could anyone have to abduct Dr. Grantby?

Whether or not the man who asked for him had anything to do with it, it looked fairly certain that he had gone between, say, two fifteen and three A.M. Wherever.

Abduct? Maddox rubbed his jaw and wondered if he ought to report this, routinely, to the Feds. Technically, any case of a disappearance must be presumed abduction after twenty-four hours, and reported to the FBI.

But— A responsible adult. Who wouldn't walk off the job. You never knew *what* people would do, thought Maddox. As any experienced cop could say.

He sighed. He hadn't had much breakfast, oversleeping,

and it was five to twelve. He thought he'd like some company for lunch. He sought the Maserati in the lot and drove the six blocks back to the station.

Downstairs, standing round the desk talking, he found the Fed, Brandon, Lieutenant Eden, and Sergeant Ellis. O'Neill was leaning back admiring something held up to the light.

"Beautiful work," said the Fed. "Beautiful. I thought there was something familiar about it, the first one I saw, and now Washington halfway backs that up. Probably the old man's work."

"You let me keep this one, boy?" O'Neill grinned. "With any luck I could pass it easy, and I can always use—"

The Fed grabbed at it in mock alarm. "That's evidence, my son. At least we've identified one of the passers, and if we get fliers out on that— We need all the evidence we've got."

Ellis spotted Maddox and raised a hand. "You seen one of these yet?" He took it from Brandon and handed it over; Maddox examined it curiously.

"Looks absolutely kosher. A nice twenty." He weighed it, rubbed a finger over it. "Just a little something about the feel—"

"Yep. You look at it close, you can see. But at first glance —lovely work," said Brandon. "Some of old Pete Gunnarson's work. Damn it, you've got to hand it to the old boy, he's got to be nearly eighty. The first few of these I saw, they rang a little bell in my mind—I'd seen the exhibit of fancy fakes back in Washington just recently—and when the experts back there had some more to look at, they backed me up. Old Pete Gunnarson—or somebody he trained, I suppose. The last time he got picked up, before my time, was in nineteen forty-nine—and there wasn't enough evidence to hold him. He was sixty then. Did about five years back in the thirties for it—they got his plates that time. Quite a cute old guy."

"But the actual makers never pass the stuff," said Eden, massaging his bald head. "Now we've got a make on one of the passers—"

"That Tellman. Done a little time for kite-flying, which figures," said Ellis thoughtfully. "If he's still here—"

"Let me see the pretty thing again," begged O'Neill.

"You watch out, he'll lift it," said Maddox, turning to the stairs.

"Ah, Sergeant, now how could you suspect me of such a thing?"

"It's easy," said Maddox. He went upstairs. Voices issued from the first interrogation room down the hall. He eased the door open.

"—For God's sake, I didn't I didn't I didn't! It wasn't me—or any of us! Sure, sure, we pal around together some—"

"And you pulled one caper with Tom Carney before, didn't you, Bill?" Rodriguez' deep voice.

"Yeah, I did, but that was three years ago and neither of us want any more of it—we been clean since we got out, I swear to God! And so Jimmy did a little time too, he feels like we do, never again. It wasn't us! It wasn't—"

"You know we've got a warrant coming through for your room, Bill. Are we going to find anything interesting?" Feinman.

"No, you ain't! You can look all you want! I ain't saying it's been easy—some people don't want to hire ex-cons, and I don't have much schooling, but I *try*—I pick up this 'n' that, yard work and like that, I got a kind of offer of regular work from a guy does tree trimmin'—but anyways I don't want *no more* bein' shut up. I made up my mind, stay clean, and I have. You damn guys—"

Maddox poked his head inside. The man in the straight

chair was about twenty-three, not bad-looking, big and blond. Rodriguez looked hot and tired; he had pulled his tie loose, and for once didn't look his dapper self. Feinman just looked resigned. Rodriguez saw Maddox and came over.

"You like to knock off for lunch a little early? Are you getting anywhere?"

"Well, we thought we were," said Rodriguez. It was very hot in the precinct house; the old building was baked through. "The place they hit last night—an elderly widow, deaf, living alone up on Del Mar. Same general area as the Vedder place, and the old lady kept her head—gave in to 'em, and they just knocked her around a little. She gave us a better description than Vedder. Three men this time. Young men, early twenties. One blond. One with a tattoo on his right arm. No make on tattoo. But this Bill Giese, who was one we talked to before, looks possible. No alibi— he was out with these two pals just riding around, he says— they stopped at a drive-in but it was busy and nobody there backs them up. So we drag him in again—and we'll talk to the pals—but you heard him."

"I did. He sounds a little bit convincing," said Maddox. "Just occasionally, César, the first trip in does have that— um—sobering effect, and they get, in the jargon, rehabilitated."

"Occasionally," said Rodriguez. "Very occasionally. It does happen. We'll see what the pals have to say. We've got nothing to hold him on. And I will say, he's only got four eighty-five on him, and whoever pulled the Vedder job ought to be more flush than that."

"Yes. Come and have lunch."

"O.K. Give us five minutes to wash—we've had a session —meet you downstairs."

Maddox drifted downstairs again and stood in the door. The big blond bolted past him a minute later, anxious to be away from the fuzz. Sue Carstairs came briskly across the street from the parking lot and said, "Hi. I feel as if I need a bath. Those people! Honestly, people! That Jill Shafter. They hadn't worried when she didn't come home last night—figured she was with some girl friend."

"As you say, people."

"Sitting guzzling beer and watching TV. The mother was half tight. They're on welfare."

"Slight correction," said Maddox. "On my neck and yours. And the rest of the citizenry who work for a living."

"And five other kids from fourteen down," said Sue. "How will they turn out?"

"We can have an educated guess."

"Honestly!" said Sue, and went past him.

"Ah, there, Beautiful," said O'Neill's caressing soft voice. "Now, Johnny—"

Maddox didn't turn. There was a little exchange of low-voiced talk, and then Sue's footsteps started up the bare stairs. "I'll pick you up at seven, *agrah*," called O'Neill after her. "We're both off tomorrow, we can make a night of it."

Sue laughed. "I've got a few things to do on my day off. See you, Johnny. . . . Hi, César."

Why, that goddamned Irishman, thought Maddox, seething. It wasn't—well, professional conduct. It wasn't— Making up to one of the women officers, as if—

"And what's bitten you?" asked Rodriguez.

"Nothing!" said Maddox violently. "Nothing at all. Where's Joe?"

"Right behind me." Rodriguez looked at him curiously.

That damned— It was just, thought Maddox vaguely, that Carstairs was a nice girl, a good officer, and to see her falling for that blarney—not meaning a damn thing, and at that he wouldn't have put it past that damned fellow to palm that queer bill.

"What?" he said. "Oh, the Grotto, I suppose. I want a drink."

"Don't we all," said Feinman. "Adding insult to injury, the first real heat this early."

After lunch, Maddox (still, when he thought of it, seething at the impudence of that damned Irishman) called the hospital to check on Marian Dickerson. The hospital told him that Mrs. Dickerson was out of danger, coming on fine, and would be discharged in a few days. Visiting hours two to four, and hospitals constitutionally averse to changing the rules, but Maddox pulled his rank and at half-past one was looking at a pale, rather childishly pretty blonde young woman flat in a hospital bed with a screen around it.

"You mean I can say about it? About you putting him in jail?"

"That's right, Mrs. Dickerson. About wounding you, that is. If you want to prefer charges against him—"

"I don't guess," she said in a thin voice. "Bob never meant to hurt me. He wouldn't."

"He did shoot you, Mrs. Dickerson."

"It was an accident. He didn't mean to. I'd made him mad. It was just— I didn't want to move back East, but I guess if he's got a job there we'll have to. You won't keep him in jail?" She looked up at Maddox anxiously.

"If you don't want to charge him, all we've got on him is carrying a concealed weapon and discharging it to the public danger. He'll get a fine and probation most likely."

"Oh well, then, that's all right," she said. "Bob never meant no harm."

Lucky for Thorsen, reflected Maddox. And so probably the next time Thorsen lost his temper, it'd be back in K.C. and up to the boys on the force there. Maddox wished them joy of it.

He went, tiresomely, to see the contractor Harry Arthur had worked for, to talk to the men who had worked with him. He got nothing but more of the same. Harry a good worker, conscientious. Got on fine with everybody. No fights. Quiet fellow, but a sense of humor. A fellow you could count on.

"Listen," said the contractor, "I had a job I wanted done right, I give it to only three-four of this crew, and Harry was one. Not often you find a young guy, these days, that's a real perfectionist kind of worker, but he was. Some just made that way. I just can't figure what happened—terrible thing, him getting killed that way—it musta been an accident some kind, because nobody'd have any reason, on Harry—"

By the time Maddox got back to Rex Slaney, he was feeling slightly annoyed at Harry the paragon. Slaney was a mechanic at a Chrysler agency garage in Beverly Hills, and the manager let him talk to Maddox in the garage office. It was very hot and airless and smelled strongly of gasoline. "Listen," said Maddox bluntly, "I'm willing to swallow that Harry was a good guy, but he wasn't an angel, Slaney."

"Nobody said he was, damn it. I just—"

"Well, all right. Are you going to tell me he never laid a girl, or got tight? That he was immune to temptation? He was only twenty-one, after all, and he must have had *some* fun. All work and no play—"

"What the hell are you driving at?" asked Slaney angrily. "I'm not telling you anything like that!"

"What I'm getting at, it couldn't have been all sweetness and light. He never had an argument with anybody, over anything?"

"Well, sure. Who doesn't? All I'm telling you is," said Slaney, "there wasn't anything like that recent." He was silent, lighting a cigarette, and then he said in a calmer voice, "Look, I didn't mean to go up in the air, Sergeant. I know you've got a job to do, have to ask the questions. And you didn't know Harry. So all right, no, he wasn't a sis—like you said. Girls, sure. A couple of the easy ones, back in high school—after. Sure. He liked a beer, relax a little. But not the hard stuff—a little reached him, and he didn't go for it. Partly on account of the money too. We were all through school together, all our lives— I knew him! Inside and out I knew him. I can only tell you. I don't want to—to give you the impression he was a *prude*, for God's sake. No. But he'd been raised right—Episcopal Church—my God, he used to lecture me because I don't get to Mass oftener! He was *straight*. About the big things. Like with Ruth. Girls, sure, but not after he got engaged to Ruth. There'd be nothing like that. I just—" Slaney drew deeply on his cigarette and shook his head helplessly. "Unless it was some nut, like I said to you, I don't know what could have happened. It just doesn't make sense."

"Well, you've filled me in a little," said Maddox.

"Besides, for God's sake, you thinking he maybe got himself in some mess—a girl, liquor, gambling—to give somebody a reason. Look, Sergeant, where'd he have the time? He was working six days a week eight to five, and six nights a week eight to eleven. He had to sleep. Where'd he have the time to get mixed up in anything?"

There was that. Harry had had a full schedule. And nothing made sense. Anywhere.

"We were going to the beach that Sunday," said Slaney. "Last Sunday. Harry and Ruth and me and Selma, my girl. I said I'd pick them up about nine."

So, even if the casual pal had dropped by and asked him to a party Saturday night, Harry likely would have turned him down. Getting up early next day.

Maddox didn't like these up-in-the-air things. They annoyed him. The offbeat plots, the real mysteries, he could find enjoyable between book covers, but in real life they were frustrating.

And of course—on either Harry or Dr. Grantby—it could have been the ultimate nut, the unpredictable nut, who might do anything. Anything at all. But because you didn't as a rule get more than one of those at a time, even in a place as big as L.A., Maddox felt that there had to be a halfway rational explanation on one case or the other—or both.

And also on Madame Sylvia.

He thanked Slaney and went back to the office. It was four forty; he'd had to drive clear up to La Crescenta (the valley ten degrees hotter) to see the contractor.

Nobody else was in. O'Neill was sitting with his feet up, doing a crossword and whistling "The Patriot Game" softly between his teeth.

There was a report from the lab on Maddox's desk. The Hi-Standard .22 given to ballistics this morning was the gun that had killed Mrs. Sylvia Brown. The serial number had, in ordinary routine, been checked against their records and relayed down to Central. Central had the gun registered. It had been registered, as a new gun, in 1950, as owned by Dr. Adam Hildebrand, office address on Wilshire, home address on Franklin in Hollywood.

"For God's sake," said Maddox blankly to the empty office. Of course, 1950—quite a lot of water under a lot of bridges since, and the gun could have changed hands. But a place to start looking.

He looked in the phone book. No office address on Wilshire for Dr. Hildebrand. But the address on Franklin still listed.

He picked up the phone, as Rodriguez and Feinman came

in. "*Nada absolutamente* from the warrants," said Rodriguez mournfully. "None of the loot showing. And they looked so nice for it too."

"Way the ball bounces," said Feinman philosophically.

Maddox started to dial. And into the office marched a big beautiful blonde looking dangerous and determined. She was about five seven, with a movie-star figure, and real flaxen hair and sparking blue eyes and Grecian features, and she was wearing a very ladylike white summer suit and low-heeled pumps, a modest amount of jewelry, and she said in ringing tones, "*Who* is in charge here?"

"*¡Caramba!*" said Rodriguez in awed admiration, *sotto voce.*

Maddox stood up. "You?" She made for him purposefully. At close range, they all saw Maddox have his usual effect on anything female, but she was high-powered female and hesitated only momentarily. "I want to know what is being *done* about my father! What has happened to him? The police said—but of course I had to come! What have you found out? What happened? What are you *doing* about it?"

"Mrs. Diana Pierce?" said Maddox. "Yes—well, we—"

"Let him try to get out of this one," murmured Feinman interestedly.

D'Arcy spent the day puttering around. He mowed the lawn in front of the old house, admiring the nice view over Silver Lake Reservoir, and completed the job by refiling all his old negatives. He didn't do any wondering over Madame Sylvia. There was a little breeze off the lake and he just felt sorry for the rest of the boys wandering around on the routine.

At seven o'clock he showered and shaved and took himself out to dinner, without a drink beforehand, and at nine o'clock he dropped into the Café Royale, where Sheila Fitzpatrick was the official photographer, snapping souvenir photos of the reveling couples. She waved at him across the room, and came and sat at his table at intervals, and D'Arcy nursed one drink along and gazed at her fondly.

His Sheila was quite a girl.

Maddox got home at seven o'clock, feeling morose and put-upon. Everything happened to him. That overwhelming blonde Diana Pierce—"What you are telling me, Sergeant, is that you've done *nothing*—absolutely nothing—about my father's disappearance! I should like to see your superior officer—"

He had an appointment at eight thirty with Dr. Hilde-brand, at the Franklin Avenue address. Dr. Hildebrand, over the phone, had sounded autocratic. The Grand Panjandrum, thought Maddox. He put a TV dinner in the oven.

The phone rang as he wondered if he had better shave again. It was Sally Scott. "Ivor, darling, I'm having a cock-tail party—Saturday, dear—and I thought dinner afterward? Just you and me? Do say yes—quite ages since I've seen you."

"Well, I don't know," he said. "We're busy."

"But not that busy, darling?"

"Well, I'll try to make it."

"That's my boy. See you, dear."

He went into the bedroom and regarded himself in the mirror. Definitely should shave again. The females chasing him. Another little mystery: he'd never know why. Un-handsome, thin dark Ivor Maddox, no charm, no gift of gab.

Things slid through his mind. Episcopal Church. What the hell anybody named O'Neill was doing— Harry the paragon. Well, maybe. The big blonde. Dr. Charles Grantby. Offbeat, all right.

That .22. Very funny.

The blarney. That goddamned Irishman. Not professional conduct—

He woke up and went to shut off the oven, rescue the TV dinner. It was too hot to eat immediately, and he made himself a drink.

He wondered where O'Neill had taken Sue for dinner.

six

"Do you mean to tell me," asked Dr. Adam Hildebrand, "that *my gun* has figured in some crime?" He looked pleased and excited about it. Dr. Hildebrand was nearing eighty, about five six and very thin and erect, with a trim white Van Dyke and clipped mustache. He was clad quite unself-consciously in a gorgeously colorful Oriental silk dressing gown. A fat matron who had introduced herself as the housekeeper had admitted Maddox to the gloomy old house on Franklin Avenue, a lowering two-story mansion above an impressive terrace; apparently Dr. Hildebrand lived in it alone. "*My* gun," he repeated pleasedly, and stroked his little beard with a fine old square hand still steady. "I do wish you'd take something, Sergeant—coffee, whiskey, a cocktail?"

"No, thanks, sir. Yes, it was. You bought the gun in nineteen fifty, is that right? A Hi-Standard twenty-two revolver."

"That is correct. There had been a number of robberies and—er—I believe the term is muggers, roundabout the neighborhood of my office. I was still in practice then, you understand." The old man lay back in his chair. "I got it for self-protection, and as a gun is no use in the table drawer at home if one is attacked abroad, I got the permit to carry it. But as a matter of fact I never did have occasion to use it, and it was never fired at all while it was in my possession."

"What happened to it?"

Hildebrand frowned. "Yes, yes, if it is the same gun in a recent crime—how do you know?—oh, ah, a serial number, of course, I should have thought of that. Then William must have sold it or given it away. How very odd. I should have thought—"

"What did you do with it?"

"Well, I had no use for it after I retired from practice, you see—in nineteen fifty-seven. As a matter of fact, just recently I have been somewhat regretful that I did give it to William, the rise in the crime rate one reads about, and I live quite alone except for Mrs. Malone, who would be useless in an emergency. I've felt I'd rather like to have a weapon in the house, but at the time I— And so I gave it to William. My son-in-law. Mr. William Guest."

"Does he live in L.A., sir?"

"Long Beach. Do you want the address?" Dr. Hildebrand watched with lively interest as Maddox took notes.

Guest, it seemed, was a lawyer; he got both home and office addresses. "This was in nineteen fifty-seven, you said?"

"It was. Dear me, what a very strange thing. To think that that old gun should— May I ask *what* crime? Was—er—someone killed with it?" He sounded almost hopeful.

People, thought Maddox. And a doctor, too. "Well, yes, there was, sir. You may have seen something about it in the papers. A Sylvia Brown—called herself Madame Sylvia." The papers, of course, had quite enjoyed Sylvia, and one columnist had published an interview with Cecilia Taylor that had made Maddox cringe for her, but probably the satire had passed straight over her head. "An—er, psychic, a medium as they're—"

Hildebrand swelled like an angry cat, or gave that effect. "That *fraud!*" he exclaimed, his voice rising; he turned a slow crimson. "That—that—! Well, really! I do not condone

82

murder, but if anyone had to be killed— Fools and sentimental idiots, Sergeant— *Imbeciles!* Only a fool can believe
in an afterlife! Afterlife! Poppycock—fantastic poppycock! A
crutch for weak minds. I am proud to say that I have never
been taken in by any of these *foolish religious fairy tales!*
As a doctor, sir, I have performed many operations—*and*
autopsies—and I have never come across the soul. Tosh! No
such thing! A medium! Fraudulent trash! *As* a doctor, I am
realistically aware that a dead man is *dead.* D-E-A-D, dead.
Permanently. And without any so-called spirit to return and
utter nonsensical messages—tchah!—into a trumpet! I cannot
conceive how there can be so many *idiots* in the world, sir!"

"No need to get upset," said Maddox, rather alarmed at
Hildebrand's color—he had gone from crimson to purple,
and was waving his arms about excitedly. "It's nothing to do
with you now, sir."

"No, no, that is perfectly true, of course, and I must remember my blood pressure. But one of my firmest convic-
tions, Sergeant, is that physical death is the end of the
matter, dust to dust, there is *nothing else,* and I am afraid
I tend to be rather emphatic in my opinions, not that I re-
gard that as an opinion, but a *fact.* The most intelligent
minds have always realized—"

"Yes," said Maddox, "thanks very much for your help,
sir." He stood up.

"Oh, you're going?" Hildebrand looked disappointed. "It's
always a pleasure to me to have someone drop in, but I suppose you've your work to do."

"That's right," said Maddox.

On the way home, absently admiring the smooth purr of
the Maserati's engine, he reflected that Dr. Hildebrand was
going to be extremely surprised one day, when he died and,
so to speak, found himself still there. Some of the more
amusing evidence in the annals of parapsychology were the

indignant denials of former convinced atheists that they were dead at all.

But then people, coming all sorts, tended to remain much the same on either side of the line.

At home, he tried Guest's home number; but the ringing went unanswered. Tomorrow.

When he came into the station on Wednesday morning, the desk was occupied by the burly uniformed bulk of Sergeant Buck from Communications. O'Neill's day off. Maddox wondered where O'Neill had taken Sue last night, and was still frowning as he went upstairs to the detective bureau.

Brougham had left some notes on the desk: more tips called in about Grantby. Since the press had given that some publicity, people had been calling in from all over the county—which was par for the course—but so far all the reports that Grantby had been seen had turned out to be duds. But every tip had to be checked out, just in case.

He wondered how Eden had coped with Diana Pierce, yesterday afternoon.

The autopsy report on Sylvia was also on his desk. There was nothing in it they hadn't known except that she'd been a healthy middle-aged woman with no physical history of chronic disease or use of alcohol. The body would have been released yesterday; he wondered what Cecilia was doing about the funeral. Poor Cecilia.

Voices and steps up the stairs, Rodriguez and Feinman.

"¡Un millón demonios! ¡Mil rayos—es el colmo! Me!" said Rodriguez. He marched in with Feinman behind him laughing. "And the bank, for God's sake— Like the innocent babes in the woods—"

"What's bit you?" asked Maddox. Rodriguez sat down and picked up the phone.

"At least I'll let those blockheads, *hombrates, estupidos,* know what—"

"The bank doesn't open till ten," said Feinman, still laughing. "He got stuck with one of those fake twenties."

"From the *bank*, my God. So it doesn't. Hell." Rodriguez snapped his lighter angrily. "Cashed a check yesterday, and when I handed over the damn bill to pay for breakfast just now at Mannings', they called the damn manager and he nearly held me while he called up a squad car—cross-questioned me as if I was a Soviet spy and even had the gall to ask if I'd bought the badge at a pawnshop—"

Maddox exploded into mirth. "Yes, laugh! Go on and laugh!" said Rodriguez bitterly. "It didn't happen to you." D'Arcy wandered in and wanted to know what was up. Maddox and Feinman enlightened him, and he began to laugh. "*So* very damned funny," said Rodriguez. "Me, getting stuck with—at the *bank!* I will be damned."

"Well, Eden said they were damned good forgeries," said Maddox. "The one I saw, I'd have taken it without question. At first glance. I suppose the bank'll credit you. After all, it was their fault."

Rodriguez snarled. "Oh, will they? I won't take any bets."

Dr. Bergner came in and asked what was going on; informed, he grinned. "Understandable error, César. Even the legal tender is just pretty engraving, and getting more so all the time."

"If it'll cheer you up any," offered D'Arcy, "you can come with me to see the medium. I've got to find out about the funeral." Often a waste of time, but sometimes an X did show at a victim's funeral.

"All right," said Rodriguez gloomily. "The exotic case. After the hoods. I've about given up on the hoods. I'm thinking now it could be a bunch with no pedigrees at all.

That Giese and his pals are clear—the widow looked at him and said definitely not the blond of the bunch who robbed her. Damnation."

"All in the day's work," said D'Arcy. "Come on." They went out together, Rodriguez still grumbling.

"Thought you'd like what I've got on Arthur right away," said Bergner, hoisting one fat hip onto the corner of Maddox's desk. "Official report up sometime today."

"What did you find?"

"Well, a very healthy specimen," said Bergner, bringing out a cigar. "Everything shipshape, excellent condition, organs sound and healthy. No traces of alcohol, by the way."

"I knew he was healthy," said Maddox. "How did he die?"

"There was a massive blow to the forehead—put it in lay language—causing a skull fracture. I would deduce he was knocked violently down, from behind, on—"

"A cemented area. I'd deduced that too, or rather Joe Rowan did."

"Oh? That'd account for the little grains of cement embedded in the surface wound. Also traces of grease and oil. But that wasn't what killed him," said Bergner. "He'd likely have recovered from that, with treatment. It probably knocked him unconscious at once, and he'd have begun to bleed, from nose and mouth. But he lived, I think, about an hour after getting that blow. That's judging from the amount of blood amassed beneath the contusion, and so on."

"So, what did kill him?"

"More blows delivered later. To the top and back of the skull. With something like a wrench," said Bergner. "I think, from the sparsity of bleeding and a couple of other things, those blows finished him off almost at once. Within five minutes, anyway. He hadn't bled much from those—and two of 'em tore the scalp open to the bone. As for the time —well, he'd had a meal about five hours before he died.

Ground beef, carrots and peas, potatoes, something with chocolate in it. I'd put the time of death between eleven and two on Saturday night."

"Oh," said Maddox. He had lived an hour, from the time he had been (probably) struck down at the station until the final killing blows were given. Still at the station? He didn't think so. Mr. Bell had something with his point about the lights: most businesses along there left their signs on all night, closed or not, and even with the station lights off, the street lights and others would make the station area fairly visible to the occasional passing cars, on that main drag. Maddox didn't think Harry had lain there on the cement at the station for an hour, bleeding, before he'd been finished off.

A vague outline took shape in his mind. Somebody hitting out in sudden temper, at Harry's back—as he was heading toward his car. Harry, maybe caught off balance, falling forward onto the cement, unable to save himself, arms flung wide, tossing the keys away inadvertently. Harry unconscious, injured how badly X couldn't know. And then the quick bundling of Harry out of sight, in panic that that had been seen by someone passing—out of sight into somebody's car? Almost definitely, with the station office and the garage locked; Harry had had the keys, but they'd landed behind that can. Even if X had looked for them— And then, maybe, the frantic casting about for a place to stash the body. And the idea of the park. And then, up there, as X hauled Harry out to roll him down that hillside, the discovery that he was still breathing. So, the quick hard blows with something like a wrench to make sure.

It could have gone like that. And a wrench or whatever, nothing from Mr. Bell's station: the lab had looked that over thoroughly by now.

He thanked Bergner absently. "Thought you'd want to

87

know," said Bergner. "Pity, healthy young fellow like that."
He stumped out.

And all that might make pictures in Maddox's mind, but it said nothing as to who.

It was nine o'clock. Was an attorney in his office by nine? Maddox tried the office number of Mr. William Guest and found that this attorney was. "Excuse me, but we do prefer an appointment to be made. May I ask—"

"This is police business—Sergeant Maddox, L.A.P.D. I'd like to talk to Mr. Guest personally."

"*Oh*," said the female voice. "*Police*—well, I'll tell him, sir." And presently a firm masculine baritone came on the line.

"William Guest speaking. Did I understand from Dolly that you're *police?* What's happened? What—"

"That's right, sir. Nothing to be alarmed about, just a routine matter. Sergeant Maddox, L.A.P.D. Some years ago, Mr. Guest, your father-in-law, Dr. Hildebrand, gave you a revolver. A Hi-Standard twenty-two revolver. You recall that?"

"Why—yes. This is about the gun? That gun? But why? I don't have it any longer. Why are the police—"

"We know that, Mr. Guest. The gun has just figured in a crime here, and we have it in our possession. We're trying to trace it back. Did you sell it, give it away, or what? Do you remember to whom?"

"Well, naturally," said Guest. "Well, I'll be damned. It *has?* I will be damned. I kept it around for a while, but I hadn't really any use for it. I don't think much of a twenty-two for self-protection, I keep a Police Positive thirty-eight in my office and another at home—and I finally sold it for fifteen bucks."

"Do you remember to whom?"

"Yes, of course. The kid next door, Terry Lord. I say kid,

88

time does get away from you. He was twenty-one, twenty-two, then—in college."

"Oh. Do you know if he kept it, or—"

"No idea," said Guest. "But obviously he hasn't had it in a while, if it was just used in a crime here. Terry's up in Portland, Oregon, now. His parents still live next door to us, they tell me he's doing very well, married, a couple of kids now. He's partner in a Chrysler agency up there."

"Oh. When did you sell him the gun?"

"Less than a year after the old man gave it to me. Maybe early nineteen fifty-eight, closest I can say. I will be damned," said Guest. "This is a funny one. I suppose you're sure from the serial number."

"That's it. Well, thanks very much," said Maddox.

"Glad to be of any help, Sergeant. I'll bet the old man was interested," and Guest laughed. "Good luck on it."

Portland. Well, 1958—a lot of things could have happened to the gun since then. Round and round on the merry-go-round. Maddox got the desk and asked to be connected with police headquarters in Portland. There, he got an obliging Captain Drummond, who took down the particulars and said he'd get right on it, not much in this morning, business was slow. "I wish I could say the same," said Maddox, and Drummond laughed, and said he'd call back when he got anything. "Thanks so much. We do appreciate the cooperation."

Was this the same gun? Had Central Records slipped up for once? Well, they never did, actually.

It was now nine thirty, and the thermometer read ninety-nine degrees. Adding insult to injury, on June twenty-fourth.

D'Arcy and Rodriguez ran into a little contingent of the true believers at the old house on Rosewood. Cecilia Taylor, gaunt and dowdy in an overlong black dress, introduced them incoherently. "Such a relief to know the police are trying—Mrs. Meeker, Mrs. Peebles—Mr. Krueger, and our faithful Miss Allgood—er—I'm not sure of your names? So good of them all, help me make the arrangements. I really wouldn't know what, except that dear Sylvia was so fond of 'Rock of Ages,' that must be played—"

"Haven't you found out who did it yet?" Mrs. Meeker, a stout popeyed matron with a sharp voice. "I should think by now you'd have some idea—a terrible thing! I've read about the rise in the crime rate, but this—innocent woman in her own house. We all feel just lost without her. *Lost.* I can't tell you what comfort she'd brought to me—*knowing* my own dear little girl was still alive, really and truly—only translated. If only more people would realize—"

"She helped a lot of folk, you got to remember," said Krueger gruffly. "Before she was taken. Least we can do for her is see she has a nice funeral."

"And I really do think we must *try*," said Cecilia. "Try to *contact* her. My own poor powers— I'm not developed as far as Sylvia, but we can *try*. Because of course she knows who did it, and if she could get a message through to us, perhaps with the help of one of the wonderful people on the Other Side, we could tell you," and she beamed vaguely at D'Arcy and Rodriguez. "And you could arrest whoever it was."

"That would be very helpful," said Rodriguez gravely.

D'Arcy said they'd like to know about the funeral.

"Oh, would you? How *very* nice of you to want to come. I'll remember. Dear Sylvia, it would be wonderful if she could go on helping us now, in such a practical way."

"She helped so many people," said Mrs. Peebles, wiping her eyes.

"And we shall try—tonight. But we do have an appointment with the mortician—" Cecilia turned her beam on

Krueger. "So kind of Mr. Krueger to drive us. It will be quite all right if you want to stay, but if you should leave before we get back, would you mind just banging the front door? Hard? That will catch the lock. But mind you bang it hard."

They watched Mr. Krueger's ancient Ford back out of the drive, and Rodriguez said, "¡Caray! What a bunch. And they really believe it."

"I told you. Ivor says Sylvia was on the level—this one too—just fooling themselves. I don't know. But whether or not, they weren't exactly making a fortune at it, you can see. This rented hole of a place. Come see the séance room." D'Arcy led him back to the room where Sylvia had died. The crystal ball was still on the table, the fallen chair set upright. It was all tidy and the powder the prints men had scattered all around had been cleaned away. "Every last thing we've got, some fellow seen coming up the front walk about one thirty, which is roundabout the time she was shot. Not even a vague description of him. Nothing but Sylvia shot. The small-time con artist, even if Ivor's right and she didn't know she was."

"The unexpected visitor. She hadn't offered him coffee, tea."

"Nothing, I told you. Not even a cigarette stub in here. Or prints, except for hers and Cecilia's."

"Oh. But wouldn't there have been?" asked Rodriguez. "If she used this room for her clients?"

D'Arcy shook his head. "We can't even say that. Cecilia tells us dear Sylvia was most particular about the clients' room, and was always dusting and tidying up in here. He may have wiped off prints, or he may not. May have posed as a client, rung the bell and she let him in, took him back here, and bingo. Or he could have just walked in the front door—Cecilia isn't sure whether it was locked—and looked around and found her. We don't even know if he'd ever been here before."

"All up in the air. Very funny. And I don't suppose she was much loss. What a thing," said Rodriguez.

Maddox had gone up to Hollywood Receiving to see Dr. Prince, and found Dr. Prince closeted with Mrs. Diana Pierce. On the Napoleonic principle that attack is the best defense, he cross-questioned Mrs. Pierce about her father, his personal habits, general routine, and everything else he could think of. Dr. Prince helpfully chimed in when her knowledge failed, and Maddox learned a good deal about Dr. Charles Grantby, but none of it said anything at all about Grantby's sudden and mysterious removal from among them.

He liked the night work. He liked a cocktail before dinner, but was a very moderate drinker, usually either a Martini or bourbon-and-water. He dressed quietly. He liked dogs and used to keep Golden Retrievers. His hobbies were chess and golf. He didn't like electric razors. He was over-indulgent with his grandchildren. He smoked Chesterfield cigarettes. He had invested in real estate. He went to the Presbyterian church when he attended church.

It was interesting to know, but it hadn't any remote bearing on what had happened to Dr. Grantby, or if it had, Maddox wasn't smart enough to spot it.

"But of course I must stay until we find out," said Mrs. Pierce energetically. "I couldn't dream of leaving."

"Dear lady, I appreciate your natural feelings, but nothing may come to light for some time." Dr. Prince evidently found Diana Pierce as overwhelming as he did, deduced Maddox.

"I'm staying," she said decisively. "If only to keep an eye

on the police—whatever they *say* they're doing about it," and her gimlet eye rested accusingly on Maddox.

"I'm sure they're doing all they can," said Dr. Prince feebly. "It's all very mysterious."

And the police, who did not generally come up against the pure mystery, were not equipped to handle such, thought Maddox sadly. He had a general notion of how Dr. Grantby had gone (whether voluntarily or otherwise)—via the ambulance entrance; but as to why or where, there just wasn't a clue.

He came back to the station at a quarter to eleven to find Mrs. Arthur and Ruth Snyder talking to Sergeant Buck, who beckoned him over.

"Maybe you'd know more about what the ladies are asking."

"We were just wondering about—the arrangements," said Mrs. Arthur. "The—his body. Nobody told us—"

"Yes, Mrs. Arthur. The body can be released at any time now and you can go on and make the funeral arrangements. Would you like to come up to the office? As long as you're here, I'd like to ask you a few more questions." They trailed obediently upstairs ahead of him; nobody else was in. He found chairs for them, sat down at his own desk.

They were both in black: two forlorn grieving women, but calmer now and resigned. To the loss of Harry. Harry the paragon. Well, by all Maddox knew about him now, so he had been. If human. One of those the world could ill afford to lose: and just how had that happened?

Generally speaking, anybody who got violently dead had done this or that to invite it. Gone strolling at midnight in a bad neighborhood. Got mixed up with the violent people. Picked up a stranger. Got tanked up and climbed behind the wheel of a car. Like that. Just occasionally, they got somebody violently dead by no fault of his own, and it seemed that Harry was one of them. A shame. But they would like to find out how, and who.

"I'd like to ask you," he said, "and I know I asked you before, but—about anything, any little thing, no matter what—that you remember Harry saying or doing lately, that was—different. To say he'd had an argument with someone, or—trouble of any kind. Anything."

Mrs. Arthur shook her head. "There wasn't anything like that. The only thing I can think—what Rex said. How it could have happened. Harry minded his own business. He was easygoing."

The girl drew a little breath, and Maddox looked at her. A rather plain girl, he'd thought at first, and she dressed badly, ungracefully, if her skirt was a modest length and her clothes neat; but now he saw that she had a flawless white skin and long lashes; a quietly pretty girl, and she'd probably be a good wife and mother. Now, for somebody besides Harry.

"Yes, Miss Snyder? You've thought of something?"

Her hands clutched each other tighter. Her engagement ring, it would be, still on her left hand: a small square amethyst set in gold. They'd been saving up for the down payment on the house. "Not—really," she said. "It wouldn't be anything to do with Harry getting *killed*. It was just—he *was* mad at that boy. Next door. He said he'd be getting into trouble."

"What was that, Miss Snyder?"

"Oh—that," said Mrs. Arthur dully. "They don't mean any little thing like that, Ruthie."

"But I'd like to hear about it," said Maddox. Something?

"He said anything, Mrs. Arthur. And I just thought about that."

94

"A boy next door?" prompted Maddox.

"We don't know them—they just moved in a couple months back," said Mrs. Arthur. "The apartment next to us, the place next door." The Arthurs lived in one side of a duplex, and there was another duplex next to it, a driveway between.

"Why was Harry mad at the boy?"

"Well, he caught him trying to steal his car," said Ruth. "He thought. He told me about it on the phone that night. He'd left his car in the drive, while he had supper—it was—I think it was last Wednesday night. He called me before he went to the station, he did most nights, and he just mentioned it then. How this boy next door had—he'd heard the car door slam, and looked out, and this boy was in his car trying to start the engine, the way they do, you know, crossing wires or something. And Harry went out and dragged him out of the car and went and told his parents. Next door. He said the boy claimed he just wanted to look at the car or something, but Harry said he'd get in trouble, go on like that."

"I remember," said Mrs. Arthur. "He was mad all right, but that wouldn't—"

"What's the boy's name?" asked Maddox.

"I don't know them," said Mrs. Arthur. "Their name's Walsh. They've got just the one boy, about seventeen he'd be."

"Well, we don't know what might give us a lead," said Maddox.

"But a young boy—just fooling around. Harry was mad, but men are funny about their cars." The older woman stood up heavily.

The girl stood, looking at him fiercely. "You'll find out?" she said. "You'll go on looking? For whoever— Because it—

it isn't *right* that a good honest man like Harry—just for no reason—and he was only twenty-one, and we had *plans*— When there're so many people just *worthless*, walking around—"

"We always keep on looking, Miss Snyder," said Maddox. "We want to find out too. We'll be looking."

She turned away quickly, eyes full, and led the other woman out.

Anything in that? The neighbor boy, trying to sneak a joyride? Well, you never did know. Another something to look into at least.

The phone rang and he picked it up.

"I got a long-distance call for you. Portland. A Captain Drummond, headquarters there."

"Put him on." Drummond had been as good as his word, prompt. It was eleven twenty-seven. Maddox waited; there was a series of clicks in his ear.

"Sergeant Maddox?"

"In person. You really got on it. What did you get?"

"Well—" Drummond sounded apologetic. "I don't know but what it adds up to a dead end for you, Sergeant. I know that agency, went right over. Young Lord was there. I asked him about the gun, and he said right off, sure, he bought it from Mr. Guest, had it a year or two while he was in college. Used it a little at target shooting, for fun, but then he got engaged and all, sort of lost interest in that. He—"

"So?"

"I'm getting there. He says he sold it for ten bucks to a friend of his. Another fellow in college with him. This was just before he got married, in May nineteen sixty. The friend was Jimmy Grierson, he lived in Glendale. I've got the address, but it'll likely do you no good, Sergeant. Grierson was killed in an accident in August that same year—nineteen sixty—his mother was a widow then and Lord's got no idea what might have happened to the gun. And that was years back, Sergeant, she could have moved or died."

"Hell!" said Maddox. "Well, I'll take the address anyway, and thanks very much."

97

seven

Maddox thought for five minutes about what Ruth Snyder had told him, and then got up. Twenty-five to twelve. He left a note for D'Arcy outlining the latest on the gun, giving the address in Glendale: better follow it up. Conceivably the woman could still be living there.

He went out to the lot and drove down to Leland Way, a little narrow residential street just below Sunset. There were few single houses on this block: a number of duplexes, a couple of small apartment houses; the single houses mostly had rental units in the back yards.

The duplex Mrs. Arthur lived in was identical to the one beside it: built by the same contractor, years ago: flat-topped stucco boxes with tiny front porches. There was a narrow driveway between them, twin strips of cement with brown grass in the middle. Maddox went up to the right-hand front door of the other duplex: the name on the mail slot was BARTON. He tried the left-hand door and found no name in the slot at all; he pushed the bell. He thought these places must be like ovens in this heat: not even a screen door so the front door could be left open.

The door opened and a draggled-looking woman about forty faced him. "Yes?"

"Mrs. Walsh?"

"Why, yes. What was it?" She had, some time ago, given up taking any trouble over her appearance, Maddox thought.

Decent and clean: a faded wrap-around cotton dress, her dark hair pinned back out of the way, no make-up, thong sandals.

Maddox introduced himself and her eyes widened. "What's the trouble? My husband—"

"Nothing like that. But do you remember, last week, when Harry Arthur next door complained about your son— something about Arthur's car?"

"Oh," she said. "Oh. But Harry Arthur's dead. He got killed. It was terrible—terrible for that poor woman. I don't know her, but Mrs. Barton told me. He was so good to her. She's all broke up. That—about Don and his car—it was last week. Did he go to the *police* and you're just now—? It wasn't anything much. Don didn't mean—"

"Well, I'd like to see him, if he's home, Mrs. Walsh."

"Don? About that? But now Mr. Arthur's dead, I should think— Yes, he's home, school's out, you know." She licked her lips, staring at Maddox, and then stepped back and shouted, *"Don! Come out here! . . .* Makes you wonder why you try, sometimes. Guess I'm soft with him, but the only one, and his dad's so awful strict." She gave Maddox a timid smile. "That poor Mrs. Arthur, though. Awful, him getting killed like that. By a robber or something. Mrs. Barton says she never saw anybody so hard-working and all, helping out his mother even when he was just a youngster. She was left a widow real young. Mrs. Barton—"

"So whaddaya want?"

Maddox looked with interest at the kid slouching up to the door. Sixteen, seventeen, tall and hefty, if still awkward. His long face, unprepossessing with snub nose and buck teeth, was spotted with acne, and he looked sullen.

"Don, it's a police officer, about that—that time last week when Harry Arthur— I guess he, before he got killed, you know— I told him it wasn't nothing, but you know your dad." She looked back at Maddox. "His dad, he belted him for it then."

"Harry Arthur!" said the boy. His voice went high. "He's dead. He got killed."

"Yes, but this was before that, wasn't it?" said Maddox. "When you tried to steal his car. Last Wednesday night."

"His dad had to work late that night, he wasn't here, but he come home while Mr. Arthur—"

"I never did! I never did that! I was—just—sittin' in it," said the boy. "I told him that was all. What's so great about his ole Ford? I was just—"

"You know how to drive, Don?"

He gave Maddox a scornful look. "Course I can drive."

"He'd like a car of his own, but like his dad says—"

"Oh, for gosh sakes, haven't I heard it enough times, a job, *he* went to work at twelve, for gosh sakes, back in the dark ages or somethin' people did, and— That jerk comin' over, just because I sat in his ole car, callin' me names, and Dad would have to come in right then and I told him for gosh sakes—"

"Harry Arthur?" said Maddox. "What names did Harry Arthur—" And the boy uttered a frustrated sound that was between a sob and a curse, and turned on his mother.

"*Harry Arthur!* Ever since we moved in here I hear it, alla time, you and that damn Mis' Barton, this Arthur, what a wonderful guy, he's got wings maybe— Dad goin' *on* at me, example, and why don't I this, that, and the other like *Harry Arthur*. An' that damn jerk callin' me a lazy no-goodnik for Dad to hear as if he ain't said worse himself and I about had enough—for gosh sakes I'm just a *kid*, I got to go to school and kids aren't *s'posed* to hafta work—"

"Now don't get all upset, your dad just means it for your own good, Donny."

Maddox's interest in Don Walsh grew. He could see how

it might be annoying to one like Don Walsh, the example held up before him—Harry the paragon. And yet how natural. Odd, the working-out of patterns: Mrs. Arthur didn't know the Walshes, but evidently Mrs. Barton next door had been the catalyst. But could this possibly be anything to do with his case?

"So you didn't like Arthur, Don?" he asked gently.

The boy had relapsed into sullenness again. "I didn't know him. It was just— Ah, forget it. But he didn't have to make a big thing, call the fuzz down—and anyway I didn't do anything."

"Did you mean to steal his car?"

"Who's talkin' about steal? No—I was just—"

"Where were you on Saturday night?" asked Maddox very softly.

"Saturday night? What's with Saturday night? Somebody do something then and just because you think I— It ain't none of your business where I was."

"Oh Donny, you didn't ought to be so impolite. Young people, they're generally out weekends, some place, you know, sir. And with school out now— But I don't see, come to think, why you should come here, bother Don about that little thing. I'm surprised Mr. Arthur'd do such a thing, tell the police. It wasn't anything. And—my husband, he'll be home for lunch any minute. He'd be wild find a cop here— he fusses so about Don—" Her eyes begged him to go.

Maddox took another look at Don. "Yes, well, thanks very much." He went down to the Maserati at the curb, got behind the wheel, and ruminated.

Don would have had a couple of inches on Harry Arthur, and maybe ten pounds too, even if he was still a little awkward with youth. An unstable kid—and he could deduce this and that about Don Walsh: as Harry had said, very probably, the lazy lout, spoiled by the mother and bullied

101

by the father, who'd like to see him straighten up. Don knew how to drive and wanted a car. Given Don's type, that was just one short step away from hopping a car. Harry had said, trying to cross the wires: so, did he know some kids who knew how to do that? Or had he just heard about it? And—he had a kind of reason, a kid's reason, to dislike Harry.

It might add up to four or a hundred and four, thought Maddox. It was kids like that who went off the rails sometimes; and lacking imagination, self-centered, they sometimes got violent.

And he was thinking now, quite apart from Don Walsh, that it could have been a very small reason, on Harry. Some quite insignificant motive, to a mature and reasonable mind, that had triggered that violence.

What about Don Walsh? If he wasn't a loner, if he ran with a bunch his own age, ten to one one of them had a car, or access to one. Or Don could have succeeded in hopping one. Saturday night? By what Mrs. Walsh said, she didn't know where he'd been. To what hour?

The lout Don, maybe seventeen—did he know where Harry worked at night? Would Don have had enough wit, after striking that first blow, to think of Griffith Park? Why should he? What reason would Don have to hide the body? Well, what reason had anybody? Don probably had the strength to haul Harry's body around. . . .

Maddox shook his head. One way he could see it, another way he couldn't. It was *possible*. It wouldn't do any harm to look a little closer at Don Walsh. And, Don being still a minor, that would have to be done rather carefully too. Haul him in to question, and doubtless get the parents roaring Police Brutality.

He drove down to the Grotto, which was air-conditioned, and gratefully stepped into the chill air inside. Ellis and

Eden were sharing a table in the middle of the room and he made for it, pulling his tie loose.

"Did you hear that César got one of your funny-money twenties?" He sat down and the waitress hurried up.

"No!" Eden laughed. "Don't tell me. Where? At the *bank?* Well, you would think somebody'd have spotted it there, but they're putting up with inefficient help too these days. The Feds are really working it, but it's a bastard to trace the stuff back, so many people involved in the job. The last anybody heard of that old Pete Gunnarson, he was living with a married daughter in Meadville, Pennsylvania, but it seems she's moved and nobody knows where or whether he went with her. And the Feds are saying now it doesn't have to be him making the stuff—maybe somebody he trained, or maybe somebody just got hold of some of his old plates. And God knows how many in the gang passing them—they're turning up in Pasadena and San Berdu and all over. And, by the way, as if I hadn't enough on my mind—you turning that—that godawful woman loose on me! *What* a time I had with her! Couldn't get a word in edgewise."

Maddox laughed. "Quite a looker."

"Oh, indeedy," said Eden, "and the general character of a Prussian general. And what *about* that funny case, anyway? Anything new on it?"

"Nothing," said Maddox. "He's just gone." He passed on details, which Eden would have seen in reports but were new to Ellis. "Nothing says abduction, no ransom note, and there's no big money in the family. No quarrels with anybody, no trouble. And not really anything more for us to do on it, but try explaining that to Diana Pierce! Except keep the fliers out. The papers have dropped it now—yesterday's news. And we may never know any more. Once in a while somebody does just drop out of all ken, so to speak."

"Yes," said Ellis, "but damn it, such an ordinary man—and it doesn't happen all that often, Ivor."

"Oh, I know. But we've done every last thing we can on it, that I can see."

"And these other offbeat cases," said Eden. "That medium. Funny about the gun showing up. I wondered, have a look at the general area where it did? Does anybody living around there have any connection with the medium?"

Maddox considered and shook his head. "I shouldn't think that'd turn up anything. Practically everybody's got access to a car nowadays. Somebody tossing the gun away, not to be connected to it. Funny too. That old a gun, whoever used it on Sylvia wouldn't have had any idea, probably, that it had once been registered. That we could try to trace it. Just so far, maybe—we may have come to a dead end on it now." He told them why. "We'll see what turns up, but even if we can locate this Mrs. Grierson, she might have given it to the Salvation Army or sold it through a classified ad, and that long ago—" He shrugged.

"Frustrating," said Ellis. Their sandwiches arrived and he finished his drink.

"What about that Arthur?" asked Eden. "Any leads?"

Maddox's hand crept up to his jaw. "I really don't know," he said. "I don't. That lout. I wonder."

D'Arcy came back to the office at one o'clock and found Maddox's note. Glendale, he thought, depressed. Over in the valley. And a very small chance that this woman could be found. But the routine had to be done.

Rodriguez and Feinman were back at the routine in Records, looking for another set of possibles on the burglars.

Quite often, D'Arcy wondered why he had picked this particular job.

And as he drove over to Glendale, he also wondered what

the hell he was going to do about Sheila Fitzpatrick. She was a persistent girl. When he'd first said, "Just call me D'Arcy," she had been intrigued right off. "First, last, or middle? What's the rest of it?" He'd been firm, but a curious female— "Look," she had said on their latest date, in a reasonable tone, "you call me Sheila. Lots of people have unusual names. I wouldn't laugh, honestly I wouldn't."

But she would, of course. D'Arcy sometimes thought it was very funny he hadn't acquired a whole set of complexes, as well as an undying hatred for his parents, at having saddled him with such a first name; there was probably something lacking in him, that he hadn't. He'd got on fine with his parents, and grieved when they were killed together in the accident. Nobody had called him by his first name since. He'd got the boys trained never to mention it; but the once or twice he'd succumbed to blandishment and told some girl what it was, she'd had fits, and who could blame her?

Of course Ivor understood, having a sort of funny first name himself. But most people—

Well, people, thought D'Arcy, stopped for the light at Los Feliz and Riverside Drive. They tended to have foibles. Even the best of them, at times. Take Johnny O'Neill—very nice fellow, livened the station up a bit, everybody liked Johnny. But for some reason he seemed to have rubbed Ivor the wrong way from the first minute he'd been at Wilcox Street; and for no reason that D'Arcy could see. Only Johnny O'Neill, who was a lot smarter than he made out to be, D'Arcy suspected, saw that and went needling Ivor deliberately. Johnny talked a lot of blarney to everybody, it was just Johnny, and nobody else minded. It wasn't as if Ivor didn't have a sense of humor, either.

Johnny, thought D'Arcy a little sleepily, sort of making up to Sue Carstairs. Nice girl, Carstairs. Pretty little thing, and also an efficient policewoman. Ivor seemed to think, something wrong about that. D'Arcy couldn't see what. They were both free and over twenty-one after all.

And that was a little funny too, because Ivor— Well, no man could see what made for it in another man, God knew he wasn't a movie star for looks, but anything female seeming to find Ivor irresistible, chasing the hell out of him. All over him. Not that he did much talking about it, but D'Arcy knew what a nuisance it was to him: and occasionally, useful on the job with a female witness. Only, not Carstairs, that nice girl and good policewoman. Once or twice just recently it had occurred to D'Arcy that Carstairs maybe wasn't immune to whatever it was about Ivor. And now here was Ivor, who'd always gotten along casually with the females in the department, annoyed at Carstairs because Johnny talked the blarney to her too, which was senseless. Even an ordinarily sensible man like Ivor having the foibles.

And where was this address? Kenneth Road. D'Arcy pulled into the curb and consulted the County Guide, and found it. Glendale was a quiet town, largely residential, the third largest town in the county; and Kenneth Road turned out to be a very good but older street of largish houses.

He found the address, but no Mrs. Margaret Grierson lived there. "We bought the house from a Mr. Roth," said the middle-aged matron at the door. "But the Freemans next door have lived here for years, they might know."

D'Arcy tried the Freemans next door, thinking, a dead end, of course. D'Arcy tended to be pessimistic. But Mrs. Freeman said at once, "Oh, yes, after her husband died Mrs. Grierson sold the house and went to live with her other son— he's married and has a family. She lost her younger son, killed in an accident, such a tragedy. That was in nineteen sixty-three—that she moved, I mean. Do you want the address? We always exchange Christmas cards."

The address was in La Cañada, which was a very expensive, exclusive suburb indeed, and would be some five degrees hotter than Glendale. D'Arcy drove out of Glendale past Montrose and through part of La Crescenta, into La Cañada, and presently found the house: a rambling ranch house built on about three lots (Mrs. Grierson's older son must be doing right well for himself). He got, first, the younger Mrs. Grierson, who was pretty and dark, and then the older Mrs. Grierson, who was a nice plain down-to-earth woman D'Arcy warmed to.

"Well, I've never met a police officer before—I mean a detective," she said interestedly. "I can't imagine why you'd want to see me, but if I can be of any help, I'll do my best."

And she remembered about the gun. "Oh, of course," she said, and her face saddened. "When Jimmy was killed—it just didn't seem right or fair, you know—such a bright good boy, only twenty-two—just a senseless accident, not even his own fault—the other driver was drunk. But just God's will, and I've come to be thankful I've still got John, and he's doing so well."

In spades, thought D'Arcy, looking around the expensively furnished living room.

"And the grandchildren, of course. But you were asking about Jimmy's gun. I remember. When I came to go through his things—my husband was very ill then, I had it all to do—sort out his clothes for the salvage and so on, I came across the gun, and I hardly knew what to do with it. I don't like guns, don't know anything about them. But I supposed it was worth something. I thought of selling it, and then Alden asked if he could have it and I gave it to him. My husband—" she shook her head. "He hadn't been well, and Jimmy's death was a terrible blow to him. I think he just gave up after that."

"Alden?" said D'Arcy.

"Alden Grierson, Jimmy's cousin. He was older than Jimmy, of course. He was living in Santa Ana then."

My God, Orange County, thought D'Arcy. In this weather. Fifteen degrees hotter over there. "May I have the address?" he asked resignedly.

"Oh, he lives in Santa Monica now. He's married now and working for a big company, he's an electrical engineer. But I haven't the slightest idea whether he'll remember about the— Well, you said the police had it, so of course he must have sold it or something. Yes, I've got the address, of course—just a minute."

Round and round the mulberry bush, thought D'Arcy. The tiresome routine. He thanked her, took down the address, and started back for Hollywood.

At the office, he looked up phone numbers and got the Grierson household in Santa Monica. The pleasant female voice which answered turned suspicious at his questions and said, *"Police?* Whatever do you want with— I'm afraid I couldn't give you any information unless I'm quite certain—"

"I *am* police? Quite all right," said D'Arcy. If more people took common-sensible precautions, there wouldn't be all the con games pulled. "This is the Wilcox Street precinct in Hollywood, Mrs. Grierson. You can look up the number in the book and call me back—Detective D'Arcy."

Five minutes later she called. "I just wanted to be sure," she said apologetically. "Anybody could say, Police. But what's it about? My husband— Well, I can give you his office number, of course."

And five minutes after that D'Arcy was talking to Grierson. It was tedious, having to explain his business again every time, but he explained, and Grierson said, "Well, I'll be damned. That gun? Jimmy's gun? I haven't had it for years. That's a funny one, turning up in police business."

"What did you do with it, you remember?" asked D'Arcy.

"Sure. I thought I might have some fun target shooting with it, but as a matter of fact I never did use it much. I got married a little while after Aunt Margaret gave it to me, and the gun just knocked around, I sort of forgot it was there. Then, it must have been—time goes by, God, it'd have been nineteen sixty-four—or was it the summer after— No, no, nineteen sixty-four because Bobby was just walking and into everything, climb like a monkey, and Ann got nervous about having a gun around. And besides I remember he always said he was just as old as the century, and he retired a year early—he had a place up in the mountains, and he wanted a twenty-two for small game."

"Who's this? Bobby—"

"What? Oh, no—" Grierson laughed. "I was just thinking out loud, sorry. The old fellow I gave it to—sold it to—when he said that I remembered the gun, and rummaged around for it."

"Who, Mr. Grierson?"

"The old fellow did our yard work. We sort of inherited him when we bought the house, he did yard work for several people on that block. Then he retired, and—"

"His name?" asked D'Arcy.

There was silence at the other end of the line. "Damn, the name's right on the tip of my t—— Frawley? Freeley? No, that's not right. Frohler— Damn, I know it—"

"Would you have a record of it anywhere? Receipts for wages, maybe?"

"I do remember," said Grierson, "that he wouldn't let me give it to him. Insisted on giving me five bucks for it, and he gave me a receipt. I might still have it. I'll look in my desk when I get home, O.K.?"

"If you would. And give us a ring with whatever information you have. Any address you might turn up, too."

"Well, I will," said Grierson. "What a hell of a peculiar thing. Jimmy's gun! I'll look."

Maddox went back to the office after lunch with Ellis and Eden, but as they came in Sergeant Buck beckoned them.

"Call just in from a pawnshop in Beverly Hills. He's got some of the Vedder loot—a little jewelry."

"Well, that's something we hadn't expected," said Eden.

"Rodriguez or Feinman in?" asked Maddox.

"Nope."

"Hell, then I'd better take it. What's the address?" Maddox went back out, to the lot.

The pawnshop was on Santa Monica Boulevard in Beverly Hills. The detailed list of the loot taken from the Vedder house and the elderly widow had, of course, been circulated to all pawnshops in the county, as ordinary routine; but they hadn't really expected anything to come of that. That something had now told them something more about whoever it was had pulled those jobs.

The pawnbroker's name was Smith, and he was extremely annoyed.

"Twenty-four years I've been at this location, Sergeant, and never any trouble. I've maintained the integrity of my business, through ups and downs, and I may say I've always cooperated fully with the police. Naturally, in this business, it's necessary to protect yourself, and it's a very great help to all of us in this business, Sergeant, to have the hot lists circulated to us from the police. Even if your average pawnbroker wasn't an honest man—which he is—what's the profit in taking in the loot some victim can quite legally claim back without paying for it? And I *thought* I could trust my own son. The good Lord knows he's had it dinned into him about having a good thorough look at every hot list we get from you."

The young man with the scrubby mustache who was

standing nervously behind his father's chair said in something like agony, "I had, I *had*. But there was so much—and all sorts of different things—and this fellow looked absolutely O.K., looked like a college fellow and sometimes they get strapped and—"

"*And*," said Smith, "you had a date with that blonde the day the newest list came in and you just glanced at it. Don't tell *me*. You'll never keep this business twenty-four *days*, you don't pay more attention *to* business. *My* son. Seventy-three bucks he pays out over the counter. For the loot. I," said Smith, "was out to lunch."

"Well, my Lord, Pop, nobody could memorize that damn list! I vetted the stuff careful. All old stuff, and the diamonds chips except for the ring with a forty-five pointer. That was what I paid the forty bucks for, it's an old mine cut and not as— I was careful! I never—"

"And so soon as I saw that little collection, the bell rings in my head and I look at the list. My God!" said Smith. "And being an honest man, Sergeant, I call you." He looked at his offspring coldly.

"Well, let's see it," said Maddox.

It was from the Vedder loot, all right. Mrs. Vedder had made up a detailed list. Some of what was taken—the most valuable jewelry—had been modern, and the rest old family things, none of them very valuable, she admitted, but of sentimental interest. And except for Vedder's Bulova watch (at least, *a* Bulova watch, and probably his), that was what had been hocked here. An old bar brooch, enameled, with five diamond chips. A solitaire diamond ring set in white gold, with the forty-five-point stone. An eighteen-karat bracelet, with a true-lovers' knot on top. A garnet ring with two chip diamonds. A Masonic ring with a chip diamond; a garnet cross; an enamel brooch with seed pearls on it.

"All right," said Maddox, "can you tell me what he looked like? Only one man came in?"

"That's right," said the young man miserably. "A young fellow—blond."

"A college kid, he thinks. With the antique jewelry. Did you think at all?" said Smith savagely.

"Well, my Lord, Pop, I thought maybe his mother had let him—or it was family stuff he had, lots of people might have the—" Smith just shut his eyes.

"Try to describe him," said Maddox patiently. Young Smith did his best. A fellow about twenty-three, blond, ordinary-looking, maybe five ten, blue eyes maybe. Ordinary clothes—a white shirt. "Did you see him get out of a car?" No, he hadn't. There could have been a car or not; young Smith couldn't say.

Vaguely it matched the little they had—a blond young man in the gang.

And otherwise, of course, it said something else. That they weren't pros, using the pawnbroker. Pros, before going to the trouble of doing a job, would know a fence. So probably César and Feinman had been wasting time in Records. Probably these boys hadn't yet acquired any pedigrees—it might be first time out for them. Which was discouraging, because where could they look now?

All the same, also puzzling: why were they hocking the valueless old stuff—seventy-three bucks, for heaven's sake—instead of the more expensive modern jewelry?

Maddox came out to Santa Monica Boulevard to find the traffic frozen, both directions, while a siren screamed ever nearer.

An emergency. Somewhere. The red ambulance went shrieking past like a banshee, and Maddox thought, Emergency. Dr. Grantby, the sane and reliable supervisor of the Emergency Ward at Hollywood Receiving. What the hell had happened to him?

And more reports to type up, on the continued routine, all the cases.

112

He wondered if the city fathers, who poured the money out so generously into everything else, would ever get round to remembering the cops and install air conditioning in the precinct houses. Talk about wishful thinking.

He wondered if D'Arcy had got anything on the gun. He started back for Hollywood and again his mind dwelt on Don Walsh. The lout. The very immature lout. Possible? Conceivable?

Maddox was still typing a report on Grantby, D'Arcy a report on Sylvia, and Rodriguez (who had sworn mightily over the pawnbrokers' evidence on the burglaries) on the hoods, at four forty, when a stranger came briskly into the office, a big spare man in a rumpled gray suit, and said, "Desk man said to come up. Sergeant Laccia, Beverly Hills."

Maddox abandoned the typewriter without regret. "What can we do for you, Sergeant? Maddox. D'Arcy—Rodriguez. Sit down."

"Understand you had this Richard Hardig in here for something the other day—transferred to the hospital at the county jail, later remanded to parents. A juvenile."

"Hardig?" said Maddox blankly.

"Those j.d.'s the other day," said D'Arcy. "You were telling me—"

"Oh. Richard? Ritchie!" said Maddox. "Oh, yes, indeed, Sergeant. If that's who you mean. The one had the LSD backfire on him and threw a little fit. Oh, yes, I remember vividly. What about him?"

"Nothing any more," said Laccia. "We just like to keep the records straight and get everything in. On the acid, was he? That may help the doctors. He killed himself and four other people about an hour ago, out on Santa Monica on our beat. Weaving around about ninety per in an old beat-up Falcon, rammed head-on into another car."

"¡Vaya!" said Rodriguez. "No loss."

"No," said Laccia evenly, "but in the other car were four innocent citizens. Parents twenty-nine and twenty-seven, and two kids four and two years old."

"It does happen," said Maddox. "The innocents. Respectable upright people, Sergeant?"

"Very much so. You *had* him," said Laccia.

"But don't ask, why didn't we hang onto him?" Maddox's voice was softer than usual; he looked angry. "Because you know why. He was a minor—mustn't be mean to the kiddies —just expressing their high spirits. The parents?"

Laccia said economically, "The father's a junior executive downtown. Mother's a club woman. Bridge and good works. Young people from our class don't get into trouble, Officer. As you say, just youthful high spirits."

"Oh, yes," said Maddox. "Oh, yes. We get some of it too."

"I don't know what you think," said the Beverly Hills man, "and I never would have said I was so religious—but just lately, I've taken to wondering about all those prophecies in the Bible. Because it does seem like it's Sodom and Gomorrah all over again."

"It does, doesn't it?" said Maddox. "And that other passage too—forget where it comes—Will there be ten righteous men to save the city?"

"We can wonder," said Rodriguez; and the inside phone rang on Maddox's desk.

"It was one sweet bloody mess," said Laccia, grimacing. "Maddox. What?"

"A new body," said Buck. "But just a domestic accident, what I gather. Up on Franklin Avenue."

eight

When Maddox pulled the Maserati into the curb at the address on Franklin, Rodriguez said, "The ambulance beat us." The ambulance was empty: the squad car was parked beyond it. This was one of the big old houses on Franklin, above a high-terraced lawn with a long row of steps up to the entrance. They toiled upward. The squad-car man, Carmichael, was waiting for them at the open front door.

"Woman fell downstairs and broke her neck," he said laconically. "No mystery. Husband called the ambulance first, thought she was just hurt, and the interns called us. Straight back, sir—it was the basement stairs, the door's in the service porch."

There was a wide square hall inside the front door, narrowing to a long hall through the house. On the shabby old velvet love seat at the back of the front hall sat a man with his head bowed and hands clasped before him. He was a big man, and what they could see of him looked distinguished: iron-gray hair, a good dark suit, polished shoes. The husband.

The glimpse they had, at living and dining rooms down the hall, this was very typical of the older houses up here. Old, formal furniture, high ceilings, a very well-bred look. The kitchen had been modernized to some extent: the electrical gadgets stood around, and the stove was new. In the

115

service porch, off the kitchen, a door stood open opposite the rear door of the house and steps led down.

"Well, well," said Maddox, surveying the scene. Very likely when the house had been built, unlike most California houses with a basement, the basement stairs had been narrow and wooden. New cement stairs had replaced them, with a sturdy metal railing on each side: the stairs a good five feet wide. The basement down there was well lighted by a bright overhead light. The woman's body was sprawled directly at the foot of the stairs, and the interns were standing a little way off, talking. Maddox started down the stairs, not touching the railing, Rodriguez after him.

"Routine," said one of the interns in a bored tone. "Pure accident."

Maddox said nothing. He bent and looked at the woman. A stout middle-aged woman in a fussy silk housecoat, pink with lace. She had on blue leather mules with Spanish heels. Easy enough to trip in those. She had light-brown hair plentifully streaked with gray, and in death her face was fat and foolish-looking, with wide fixed eyes. She had probably cracked her skull, probably broken some bones; a little blood had soaked the hair.

"What time do you guess?" he asked the interns.

"Hour and a half, a little more. Husband got home about twenty minutes ago, found her—when we got here he was beating his breast, all his fault she came down here, poor Lorna, couldn't we save her, et cetera. I'd guess she was killed more or less instantly. I don't suppose you'll give it the full treatment—can we take her?"

Maddox looked around the basement. A clean and tidy basement: a large corner of it had been partitioned off, evidently for a work room. He walked around the body and went over there. A large drafting table, an upholstered desk

116

chair, everything to hand, T-square, ashtray, drawing pens. An architectural blueprint was spread out on the table, and on top of it rested a man's ring—a large, heavy gold ring with a good-sized diamond solitaire. "Um," said Maddox, and came back. "If you don't mind, I'll talk to friend husband first."

"What bee have you got in your bonnet?" asked Rodriguez.

"Occasionally I have a fit of caution," said Maddox. He led the way up the stairs again, and three-quarters of the way up he stopped, got out a pocket flash, and minutely examined the metal posts supporting the railing on both sides.

"Now really," said Rodriguez. "You've been reading too many detective novels, *amigo*. I like them too, but let's not carry over the complex plots into real life."

Maddox put the flash away. He went on upstairs, back to the front hall. The gray-haired man was still sitting there, head bowed. Maddox drew Carmichael aside. "You didn't tell me the name," he murmured.

"Oh, it's Halliday—Mr. Howard Halliday. They lived here alone, no family. The maid's day off, so Mrs. Halliday was here alone."

Maddox moved away, back to the still figure on the settee. "Mr. Halliday? Very sorry to disturb you, sir, we're detectives from the precinct, there's certain information we have to get. I know you're upset, sir, I'm sorry." He sounded friendly and sympathetic, and Rodriguez glanced at him; when Maddox sounded that genial, he was most dangerous.

Halliday raised his head slowly. He was a good-looking man with regular features, and he had kept his hair and his figure. He was impeccably dressed in Oxford gray suit, white shirt, dark tie neatly centered. He said sadly, "I can't help blaming myself. Yes, yes, I know you have to—get all the details, it's all right. I must get hold of myself." He sat up straighter, found a handkerchief, and wiped his eyes and blew his nose. "It's all right, whatever you want to ask. But I can't help blaming myself. Of course I couldn't know— You see, what happened is that I suddenly remembered I'd left my ring in my den last night. I often take it off when I'm working—I don't always wear it—but I like things put away properly and—and safely. I have a little study fixed for myself in the basement, it was there. As if it mattered! As if it couldn't have waited until I came home! But habits— And we were both going to be away this evening, I had a business dinner appointment, and Lorna was going to a club meeting, so the house— And I remembered, and called her from my office at about three fifteen—I should say, I'm an architect—Halliday and Forster, Hollywood Boulevard—my secretary would know the time, she was there when I—and asked Lorna to get the ring and put it in the safe with the other— Stupid, stupid, as if it was important, but I couldn't foresee—" He groaned, bowing his head again. "And then at the last minute I decided to change to another suit for dinner, and came home after all, and— God, I should call Chalmers and explain I can't— But who could have—"

Maddox stood looking at him, head cocked, for a moment, and then went back to the kitchen, where there was a wall phone. It was five minutes to six. "Night shift in yet?" he asked, having got Buck. "Mmh. Well, chase Brougham and the lab up here. Pronto."

"Really, Ivor—" said Rodriguez.

Maddox shut the kitchen door, pushed the basement door shut. "It was a nice little death trap, César. And we'll look, but unfortunately I don't think we'll ever be able to pin it on him."

"So what brainstorm did your little gray cells work up?"

Maddox leaned on the tile counter and shut his eyes. He said dreamily, "He hadn't even pulled his tie loose. And he can't act worth a damn. And he came home after all. And he's still a nice-looking fellow, while she'd let herself go. No family to maybe compensate. Did you notice what a nice freshly ironed hankie he pulled out for our benefit? Oh, he set it up. I'd lay odds. He knew, probably, that at that hour she'd be in the housecoat and mules. . . . And he waited, after making that call to send her into the trap, an hour, an hour and a half—on tenterhooks maybe that the casual visitor, the maid, would walk in and find her prematurely—while the little wire was still stretched across the stairs—before he came home and discovered her. And hey presto the wire whisked away—and damn it, those metal posts'll never show any traces—to the phone for the ambulance, my poor darling wife."

"You have an imagination," said Rodriguez thoughtfully.

Maddox opened his eyes and grinned. "Oh, I can imagine a lot more than that. That Mr. Halliday has, maybe, a more pleasing prospect for spouse—younger and prettier and possibly with some money. That the deceased Mrs. Halliday might have been annoying him more actively than by just being there, fat and forty. That obviously he wants to keep his reputation nice and clean. Sad accident instead of a trip to Reno—and he might not have had any legal cause, anyway. But he set it up, César—I swear it. And we'll never in this God's world pin it on him, but we can have a good look at least."

"¡Por Dios!" said Rodriguez. "Your wild Celtic imagination—I can see all that. He could have all right. You really think so?"

"It smells that way to me. I want Bergner to take a really close look. We'll just see. We'll brief Dick on it and then we can go home."

Occasionally Maddox did get the hunches. This could be one of them.

Maddox stopped for a meal at a coffee shop on Vine, and got home at eight o'clock, still ruminating on the cute Mr. Halliday. But with everything looking like the sad accident, Mr. Halliday would probably get away with it.

He even wondered if it was the first time that Mr. Halliday had set the little death trap. The phone rang and he picked it up, Halliday still in his mind, and a cooing female voice said, "Ivor? This is Cindy, darling." That redhead from Texas. "I'm having a li'l party on Saturday night and I do want you—"

"No, I can't make it, sorry," said Maddox. Supposed to be going to Sally Scott's party on Saturday night, damn it. Parties bored him, and the females all over him—God knew why.

"Ah, Ivor—I was countin' on you. Can't you try?"

Maddox sighed. Whatever mysterious attribute drew the females, he sometimes wished he had less of it. Which might seem madness to the average man, who didn't have to live with it. A good many females rather silly people, and Maddox had never suffered fools gladly.

Of course, some females—just a few—were sensible human beings you could talk to. Like the junior division—but of course those you didn't connect with—

D'Arcy went home and picked up a scratch meal from odds and ends in the refrigerator. He was finishing his second cup of coffee when the phone rang; it was Sheila, asking him to dinner on Monday. When the night club was dark and her father would be home too. Just potluck. D'Arcy was pleased; he liked Sheila's father, a sensible old fellow. He said if nothing came up he'd try to be on time. Seven, yes.

"Fine," said Sheila. "You're absolutely determined you won't tell me?"

"What? No," said D'Arcy firmly. "It's none of your business."

"You know, I suppose, that it's fatal to arouse a woman's curiosity. I won't give it away. *Can* it be Percy?"

"No, it's not," said D'Arcy. "Listen, what does it matter?"

"It doesn't *matter* if it's Archibald or—or Hezekiah," said Sheila. "I'd just like to know."

"Well, you'll just have to go on wanting," said D'Arcy. "I'd rather you just forgot it."

"But you must have to sign your name sometimes—checks and—"

"With initials. Listen, forget it."

"I won't, you know. Is it Zachariah?"

"No, damn it, why do you have to—"

"I'll see you Monday," said Sheila, with a laugh in her voice.

Maddox came into the office at five to eight on Thursday morning. Johnny O'Neill was already at the desk, and gave him his disarming crooked grin. "Good morning to you, Sherlock. I hear it's going to a hundred today. And the nice smog promised. Come to sunny California and enjoy life."

"Pollyanna," said Maddox. "Are either of the girls in yet?"

"Don't tell me now you've at last got round to noticing the feminine pulchritude among us? No, not yet. Will I say eeny-meeny-miney-mo when they do, or do you have a preference?"

Maddox repressed a sudden impulse to biff O'Neill a good one, and said austerely, "It doesn't matter."

"I'll send up the first one shows," said O'Neill cheerfully, "though, mind you, I think you're making a mistake. Aunt Daisy a very nice woman, but our Sue—" He was whistling "The Rising of the Moon" as Maddox went on upstairs. That damned Irishman.

On Maddox's desk was a note from Brougham. "Tend to agree with you *in re* Halliday, he smells to me too, but very slick setup and absolutely no evidence. Left note for Bergner to look close. But I don't think we'll nail him. Very cute idea, wonder if first time round?"

So. They could look, but probably nothing would show to make any charge.

He heard the two women coming up the stairs talking; he had left the door open. Daisy: "—Until they know, but—"

"Really? I didn't know that—how awful."

"Maybe I shouldn't have told you, he doesn't like—" Daisy poked her blond head in the door. "We understand you want some female help?"

"Not right now. I've decided to poke around some at this Walsh kid, try to set up an appointment with parents present—sometime today. Either of you, just to underline the fact that we're nice gentle people not persecuting the dear children. I'll let you know."

"O.K.," said Daisy. She and Sue went into the office across the hall. D'Arcy and Rodriguez came in. It was Feinman's day off.

"At least," said Rodriguez, "the bank did credit me with that twenty. Small favors. And having worked me out of a job, now we know the burglars are probably amateur so nowhere else to look, what should I do today?"

Maddox passed over Brougham's note. "There was some more vandalism last night." He was reading a report signed by Ken Donaldson now. "Parked cars along several streets between Hollywood and Sunset had windows broken, paint thrown on them, and so forth. Nice. And of course no lead. So we tell the night traffic shift to double patrol along there, tonight they hit somewhere else." He put down the report. "I might have something for you to do. I don't know about this—this Walsh kid—on the Arthur job. I may be exercising my imagination. But it can't do any harm to—" The phone rang and he picked it up. "Yes?"

"An outside call for, I quote, whatever cop it was that come to see Don Walsh yesterday, unquote."

"Oh," said Maddox, surprised. "The mother? Mrs. Walsh?"

"Masculine. Emotionally upset, and breathing heavily at me."

"I'll talk to him." Damnation, thought Maddox. The father. The strict father. To complain of the fuzz persecuting his boy. He gave himself odds that the first thing Walsh would say would be, He's a minor.

He lost the bet. "Say, you the guy talked to my wife and boy yesterday?" It was a heavy, rough male voice.

"That's right. Mr. Walsh? Yes, sir. Sergeant Maddox."

"The wife said, after Don come out with it—she wasn't goin' to tell me—about that time last week the Arthur boy said Don tried to take his car. I don't—I thought that was finished business, like. I belted him for it, that was that. Was that all you come about?"

"Well—"

"You think maybe he did something else? Listen, Sergeant —listen, if he did something, I want you guys to get him for it, good. See? I don't mind tellin' you, I been worried as hell about that boy. Talkin' to him does no good, and for God's sake I don't want my boy turn out a no good mouthy kid like a lot you see around—and like I get it out of the wife she thinks he's took money from her purse—my kid! I tried my best with him, I dunno what gets into kids these days. I swear to God. And then the cops come around. I can't get anything outta him, but—look, I don't want to waste your time, Sergeant, I know you guys are busy, you got a mean job and I got every respect for you guys, but—I like to come talk to you about Don. Whatever you think he's done. I stayed home from work today, to—if maybe I could come see you—"

Maddox recovered from astonishment and said, "That'd be fine with me, Mr. Walsh. I was going to try to contact you later, set up an appointment."

"You *was?*"

"If you could bring Don with you, maybe— Say one thirty? You know the Wilcox Street station?"

"Yeah. O.K., we'll be there. I hate like hell to think—but I always say, if these damn j.d.'s got caught up with first time and had the hide belted off them, maybe they'd straighten up. I dunno. I'll have Don there. One thirty."

"Thanks very much." It was always gratifying to find that there were some solid citizens left. Maddox went across the hall and looked into Sergeant Hoffman's office. "On that juvenile—one thirty. It's set up."

"One of us will be there to hold his hand," said Daisy, and Sue gave Maddox an absent smile.

When he came back to the office D'Arcy was on the phone. Presently he put it down and said, "More legwork. Here we go round the mulberry bush. That was that Alden Grierson. He found the receipt for the gun. He sold it to one Paul Fraynor—the retiring gardener going to live in the mountains. So what the hell use to us is Fraynor's former address on Harold Way?"

"You never know," said Maddox. "Somebody may remember him—know where he moved. We have to go through the motions."

"All for Sylvia!" said D'Arcy bitterly, and got up. "Not that there's much to choose as to the temperature, out or in."

Harold Way was a short narrow street a couple of blocks below Hollywood Boulevard. There were single houses, a

124

few apartments, and a few large old houses which had been cut up into makeshift apartments. The address D'Arcy had for Paul Fraynor was one of those. He rang a bell at random and by luck turned up the owner, a Mrs. Trask.

"Mr. Fraynor?" she said. She was a thin brisk elderly woman with piercing black eyes. "He lived here a long time, a good eight years—when he was left a widower he came here. But he moved away in nineteen sixty-four. I wouldn't know where he is now."

Just as D'Arcy, the eternal pessimist, had expected. But she went on, "He picked my place because his daughter lived just down the street. Mrs. Tronowsky. Eleanor Tronowsky. She used to bring him home baking and such, see he was comfortable. But when he retired—he did gardening work for people, had his own truck, power mower and all, he was real spry for his age—he always had a yen to live up in the mountains. He had a place up there, cabin somewheres, and that's where he went. And the Tronowskys moved that same year, he got transferred or something. She was a nice woman, Mrs. Tronowsky, she'd pass the time o' day, goin' up to the market, and me out in the yard. No, I don't know where they moved either."

End of the trail. As expected. "Well, thanks very much," said D'Arcy, and turned.

"But you could ask Mrs. Porter," she added helpfully. "She lives somewhere down this block, I'm sorry I can't tell you the address. She and Mrs. Tronowsky was real good friends, I know that from what Mrs. Tronowsky said just casual. Betty Porter. I know her by sight—a fattish blonde about forty, I see her go past now 'n' then so I know she still lives around. The Tronowskys rented the house this side o' the street third from the next corner, the little white Spanish house. You could ask for Mrs. Porter somewhere around there."

Well, as long as there was any trail to follow, you had to keep at it. It was broiling hot on the narrow little street, and unrealistically the L.A.P.D. expected its plain-clothes men to appear formally dressed in white shirts and ties, all year round. D'Arcy thanked her and gloomily plodded up Harold Way. He stopped at random at a house halfway up the block; the young woman in shorts, halter, and enormous pink hair curlers didn't know Mrs. Porter. He stopped at the next house but one, and a fat elderly woman in a kimono came to the door fanning herself with an old-fashioned fly swatter and said she didn't know Mrs. Porter. He went up three houses and rang the bell of a single frame house, and a thin elderly woman in a decent cotton house dress told him the Porters rented the house in the rear.

D'Arcy plodded up the driveway to the house in the rear. Mrs. Betty Porter was at home, a fattish blonde about forty, who looked dubiously at his badge and said, "But what on earth do the police want with Eleanor?"

"Just routine," said D'Arcy. "It's a matter of tracing some property."

"Oh. From a burglary or something? She never said anything to me about having burglars. But I suppose you're all right. I mean, we got to figure the police anyway are all right, or where are you?"

"That's right, Mrs. Porter. Do you know Mrs. Tronowsky's address?"

"Oh, sure. I'll get it for you. Her husband Tom, he works for the Parks and Recreation, and he got moved over to the Glendale branch, so they moved. It's in the Atwater district, LaClede Street. You want I should phone her you're coming, so she'll stay in?"

"Er—well, that would be helpful," said D'Arcy. "Thanks."

He walked back the long block to where he'd parked the

Dodge, and went up Western to get on Los Feliz. The Atwater area lay just over the natural pass in the Hollywood foothills to the San Fernando Valley. He looked up LaClede Street on the map; it was a little street below Glendale Avenue. It was, when he came to it, a street of newer, nicer houses than those on Harold Way, but modest houses. He found the address, and as he got out of the car he thought suddenly how strange it was, when you thought of it, how lives abutted on lives. Like the ripples on a pond, when you tossed in a stone. This one little thing, the gun, leading them to this person and that—and the only thing all these people had in common, the gun. They had had a starting place on the gun, of course, because the original owner had registered it; and all too likely, thought D'Arcy tiredly, if they should happen to track down the X who had shot Sylvia, by the gun, there would be the righteous pointing out by the press that the gun registration had solved the crime. Whereas any realistic thinking would hardly support the contention that legal gun controls prevented crime. Because it was extremely unlikely that the X on Sylvia was a pro criminal, and it was mostly pro criminals who upped the crime rate, and no gun laws ever passed would ever keep the guns out of the hands of the pro criminals. Only of the honest citizens. And there were a lot of other ways to commit violence than by guns. . . . Maybe they ought to outlaw automobiles, thought D'Arcy, you carry the notion through to the logical end. Outlaw butcher knives. And baseball bats.

And just where, he wondered, was this game of musical chairs, on this gun, going to end? Who had had the gun last?

"Oh, Betty phoned me," said Eleanor Tronowsky. "Come in. Sit down. You don't look like a detective," and she looked at D'Arcy's lank six feet four of height. He got out his badge. "Oh, goodness, I didn't mean I don't think you are. I've never met a detective. Would you like some iced coffee? I was just having some." D'Arcy said he wouldn't turn that down. He sipped iced coffee gratefully and told her, economically, about the gun. That they were trying to trace. "Your father bought it from Mr. Grierson, that was in nineteen sixty-four. I expect you've got your father's present address?"

"Why, yes. But that gun—he hasn't got it now, Mr. D'Arcy." Eleanor Tronowsky was about forty, a sensible-looking woman, dark, with a plain face that was still somehow attractive, good blue eyes, unplucked brows, and untidy brown hair. "Poor Dad, you know he always wanted to live in his mountain cabin all year round. He was brought up in the country, you see. He's got a nice snug little cabin, had it for years, up near Crestline in the Angeles Forest. We always go up there on vacations, the kids love it, and of course it doesn't cost anything. Poor Dad, he was looking forward to it so—he had some savings, and he's so independent, said he'd get on fine by himself, he doesn't hold with taking charity, like the state pension, he had it all planned out. And then the second winter he was living up there, he fell and broke his hip—wonder he didn't die before he got found. And of course we brought him right down here to the hospital. He was sixty-five then, they put in one of those steel pins like they do now, and it worked all right but he's still a little lame. Gets around all right, but not good enough for living up there in the wilderness. You like some more ice?"

"Well—"

"I'll get some. . . . Help yourself. He was mad as could be, you know. It was awfully bad luck on him. He says to me, Eleanor, I reckon it's just not meant. He's sensible enough, Dad is. He's in a nice place, a church home for older people, and he can pay his own way, they let him

128

putter around the garden. In Burbank, so we can have him here for Sunday dinner every week. He likes it fine."

"The gun," said D'Arcy.

"Oh, yes, excuse me, that's what you wanted to know, isn't it? Well, Dad said to me then, it wasn't meant, and I'd better just sort out the stuff he'd got for the mountains, winter clothes and all, and get what I could for it, he wouldn't be needing it. And when I came across that little gun, a pistol it was, I asked Tom what it'd be worth, and he said he supposed something like ten bucks or so, and he'd take it to work, ask around if any of the fellows wanted to buy it. So that's what happened to it. Some fellow in the department gave us ten bucks for it."

"You don't know who?"

"Oh, Tom will. He'll remember. You want me to call him and ask? I might get him—he said they were having a meeting like this morning, about the new plans for that park where the freeway's cutting off part—I could call and see."

"If you would."

"Sure. I hope I catch him. Let me fill your glass up. Look at the time, I better be thinking about lunch for the kids, I swear you can't keep them filled up, bottomless pits they are. You got any kids?"

"Not so far," said D'Arcy.

"Oh. We got three. Twelve down to seven. Like a pack of starving bears," said Mrs. Tronowsky. "Well, I'll try to get hold of Tom. If he isn't out somewhere on a truck. You sit and finish your coffee. It sure is hot." She vanished down the hall.

Kids, thought D'Arcy. You got married, you had to fill out the license. . . . Well, so lots of people had funny names: not quite *so* funny. Sheila was a very determined girl. And naturally, if she found *out*—

He finished the iced coffee. And if Tom Tronowsky remembered who had paid him ten bucks for the gun, where would the trail lead next?

She came back briskly. "I got him, Mr. D'Arcy. He remembered O.K. It was one of the men in the front office, one of the clerks. Bought that gun. His name's Walt Ericson. But he's on vacation right now, early. Only of course you can get his address from the department and he's due back at work Monday."

"Damn," said D'Arcy. "Monday. Well, something. Thanks very much, Mrs. Tronowsky."

"No trouble. We got to help the police," she said, friendly. "I better be thinking about lunch."

When Maddox came back from lunch at one fifteen, thinking about Halliday, about Grantby (what the *hell* had happened to the man?), about Harry Arthur—could this Walsh kid be possible, on that?—Johnny O'Neill was working a crossword and whistling "Danny Boy" softly between his teeth. "You just missed one of your girl friends, Sergeant *avic*," he said. "I do like this precinct. The exotic cases, in the wilds of Hollywood. *As* well as the glamorous junior division. . . . Quite a girl friend, asking particularly for dear Sergeant Maddox."

Maddox suffered a momentary spasm of fright that that kooky lush Maggie McNeill had been let out of the sanitarium. "Who—"

O'Neill grinned at him. "Miss Cecilia Taylor, my boy, to let you know that the little circle of the faithful haven't quite contacted Sylvia in the Great Beyond yet, but they have the definite promise of help from one of the Ascended Masters, and just as soon as they do interview Sylvia about whoever took her off they'll be in with the information."

"Oh, thanks so much," said Maddox. "It sounds so nutty. Not saying the Cecilias aren't. Wishful thinking. I suppose you think that's all crazy. The neurotics get attracted, sure."

O'Neill gave him his slanted quick grin. "Sure. Oddly enough, I have read Rhine. Only the Cecilias— And our Sue is waiting for you, Sergeant. And your j.d."

Maddox went on upstairs, pursued by O'Neill's soft whistling.

nine

"The *Arthur* fellow!" Mike Walsh
looked at Maddox in dumb horror and surprise. "You don't
think *Don*—" He was a big heavy man, shadow of a blue-
black beard even at this hour, intensely blue eyes, and he
looked uneasy in probably unaccustomed formal suit and
shirt instead of work clothes. "*Arthur*—"

"I don't think I do," said Maddox, "really. But if you'll
look at it the way I've got to, Mr. Walsh—somebody killed
Arthur. And while it isn't likely that it was your son, I've
got to find out. Don didn't like Arthur, he thought Arthur
had been unfair—at the least Arthur had let him in for the
punishment from you—and Don was out somewhere Saturday night, we don't know where. Ten to one some one of
his friends had access to a car. And kids that age are apt to
be unstable. It's an egotistic age. He could even have had
help on it for all I know. I'd like to find out for certain that
he's clear, that's all."

Walsh sat forward in the chair beside Maddox' desk, and
you could see his mind working. He was a plumber, em-
ployee of a big shop, and he hadn't finished high school,
but he was no fool. "I see what you mean," he nodded.
"You're always reading in the papers about these damn kids.
Kill people for no reason. Or they're on dope or something.
If you'd ever told me I'd be worrying this way about *my*
kid I'd've said you was nuts. But—it don't seem possible,

132

think of Don killing somebody. Don. But I tell you the truth, I dunno where I am with him any more. That's a fact." He made an angry gesture, and he looked troubled. "His ma's too soft with him."

"If we can just get out of him where he was and who with Saturday night," said Maddox, "that's all I want right now. To check it."

"O.K.," said Walsh, "I'll see you get that anyhow, I have to belt him—"

"Um," said Maddox. "If you don't mind, Mr. Walsh, I'd just as soon you let me and Miss Carstairs here question him alone." They had put Don in one of the interrogation rooms while Maddox talked to Walsh.

"You don't want me? Well, all right." Walsh looked at Sue, her neat cap of smooth dark hair, her steady blue eyes. "I guess you know your job. You want me to wait here?"

"If you don't mind." Maddox got up, and he and Sue went out. "I have an idea he's a little afraid of Walsh Senior, you know. Pity. Not the kind of boy a fellow like Walsh ought to have—no guts. I suppose he takes after the mother."

"You want me all lovey-dovey with Donny?"

"That's the idea."

Don was sitting in the straight chair, head down, and looked up to give them one resentful stare as they came in. "I don't know what this is all *about*," he said. "My own dad, haul me down here like I was a— What you think I *done*, anyway?" But his eyes were frightened.

"All I want to know from you," said Maddox abruptly, "is where you went last Saturday night. Were you alone or with some pals?"

Sue smiled at the boy and patted his shoulder. The very unattractive boy, weak chin, acne scars, rough hair, probably shunned or ignored by the girls, thought Maddox, and also probably running with others the same kind. "There's nothing to be afraid of, Don," said Sue. "We just want to know where you were so we'll know you *didn't* do something."

"What kinda double talk's that?" He looked bewildered, confused.

"Come on, come on, where were you?" asked Maddox brusquely.

Don shot a look between them, quick and furtive. "I—didn't do nothing much. Just fooled around. Who else you asking?"

Maddox wondered how to take that one. Who else? Had Don been up to something, and now thought a pal might have squealed on him? He was silent, and after a minute Don said a little desperately, "What's there to do without much loot, even the movies cost— I don't know what this is *about*. What am I s'posed to've done?"

"You tell us, Don. Saturday night. Who were you with?"

His eyes darted, frantic, and then he seemed to make up his mind. His voice hardened and he said defiantly, "Well, gosh sakes, there's no secret about it. I was with a couple friends o' mine."

"Names?"

"All *right*. Their folks aren't gonna like it, you go snooping around. They're all-right kids. Ben Schultz, Dick Hunter, Rod Gorman, and his brother. We were just fooling around."

"What does that mean?" asked Maddox coldly.

"Uh—we were in Ben's car. His dad's car. We had—uh—some malts at a place on Hollywood—and then we just walked around for a while—and we stopped another place and had Cokes. That's all."

"What time did you get home?"

"I dunno—midnight maybe. School's out, it was Saturday."

"Prove what time you got home? Either of your parents up?"

"No, but I saw the clock. What's this all about? Like I

was a hood or something—where's my dad? I'm just a *kid*, you can't treat me—"

"Now, Don, there's nothing to be frightened of," said Sue.

They went on at him for some while, but that was what they got. Maddox went back to Walsh and asked him if he knew any of the other boys. Walsh looked at the names and shook his head. "I got to say I don't. I ought to know who my kid goes with, but you're working a long day like I am, and in a big town—you lose touch. I sure hate to think Don might've got mixed into anything wrong, but like I say, if he has I want you to pin it on him good. If they get caught first time—"

"I don't know about the homicide," said Sue when the Walshes had gone, "but Don's got something on his mind, Ivor. He was more scared than he should have been, even a boy like that."

"I thought so too. No harm to look a little farther on it." Maddox lit a cigarette and added a little coldly, "You enjoy your date the other night?"

"And how did you—yes, if it's any of your business," said Sue, surprised.

"I hope you remember the oath you took when you joined. The bit about the dignity of the force."

"And just what has that—"

"Flirting with the desk sergeant!" said Maddox. "Like a—"

"I do *not*. And it's nothing to do with you anyway! Trying to tell me—"

"What's going on here?" asked Rodriguez at the door.

"Nothing at all," said Sue coldly. She went out, heels clicking, and into the office across the hall; the door shut. Rodriguez gave Maddox an amused cynical look Maddox didn't see. D'Arcy came in, sat down with a groan, and retailed the saga of his hunt on the gun.

"I've got this Ericson's address—Burbank—and one of the other men in the office said Ericson intended to be home Saturday. So we're stymied until then."

"Yes," said Maddox. "One of those things. Meanwhile, I don't think it'd do any harm to look at these kids a little. Just feel them out." He had pried some addresses out of Don; he passed them over to Rodriguez with the names. "God knows if you can locate 'em—it's vacation, and the kids loose. But go look and talk to any you come across."

"You don't want me to go?" said D'Arcy plaintively. "Please. I've got to attend Sylvia's funeral at three o'clock."

"I'll get on it," said Rodriguez. "Have a look anyway." D'Arcy got up with another groan and went out with him for coffee from the machine down the hall.

"Only it's a pity they don't dispense it hot *and* cold. If we had an ice machine, now—"

"Apply to the city fathers," said Rodriguez. "It may be just my imagination, but I don't think it's quite so hot today. Maybe it's getting ready to break."

It was hot enough. Maddox sat thinking over everything they had on hand to work, and what ought to be done, and what could be done. Funerals . . . The inquests had been formal, brief: the open verdicts. Harry Arthur's funeral this morning: he had attended it. An orthodox funeral, with the muffled sobs coming from the family room off at the side of the chapel. A little crowd of people, a good many young people. Rex Slaney, spotting him, taking him aside: what had they found out and why hadn't they found out anything? He'd thought the police here were efficient. Hadn't they found out anything?

The most efficient police couldn't make bricks without straw.

And as soon as he got back to the office, Dr. Prince calling. What had they found out? Why hadn't they found out something? The police were supposed to know how to find out—

Damn it, thought Maddox, that was the real offbeat one. Grantby. What the hell had happened to the man? He hadn't just disintegrated. Imagine the worst and say he'd been abducted and murdered—why hadn't the body turned up? How had he been spirited away, if that was so, from among that crowd of people? Well, busy people—minding their own business.

Madame Sylvia. They were on firmer ground there. The gun. So far everybody who had had the gun remembered who it had gone to next. It was a fifty-fifty chance: either they'd come to a dead end, where it had been stolen from someone or someone had sold it blind through an ad or something—or sooner or later they'd pin down the latest owner. Oh, really? said Maddox's mind belatedly. Would they? Knowing the gun had killed Sylvia, and that the cops knew it too, nobody was going to admit being the owner of that gun as late as last Sunday. It would be, I sold that gun six months ago. Like that. However, on Sylvia—it had probably been the personal motive, and if they turned up somebody who had been known to have the gun and also had some connection with Sylvia, it shouldn't be too hard to unravel. On the others—

Dr. Bergner came in, hoisted one hip on Maddox's desk, and said, "You had an idea about that Halliday woman. You get no evidence from me, sorry. Everything consistent with the simple accident. The fall downstairs. Woman was asking for it, wearing that long robe and mules with high heels. She cracked her skull and died within five minutes. Also broke a leg, a couple of ribs, and one arm. I looked for marks on the tops of the legs, but it was n.g."

"That's a pity," said Maddox. "A real pity. But that long housecoat—maybe enough to prevent marks being made. It wouldn't have taken a very heavy piece of wire, stretched tight across there, to trip her up. A fat middle-aged woman in those clothes. It's a very wide staircase, Doctor. If she was in the middle when she started down, and tripped, she wouldn't have a chance to grab for the railing—it wouldn't be within reach, either side. And even if she was close to one railing, and tripped—I suppose she could have saved herself if—" He was silent, and then said, "I think we've got to say he had some specialized knowledge of some kind or he'd never have set it up like that. He couldn't have been exactly certain she'd be killed."

"Such as what?"

"That she always went downstairs in the middle, not touching the railing. Or—well, that would do it. Because I swear he set that up, Doctor."

"You'll never prove it."

"I'm not going to waste time trying. The very cute Mr. Halliday," said Maddox. "Thanks anyway, Doctor."

"You may just be giving your imagination a workout," said Bergner, and stumped away.

Maddox went on thinking. Grantby. What the hell else could they do on Grantby? Circulate the fliers—Have you seen this man. Because you couldn't search the whole city. It was barely possible that it was a real case of amnesia and Grantby wandering away on his own—by now, who could say where?

Harry Arthur. Maybe Dr. Grantby was up in Griffith Park too. Under a bush on the wild hillside. In a detective story, of course, thought Maddox a little sleepily, the same X would be responsible for both, and some complex hidden link between them, Dr. Grantby and Harry Arthur. In real life, equally of course, things weren't so tidy and economical.

The break-in artists. Not artists. There wasn't any place to look there, either. Was there? Anybody with the pedigree and similar m.o. showing would have had a fence all picked out to take the loot to. Only the amateur would try a pawn-broker; and it was decidedly queer that the only loot yet pawned (so far as they knew) was the least valuable. That was funny indeed.

The burglary on Sunset, now, that had been a pro. No prints—he'd worn gloves; and the safe blown open by an expert. Not a line on that. They'd probably get nothing, now.

The gun, on Sylvia; maybe break that one for them sooner or later, and he was going to be interested, if it did, to find out just why the little back-street medium-by-wishful-think-ing had got herself murdered. A very unlikely murderee.

He thought César was indulging in some wishful thinking, saying not quite so hot today. But when he looked, the thermometer said only ninety-seven. He shut his eyes again.

"And I might have *expected* it!" said a loud voice. Mad-dox jumped. "What *else?* Civil servants! Sleeping peacefully in the nice quiet office—where are all the other *detectives?* Off playing poker somewhere?"

She clattered across the bare floor and stood before him, a goddess of vengeance—Diana Pierce, smart in her white suit, every blond hair in place, glittering bright as a beauty queen but with anger and scorn and white-hot bitterness. "What have you got to say for yourself?" she demanded furiously. "No wonder they say the crime rate's up, with *police* like you lying around doing nothing! Do you know *how* to go about investigating anything? Well? Who got you your nice fat cushy job, Sergeant? Maybe you know some-body in the mayor's office? And how much graft are you taking on the side? That damned desk sergeant downstairs said—"

Maddox got up slowly. Quite suddenly, the way it hap-pened with him, he was very deeply angry. He was so angry that he didn't stop to think that in Diana Pierce's present mood, anything a known cop said to her would be taken as stupid or insulting. It just went through his mind, What did that goddamn Irish bastard say, without thinking of the dignity of the—

"*Well?*" she said. "Will you tell me one single solitary *thing* you have done—supposed to be guardians of law and order!—about *my father?* Will you? Of course you can't! You don't know what to do! You—you couldn't find a—a—you—"

"Sit down, Mrs. Pierce," said Maddox very distinctly and quietly. And when she just looked at him, "Sit *down*. There. Mrs. Pierce, it's a hot day and we've both got a lot on our minds and I won't be polite. I—"

"You wouldn't know *how!*"

"*Shut up!*" said Maddox violently. He came round the desk and stood over her. "Mrs. Pierce. We've been busier, but we are busy. We've got two homicides on our hands and a gang of burglars beating up the senior citizens and a gang of counterfeiters and another burglary. The L.A.P.D., Mrs. Pierce, is the top law-enforcement body in the world. We earn our salaries, Mrs. Pierce. We are on your father's case, but we can't make bricks without straw. I don't know anybody in the mayor's office, Mrs. Pierce. Any man with rank on *this* force has got there by hard work and ability, in that order, and under *this* chief he's an honest man or he never gets on the force to start with. Do you understand me, Mrs. Pierce?"

She just stared at him, wetting her lips.

"It is so very damn easy for the arrogant civilian to come in here and call us names, Mrs. Pierce. Until you have sat our side of the desk and had to cope with all the goddamned rules and regulations hamstringing us these days, and all the goddamned senseless stupid little crime, you can damn well keep still about what kind of a job we do." His voice hadn't raised; it was soft and cold. "Do you understand *that*, Mrs. Pierce?"

She swallowed, looking at him, and said in a small voice, "Yes."

Maddox lifted his head and saw out there in the hall beyond the open door, Johnny O'Neill with a paper cup of coffee in his hand. O'Neill was grinning. He raised his other hand and circled thumb and forefinger at Maddox and turned away for the stairs.

"So all right," said Maddox. "Will you listen to me with an open mind? Your father—"

She interrupted him in a subdued voice. "I—I've been trying to—asking questions, all those interns and orderlies—Sunday night, what—"

"Oh, you have? And what did you find out?" asked Maddox.

"Nothing! Nothing! It doesn't tell you anything—just, he's gone, and nobody knows how or why or where. I can't *understand* it— There's just nothing to say—"

"You've found that out. Do you think we weren't there before you? Didn't ask all the questions, talk to all those people? Do you know how many reports I've typed on it? How many formal statements we've taken? And that's only one of the cases we're working on right now, Mrs. Pierce. There are other citizens. One of the homicides we've got right now, he was a young man, twenty-one. A very fine young man, ambitious and hard-working and minding his own business. We don't know why he was murdered, or who did it. We haven't any more leads on it than on your father. He was engaged, Mrs. Pierce. To a nice girl. He had a mother—she's a widow. Do you suppose they're less concerned about him than you are about your father?"

"I—no," she whispered. "I—suppose not."

"If you want to be crude about it, Mrs. Pierce," said Maddox hardly, "let's suppose your father's been murdered too. We don't know that, and we all hope he hasn't been. But

141

suppose it. He was fifty-eight, Mrs. Pierce, and he'd lived a good productive useful life. But Harry Arthur was only twenty-one, with everything in front of him. We don't look at it that way—we can't. Murder is murder, after all. But which was maybe the more important? No, you can't evaluate human life. Any individual as important as any other. But practically speaking, which was the most loss to the world?"

"You—"

"I don't know, you don't know—but are you telling me I ought to forget all these other crimes and concentrate on Dr. Charles Grantby, even when there's nowhere else to look and nothing to do but keep the fliers out and—" He stopped abruptly. His head had begun to ache, and the anger died in him.

She dropped her handbag and bowed forward toward his desk and began to cry. "I'm not telling you anything—but you don't know, you don't know—what a wonderful man he —so kind and good—and wise—and patient—what a wonderful doctor—and M-Mother used to be sharp with him—and so did I—everybody always says I take after Mother—impatient, and he'd only laugh. And I—and I was cross with him—the last time he came to see us—I was cross because he spoiled the children so, and I never m-meant it but I said —horrible things—to him. And now he's gone God knows where and I can't s-say I'm *sorry*—" She began to sob helplessly.

Maddox said, "Oh hell," and went across the hall. Sergeant Daisy was in, reading a report. She followed him back to the detective office and took Diana Pierce to her grandmotherly bosom, patting her soothingly.

"You come with me, dear—it's all right, don't mind about crying, it'll do you good. Let me find you a comfortable chair and some aspirin, you'll feel better in a while." She shepherded her across the hall, and the inside phone rang on Maddox's desk. He picked it up.

"I will say for the Welsh," said O'Neill, "they're like the Irish that way—tend to have strong opinions and stand up for 'em. As a nine-year veteran, Sergeant *avic*, who has taken my share of the Police Brutality bit, I enjoyed your speechifying."

"Did you ring me just to say that?"

"Not entirely. Squad car just called in. An attempted burglary—woman came back and surprised 'em. They banged her on the head and got away. Up on Vedanta Terrace."

"Oh, really. All right, I'm on it."

When Maddox came downstairs, O'Neill gave him a casual salute as he passed. Maddox hunched a shoulder and went on out.

And that new job might be rather significant, thought Maddox, listening to Mrs. Ryan. The ambulance had been before him, but Mrs. Ryan was more mad than hurt. She was a little black-haired woman about fifty, full of spunk and energy, and what she had to say might tell them something new.

"I'm usually out all afternoon, most days," she said, sitting on the couch in her early-American living room. "I'm involved in all sorts of clubs and things, the children both in college. And I went out today, after lunch, but I forgot the tickets for the Legion dance on Saturday night, I'd picked them up at the printers' yesterday and I was supposed to deliver them to Eva today. Well, I remembered them when I was at Cora's, I'd been gone from the house about two hours then—and I came right back. I was never so surprised in my life. They'd broken in the glass door in the breakfast room—the first officer found that—but I didn't see it, of course, coming in the back way. The first thing I knew, I went into my bedroom and there was this man going through my bureau drawers! Well! I was just—I didn't even have sense enough to scream, I was so surprised—I just said, What are *you* doing here, or something, and he—"

"Could you give me a description of him, Mrs. Ryan?" asked Maddox.

"I'm coming to that. Certainly I can. I was a fool, of course, but I was so— And just as I was telling the officer," she nodded at Carmichael, "there was more than one of them, because as this one came at me—I remember very distinctly—he shouted, *Look out, fellows!* And then he hit me, he knocked me down across the bed and my head hit the bedpost—and I guess I passed out. Not for long. I remember hearing a car start up in a hurry outside, but I was still dazed, I couldn't get to a front window in time to see anything. But they didn't get a *thing!*" She looked at Maddox triumphantly. "I've looked."

"So, the one you saw. What did he look like?"

"He was big, about twenty-two, and he had dark hair. Not fat—a good broad-shouldered figure. About six feet. He was really quite nice-looking. I mean, if he hadn't been rifling my bureau drawers I might have thought he was. And when he raised his arm to hit me—his right arm—I saw the tattoo. He had on dark slacks and a short-sleeved white shirt, you see, and I saw it quite plainly. On his right arm, just above the wrist—the underside of the arm."

"Well," said Maddox. A tattoo. Vedder had reported a tattoo on one of the men on that job. Couldn't say where, or what. "What was it, could you see?"

"Oh, yes. It was a coiled rattlesnake, very realistic—with its mouth open and the fangs and all—and underneath it," said Mrs. Ryan brightly, "was a name done in bright blue. *Kenny.*"

"Oh, really. You're sure of that?"

"I'm sure. Goodness, I don't know when I've had such a headache."

"That shot ought to work in a few minutes," said one of the interns.

"But they didn't get a *thing*. Of course my fur coat's in storage, but they might have ransacked the place. Henry's coin collection and— Goodness, he'd have been furious. It was lucky I forgot the tickets," she said complacently.

Lucky in two ways, maybe. Maddox called the office and asked for Dabney or somebody to come and hunt for latents. Amateurs, if this had been the same bunch, and interrupted at the job. He told Mrs. Ryan he'd like her to make a formal statement, and she agreed eagerly. Tomorrow would do. . . . A tattoo. It could say this and that, on that little bunch of amateurs. Yes, and that *Look out, fellows*—a definitely amateur ring to that.

He went back to Wilcox Street, and met Rodriguez just going in.

"Strangely enough," said Rodriguez, "I found two of the younger generation at home. Ben Schultz and Rod Gorman. What worries me, *amigo*, is what's going to happen to the country when we have to turn it over to the younger generation to run? I shudder to think."

"Let's hope these aren't representative. But look at it another way, César, could anybody do any worse?"

"There is that." They came into the office, Rodriguez sat down at his desk and lit a cigarette. "I don't think the idea that they had something to do with Harry Arthur is so hot, Ivor. The petty pilfering I could see, little things—that wouldn't surprise me. But they're not—big enough for the assault and murder. The snot-nosed kids, that's all."

"Yes," said Maddox. "They back Don up, just fooling around?"

"Oh, absolutely. They would. Whatever they were doing.

I wouldn't doubt they were up to something. Daring each other to hop a car—stealing hubcaps. Like that." Rodriguez shrugged.

"Yes," said Maddox again. "How do you like the idea that the break-in amateurs are casing the jobs? By this new one. Daylight break-in." He sketched out the facts. "She's usually gone, afternoons. And the others—the Vedders, the deaf widow—easy game, César. For the amateurs. ¿Como no?"

"¡Como sí! That is a thought. The tattoo—"

"Yes," said Maddox thoughtfully, and D'Arcy came in looking tired and sat down.

"That was the funniest funeral I ever went to," he said. "I think it was a Spiritualist minister. No kind of regular ceremony at all, and in the middle of it a woman got up from the crowd and said she could see our departed sister hovering over the coffin smiling, and everybody applauded and the minister said we should all respect those talented spirits to whom it was given to see our dear ones who have passed the barrier, and then they all sang 'Rocked in the Cradle of the Deep.' Nobody seemed very sad. It was just—"

"Well, if you grant that dying is just crossing over to a fuller sort of life," began Maddox, and heavy steps sounded on the stairs and Eden looked into the office.

"At least we've picked up one of the passers. That Tellman," he announced pleasedly. "Now we may get somewhere. If we get him to open up, he can tell us where his supply is coming from anyway. Occasionally the honest citizens are some help. Market manager spotted one of the phonies and corraled Tellman in his office, called up a squad car."

"Congratulations," said Maddox. "And damnation," as he noted the time—five minutes to six. "I've still got to type up this report on Ryan. Damn."

He got the report typed and left the office at six twenty-five. . . . A damn fool to have blown off like that to Diana Pierce. Didn't often lose his temper like that. And damn it, what the *hell* had happened to Grantby? As if he'd been snatched away by Martians.

As he opened the door of the Maserati, he saw Sergeant Daisy Hoffman and Johnny O'Neill standing together across the lot talking beside Daisy's Ford. As he looked, Daisy threw back her blond head and laughed.

That damned— And Sergeant Daisy, widow of an officer whose name was on the Honor Roll downtown, was a grandmother, damn it, if she didn't look it. It wasn't dignified, that— And just why the hell nobody but Maddox seemed to think so—

"She's a nice girl, Aunt Daisy," said O'Neill. "Not my type."

"Oh, you," said Sergeant Hoffman. "What is? You're being naughty, Johnny. All because I shot off my mouth about our little Welshman."

"Naughty? How long is it since I begged cookies after school? The man needs jiggering up. He's a good man, Daisy. She's a good girl."

"Not your type? You're a faker," said Sergeant Hoffman, laughing.

"I try to oblige you and you go calling me names. I'm just amusing myself filling in the time."

"What do the doctors say?"

"Never mind," said O'Neill cheerfully. "She's a very good girl, Daisy. Though you shouldn't have told her—ah, well. But he's a good one too. I wasn't thinking so, thought maybe for once you'd misjudged somebody. Until today. Our tough little Welshman. Though he takes a lot of jiggering up. Obtuse, some ways."

"If anybody can, you will," said Daisy amusedly.

"Get on with your blarney."

"Go home, Johnny," said Daisy. "I'm betting on you, boy."

ten

By Friday morning it appeared that Rodriguez had been right after all: the papers predicted a high of only ninety. The heat wave was breaking. Of course there'd be more, and worse, to come; but it was nice to have this one dying away.

And Friday turned out to be a busy day. Brougham had left a note on Maddox's desk: overnight there had been a tip that Dr. Grantby was registered at room such-and-thus of the Roosevelt Hotel. The salesman from Chicago, who did indeed resemble Dr. Grantby, hadn't thanked the night shift at Wilcox Street for waking him up. The mystery was still a mystery.

Maddox had hardly digested that than he had an outside call. Mr. Bell at his gas station had been inquiring of all his customers, regular and otherwise, whether they'd been in last Saturday night, and he had just turned up something. "Mr. Lombardi said he'd stay and talk to you if you come right over, Sergeant. Could you?"

Maddox got to the station on Melrose ten minutes later; anything new on Harry Arthur he'd welcome. Lombardi was standing talking with Bell; he was a stocky, dark man of middle age, and offered Maddox a firm hand. "See, I been off on a fishing trip, just got back today. So I hadn't heard about Harry. A terrible thing, that is. But when Mr. Bell told me, I recollected this and he says you figure it happened after the station was closed Saturday night, and right here —for God's sake—"

"That's right," said Maddox. The scrapings had tested out; blood, all right, and Harry's type.

"Well, I don't know if it's anything to do with it, Sergeant, but I guess you better hear. Because a nice young fellow like Harry—why anybody'd want to—well, anyway, I been a regular customer here awhile, it's handy, and I'll come by at night sometimes, not have to take time next morning get the tank filled, so I knew Harry. Casual like, you know. Last Saturday night, we was just starting off on this fishing trip, see, up on the Rogue—three of us in my car—I give you their names, you want—and we were going to drive all night, spell each other. We got started late, it must've been about a quarter to eleven I pulled in here, to get her filled up."

"Oh," said Maddox. "And how did Harry act?"

"Same as usual—just natural, there wasn't nothing different or queer. Only there was another car here then. Not getting the tank filled or anything, I mean—it was just sitting over there, with its lights off, down from where Harry's car was parked. But the station lights were on, and I just noticed it. There was somebody sitting in it too, behind the wheel."

"Oh, really," said Maddox. "Did you get any kind of look at him? Or her?"

"Nope," said Lombardi. "Coulda been a blue baboon in the car. I just noticed it standing there. And the car I can tell you a little bit about. It was a medium-sized car, oh, Buick, Olds, something like that, about three-four years old, and a dark color. It wasn't right in the lights from the station or I could tell you what it was. But the license plate started out GVL."

Maddox looked at him. "Sure about that? You noticed the car casually, but remember the plate?"

150

"Not all of it, naturally. But I couldn't help noticing the three letters. They're my initials, see? Giovanni Vincente Lombardi. Jeez, that's a mouthful." He laughed. "Anyway, that's how come I noticed. Yes, it was a California plate. And all I thought then was, maybe it was some friend of Harry's, waiting till he shut the station, maybe they were going on to a party or something—it was Saturday night. And it might not have anything to do with—what happened to him. But I thought you'd better hear."

"Yes—thanks. You didn't ask Harry about the car?"

"Nope. We were in a hurry—anxious to get away. He filled the tank, and I pulled out. About five to eleven, that'd be."

"Well, we're interested to hear about this," said Maddox. "We may ask you to make a statement."

"Any time, any time. I liked Harry."

"You think this'll help, Sergeant?" asked Bell anxiously.

Maddox said it might. Right now, it didn't, much. Impossible, of course, to ask the D.M.V. to list all the cars in the state which had license plates starting out GVL. If they ever got a solid lead on whoever had killed Harry, that might be some more evidence. But in all probability, that close to the time Harry had been first attacked, that GVL car sitting here that night had had something to do with it.

He got back to Wilcox Street to find a major party being planned. Three or four Federal agents, a couple of sheriff's deputies, Eden and Ellis, and everybody else in being briefed. The passer, Tellman, had come apart last night and parted with a lot of information, and the Feds were now about to mount a surprise raid on the address Tellman had given them here, where the phonies were being parceled out for passing. And everybody was going along, because Tellman said there were about thirty people involved altogether.

"What the hell?" said Maddox to Brandon. He'd had things to do today. "This is the Feds' case, when it gets to arrest and charge."

Brandon looked suddenly a little remote. "Ah, hum," he said, "we're a little short of manpower locally just now—we'll be very glad of any assistance." Reading between lines, Maddox deduced that something big and secret was occupying the local Feds at the moment.

They landed in force, with a search warrant all nice and legal, on the place at eleven o'clock, and picked up thirteen surprised and outraged people, six women and seven men. None of them had had any suspicion that Tellman had been nabbed, and the phonies were just being handed out for the day's work of getting rid of them, and the nice legal tender in exchange. The renters of the apartment were a Mr. and Mrs. Cardenas, a youngish couple; the name rang a bell in the Feds' minds, and during the day they turned up pedigrees on both of them for forging government checks.

Like the con men of all types, these were essentially timid, nonviolent people, and seeing they were dropped on with the evidence in their hands, no way to lie out of it, most of them resignedly told what they knew. They were all busy the rest of the day taking statements, reciting the tedious bit about the rights, getting all the warrants through, and eventually booking them in, to be transferred to a Federal jail later to await trial. They had left a stakeout on the apartment, and during the day they picked up five more people wandering into the trap, and had them to question too. They found, at the apartment, twenty-seven thousand dollars in the queer money, and that all had to be counted before witnesses, labeled, and a receipt handed over from the local Federal agent.

Maddox came back from delivering a charge to the county jail about four o'clock to find Rodriguez and Sue Carstairs chatting with O'Neill. "Nothing to do upstairs?" he said sardonically. They had, of course, kept Sue and Daisy busy with the women prisoners.

"Just bringing me up to date. All that pretty money. I saw the boxes Brandon carried out just now. Damn, I'm out of cigarettes." O'Neill fished in his pocket for change.

"You'd better get back to work," said Maddox to Sue.

As he started upstairs he heard her say, "I'll get them for you, Johnny—" and the lever of the cigarette machine pulled. For God's sake, he thought, running errands for the man now!

It was seven o'clock before they got all the paper work done on it, the last statement taken. The operation had originated back in Kansas City, where old Pete Gunnarson's plates had fallen into the hands (for a certain consideration) of a younger and more energetic man, so they had talked with the Feds and local police back there on and off all day.

Maddox went down to the Grotto and had a meal, and went home. He felt bone-tired. That kind of day was more tiring than the legwork or anything else, because it was such deadly routine. But the Feds were pleased, Eden was pleased, they had put the passers out of circulation and hauled in the funny money, and now that was all cleared up.

And maybe something new coming up tomorrow to fill the little void. Policemen and housewives, thought Maddox sleepily—their work never done.

He had an unprecedented highball, finished rereading *Between Two Worlds*, and went to bed at ten thirty.

The phone woke him. He swore and got out of bed. Bright moonlight poured in the window; the luminous hands of the bedside clock pointed to a quarter of twelve. He felt as if he'd been asleep for hours. "Maddox," he said through a yawn.

It was Dick Brougham, and he was laughing. He said to someone off the line, "Talk about retribution! Only what they deserved. —Ivor? We thought you'd like to be in at the finish. Those break-in amateurs. We've probably caught up with all of 'em, but we're holding one right here. I just called César too."

"Hell. I'd better come." He and César and the other day men had been doing most of the work on that, of course. "How'd we get the break?"

"I'll tell you when you get here. It's priceless."

Maddox got dressed again; the Maserati started like the sweet girl she was, and he throttled her down quickly, glancing at the darkened house in front of his little rear place.

At the station, upstairs, he found Brougham and Donaldson at their desks, and sitting at George Ellis' desk a tall, broad-shouldered, grim-faced, bulldog-jawed young man who would weigh in at about two hundred, six three, and all of it sheer power. He looked about thirty-five, and he was wearing regulation Marine uniform, and he had a row of ribbons across his left breast.

"Sergeant MacDonald," said Brougham, "meet our Sergeant Maddox." Maddox offered his hand with trepidation, but MacDonald only clasped it firmly and nodded at him.

Sitting slumped at D'Arcy's desk was a disheveled-looking young man, head down, looking sullenly at the floor.

"Er—" said Maddox. "What—"

Brougham chortled happily. "Oh, such nice retribution, Ivor. We had your latest note on the amateurs. How they've apparently been casing the jobs, picking the frail senior citizens who could be knocked around a little and wouldn't put up a fight. They picked one like that tonight. A Miss Elspeth MacDonald, hillside house up on Primrose Avenue.

Miss MacDonald lives alone, she's sixty-nine, and she has a weak heart."

"Might have killed her," said MacDonald. "Damn punks."

"Exactly. But Ivor, what the punks didn't know was that Miss MacDonald's nephew was visiting her. He's just home on leave from Vietnam, and family feeling, you know—"

"Oh," said Maddox. He started to laugh. "I see. What happened?"

"Heard 'em break in," said the sergeant economically. "Went to see. With my side arm out. Hadn't gone to bed yet. Three of 'em. No odds, but they ran fast. I collared that one, knocked him out. Other two ran. I got one. Give you odds—body shot somewhere. But they got away. Heard a car. Souped-up job, four-cylinder—Triumph, something like that. Blood on the sidewalk, way they ran. Enough to say he'd want a medic."

"I told you, priceless," said Brougham. "Just retribution. After knocking the senior citizens around."

"Very gratifying," agreed Maddox.

"Punks," said the sergeant. "Might have scared the old lady into fits. Thought you were supposed to be good, here —that kind loose."

"We do occasionally welcome a little help," said Maddox. He went over to the punk. The phone rang and Brougham picked it up.

"So, let's hear your name." The punk had a nice black eye just beginning to color, and by his looks— Maddox reached and lifted his right arm. He was wearing dark slacks and a short-sleeved white shirt, and on his upper wrist was the tattoo, the coiled snake and *Kenny.* "Well, Kenny," said Maddox, pleased, "you missed on the Ryan place today, so you picked another. Your mistake."

"I'm not saying anything," said Kenny defiantly.

155

"Ivor? That was Hollywood Receiving. They're holding two men for us—one fetched the other in with a bullet wound in the upper back just now."

"Hah," said MacDonald, and nodded once. "Said a body shot. Thought so."

"How gratifying indeed," said Maddox. Rodriguez came in and demanded to know chapter and verse. They all told him, MacDonald sitting like a statue, arms folded.

"God bless the Marines," said Rodriguez. "I'll see what I can get out of this one—you go fetch the others in, Ivor."

But at Hollywood Receiving, they told Maddox he wasn't taking the wounded man anywhere. "Bleeding like a stuck pig," said the doctor inelegantly, swinging his stethoscope round on one finger. "We've got plasma going now. You can have his effects, and we've got a couple of interns keeping an eye on the other one for you. Take him, take him, Sergeant—interns I can't spare in Emergency."

"Yes, Dr.—"

"Edmunds."

"Yes, Doctor." This was the Emergency Ward he'd looked around before, that morning. They were standing here just inside the ambulance entrance. The arc lights, and the light from the emergency examining room here, spilled a pool of light directly out there, but beyond the twenty-foot circle of light it was dark. As he'd suspected, looking at it by daylight. A week ago Sunday night, Dr. Charles Grantby vanishing away into that dark out there. And then? "You're the new supervisor here, Doctor?"

"I am. And just what happened to my predecessor? Have you got anything on it at all?"

"Nothing," said Maddox dismally. "Bricks without straw. Maybe a flying saucer picked him up."

"I knew him," said Edmunds. "Last man in the world to go off the rails any way. Very stable man."

"We've heard," said Maddox. "I've worked out how he could have gone—" He gestured out at the dark—"But as to why or where, that's just a mystery."

"Well, I hope to God you find out. Not so many competent, experienced physicians around we can afford to lose any," said Edmunds.

"I believe you. Where are you holding my boy?"

"In the dispensary. Go take him away. Oh-oh," said Edmunds. "Here we go." A shrieking ambulance came up the driveway, reversed and turned neatly, and backed up into the circle of light. Maddox went down the hall to the dispensary and found two interns keeping grim eyes on a young man. He was about twenty-two, and he had sandy hair, a weak chin, and light-blue eyes. They hadn't had a description on this one. Maddox took charge of him, and just as a precaution put the cuffs on him for the ride back to the station.

"Hey," he said, "hey, I'm not a criminal—you can't—"

"You are now, buddy boy," said Maddox, and stuffed him in the Maserati.

Back at the station, with the big Marine gone home after making a statement, it appeared that these two punks at least retained some human emotions. When Maddox led his capture in, the tattooed one said anxiously, "Jerry, how's Al? Did he get it bad?"

"They're giving him a transfusion or something. He was bleeding like hell," said Jerry glumly.

"Jerry and Al and Kenny," said Maddox. "We're very glad to meet you boys. Would you like to give us some additional names?"

"I got nothing out of him," said Rodriguez. "Maybe now he knows his pals are in the same boat—"

"Oh, hell," said Kenny miserably, "it all went wrong, didn't it, Jer? That damn one-man army—how could we know there was anybody there but the old lady? I guess we'd better tell them, Jer. Because—"

"Yeah, I guess so. That it was just—" They looked at each other sadly.

"That it was just what?" Maddox sat down and lit a cigarette. "Let's hear it by all means. All of it. Whatever."

"For God's sake, not before you've said the little piece about rights, or the court'll throw it out," said Brougham.

"I'd forgotten the roadblocks these days. So, hold it." He recited the little piece, and the two punks looked at each other again.

"Oh, what the hell?" said Jerry despondently. "They've got us. We might as well tell them how it was, get off the hook." He turned to Maddox. "It wasn't real, see. We weren't really doing burglaries, it was this initiation bit. For this club on the U.C.L.A. campus. We all go to U.C.L.A."

"Not real?" said Maddox.

"That's it. It was what we had to do, get initiated into this club. It was strictly a gag. It's a private club, not a frat, that's not so big any more, you know—just a private club, a—uh—social club. You know. And to get let into it, Ken and Al and I had to pull off three break-ins and get away with the stuff. Show it to prove we did. See? That's all."

"That's all." Rodriguez put out his cigarette. "An initiation."

"Yeah, yeah. God, I hope Al's going to be all right," said the other one. "We tried to plan it out so nobody'd get hurt, we—"

"Nobody get hurt," said Maddox. "You beat up old Mr. Vedder."

"What? Oh, I meant us," said Kenny. "We never thought an old guy like that'd put up any fight, but when he did—well, I didn't mean to *hurt* him, just, you know, keep him quiet. We weren't really stealing the stuff. It wasn't—and,

158

my God, Mrs. Ryan's *always* out all afternoon, she's a friend of my mother's and I knew that—of all the lousy luck! She has to come back just as we're— So we still hadn't done the three, and I thought of old Miss MacDonald, she lives just down the street from us, and how the hell could I know she had that damn one-man army—"

"I wonder if we don't make it now," said Jerry. "On account of getting dropped on. But anyway, you guys can see it wasn't real. We were going to give the stuff back. Ken really jumped on Al when he found out he'd hocked some of it when he got strapped, but we were going to get it back."

"It wasn't real," said Rodriguez gently. "You understand, Ivor?"

And Brougham said, "My God. A cop hears everything."

"It wasn't real," said Maddox. "The little ivory-tower punks will find out just how real."

"What do you mean? We were going to—" Jerry's ingratiating smile faded.

"God give me strength," said Maddox. "You didn't think there was anything wrong about pulling the break-ins as an initiation stunt. That I can believe, too many of you being what you are these days. But whatever, my buddy boys, you did it. You knocked around the senior citizens, you stole the loot and kept it, you threatened the deaf old widow, you banged Mrs. Ryan on the head. And when retribution catches up to you in the person of the one-man army—and thank God we've still got some like that on our side—you tell us it wasn't real. It's real so far as we're concerned. You're all going to be charged with robbery with violence, threatening bodily harm, assault, and breaking and entering. I hope very much that with the right kind of judge you might all go up for a one to three."

"What?" They stared at him dumbfounded. "*Us?*" said

159

Jerry. "But we told you how it was—we didn't mean—"

"But you did. Whatever your motives," said Maddox.

"But we're just college kids, we—"

"¡Santa Maria!" said Rodriguez wearily.

"College kids!" said Maddox in open contempt. "How old are you? Old enough to be called men, if you had any such attributes. I don't give a damn who you are, as far as I'm concerned and as far as the law is concerned you're a bunch of punks who've pulled the break-ins and burglaries. I'd have a good guess that the extracurricular campus club will be put out of commission for good. I hope. We haven't got quite that tolerant yet. You two will now be ferried down to the county jail for the night, and warrants for your arrest will come through tomorrow. You'll attend a line-up probably both tomorrow and Sunday, so your victims can identify you, and you'll be arraigned some time next week."

"You can't *do* that—"

"You will really be surprised," said Maddox, "what we can do, my little clubmen."

And when they had seen them handed over to the uniformed men for ferrying downtown, he said to Rodriguez, "But what is going to happen to the country, César? When? They didn't see anything wrong in the initiation bit—"

"Only hope," said Rodriguez, "as you said—not representative."

Maddox went home to bed at two o'clock.

And Saturday was supposed to be his day off, but he came in to help out Rodriguez and Feinman on getting the statements, typing up the reports, all the tedious routine on that one cleared up. They couldn't do anything immediately about the campus club, with schools and colleges out of session; but summer school would be getting under way soon, some personnel there to talk to.

In the midst of the paperwork they got, inevitably, the parents. Of Jerry White, Kenny Chester, Al Adler. Chester Senior was a stockbroker downtown, and he was the only one who blustered at them. There was usually one parent like that. If not more. Luckily, of course, they were not dealing with minors here. Kenny and Jerry were twenty-two, Al twenty-one. Kids! thought Maddox. Even *thinking* of themselves as— Something wrong with a society that—

The Adlers were just astonished, grieved, and stunned. Their Alfred. Chester blustered and called names and stormed off to get a lawyer. And the little thin middle-aged woman with white hair and a shabby dress, who was Jerry White's mother, sat in D'Arcy's desk chair and wept so bitterly that Maddox went away to fetch Sue.

"A sacrifice," she wept openly to them, "to send him to college. I wanted him to have a good education. His father would have wanted it. I saved every penny I could, all the while since John died—never touched the insurance, it was only twenty-five hundred, but something—and I put by every cent I could, never any new clothes or movies or—so he could go to college—and now—and now—"

Sue's eyes met Maddox's over the thin heaving shoulders. They were both wishing that Jerry White was here, to listen to that. But would it have reached him, touched him at all? They could wonder.

D'Arcy missed some of that. He was back at the routine today, the legwork. He had been told by the clerk at the Parks and Recreation office that Walter Ericson had intended to be back home from vacation on Saturday, and he tried Ericson's Burbank address as early as eleven o'clock. Ericson was there, still unloading the trunk of his car, two gangling teen-age boys carrying the bags into the house.

161

D'Arcy introduced himself and said his piece about the gun, the Hi-Standard.

"Oh," said Ericson. "Oh." He was a thin little man with hollow cheeks and graying hair. "Well, I did. I bought that gun—at least, a gun—from Tronowsky. I wanted a gun for protection, the crime rate going up so, and my wife home alone sometimes. Yes, I bought a twenty-two from Tronowsky. But well, I happen to know a man on our police force here, Bill Lewis, and when I mentioned it to him he said a twenty-two's no kind of gun to have, you want a heavier one, and I should take lessons how to use it. So I did. I got a Police Positive thirty-eight, and both my wife and I went to take a course. But the *police* asking—I don't underst——"

"What about the twenty-two?" asked D'Arcy. "Did you sell it?" Musical chairs. The .22 had had more owners than use since it had been manufactured. Doubtless, here was the dead end. It had been stolen, or he had advertised in the classified and had no idea who—

"Oh, I sold it to Lloyd," said Ericson. "That was why I was surprised. At your asking. I suppose he must have got rid of it since, because he wouldn't be mixed up in any *crime*. He's got his own business—air conditioning and heating—in Hollywood. He happened to mention he wanted a twenty-two for his son, just after I'd bought the other gun, and he gave me ten dollars for the twenty-two."

"Lloyd?" said D'Arcy. Musical chairs.

Ericson gestured. "Next door. Mr. George Lloyd. Very nice neighbor. You could ask him, of course."

D'Arcy swung and looked. In the yard next door, a paunchy bald man was wrestling with a power mower, looking hot and angry. He had stripped to a pair of polka-dotted shorts, and there was a mat of curly gray hair on his chest.

D'Arcy went around the hedge between the yards and again introduced himself, said his piece. Lloyd was just as happy to have an excuse to stop work.

"That twenty-two," he said, mopping his forehead. "Well, I'll be damned—police asking. You like some lemonade, or maybe something stronger? Papers say the heat wave's broken, but it's still damn hot. I'll get my wife to make some lemonade. *Marcia!* What you want to know about it? I've never met a detective before. Marcia, you want to make some lemonade or something?"

D'Arcy explained. Tracing the gun. Used in a crime. "Oh," said Lloyd. "Well, I haven't got it any more, of course." D'Arcy said they knew that. "Oh, sure. Sure, if you've got it. I'll be damned. I got it," said Lloyd, looking rueful, "for my kid. When Ericson mentioned having it. Damn it, I thought maybe it'd make a man of him—he was fourteen then—reading, reading all the time, not interested in baseball, football, any sports. I thought maybe a gun—if I taught him how to use it, go up in the woods together, and like that—but we can't all be alike, I guess. He wasn't interested in that, either. Wants to be an archaeologist, of all the offbeat— Reading all the time. Well, we come all all sorts. The wife says—and I don't like to think I'm not broad-minded, whatever the kid wants to do—"

"The gun," said D'Arcy.

"Oh, sure. It knocked around, the kid not interested, until about, maybe, last January—February. Yeah. The wife was at me to get a new suit, and I finally did. About then. I always go to the same place, it's not far off my business. I've been going there years for my suits. They've got a good alterations tailor. Kingman Brothers, on La Brea. And while I was trying on suits that time, the salesman and I were talking, and I says—all casual, you know—about the crime rate going up, and he says yes, he's been thinking about buying a gun, and I says I got one he could have cheap, and the upshot was he gave me ten bucks for it."

"Kingman Brothers. La Brea. You wouldn't know his name? Didn't get a receipt?" asked D'Arcy. Round and round. But coming closer. Yes? January, February.

But for God's sake, a clerk in a men's clothing store?

"No, I don't," said Lloyd, "but he's still there. He's been there for years—sold me a lot of suits. I was in just the other day to get a couple new shirts, and he's there. A little fellow about five five, kind of fat, not much hair, and horn-rimmed glasses. In the fifties, I guess. This gun showed up in *police* business— Well, I don't suppose *he'd* have anything to do with it, could be he sold it to somebody or had it stolen. Tell *me* the heat wave's broken—it is *hot*." He mopped his forehead.

D'Arcy, faithfully doing the legwork—it was only turned noon—drove back to Hollywood, out La Brea, and found Kingman Brothers Men's Wear Store. A rather quietly classy place, tailoring offered, the good atmosphere, carpet and air conditioning. When D'Arcy came in, two clerks were in evidence. A tall youngish man in a dark suit, smooth dark hair, and an older man, about five five, thinning gray hair, horn-rimmed glasses, a little paunch. He was wearing a dark gray suit, not so well-tailored.

"Can I help you, sir?" The younger man surged forward with a warm smile.

"Well, maybe," said D'Arcy. The older man had turned and was making for the back room, past a partition there. D'Arcy brought out his badge. "The other clerk there—can you tell me his name?"

The young man looked astonished and annoyed. "You're *police*? But what—what do you want?"

164

"I want to talk to that clerk," said D'Arcy. "What's his name?"

"Mr. *Meeker?* Mr. Meeker's been with us a long time— a very reliable— What on earth do you want with *Henry Meeker? Police?* I'm the manager here, and I—"

eleven

Maddox had just got back from lunch and was thinking of taking the rest of the day off as he was supposed to be doing, when D'Arcy came in shepherding a little man ahead of him. He sat the little man down beside his desk and beckoned Maddox and Rodriguez up to the end of the room.

"I think we've got there, on Sylvia," he said. "Though why, God only knows." He brought them up to date on the saga of the gun. "It was only four, five months ago when Meeker bought it from Lloyd, and the minute I heard the name— I saw a lot of the true believers in that damn Community of Light or whatever, and this Mrs. Meeker was one of 'em. So—"

"What have you got out of him?" asked Maddox interestedly.

"Not much. I was afraid to try. No witness, and— When I got so far, I shut up," said D'Arcy. "I asked him his name and address, and that told me it was the same Meeker— Harvard Avenue. I asked him if he owned a gun and he said no, and I asked him if he had ever owned a gun and he said no, and I asked him what had happened to the twenty-two he bought from George Lloyd and he turned white as a ghost and didn't say anything. So I did the same. Said nothing, that is. Well, I asked him very politely if he'd mind coming in with me for some routine questions, and he came. In silence."

"Yes, he looks promising," said Maddox. "But what kind of reason— Well, maybe we'll hear. Let's start work on him."

"For God's sake, don't forget to warn him," said Rodriguez.

"I won't, I won't." They led the silent Henry Meeker down to an interrogation room and Maddox opened proceedings by introducing himself and Rodriguez. "Now I am bound to tell you, Mr. Meeker—" and he recited the required piece. "Do you want to call a lawyer, Mr. Meeker?"

"I don't see that I need one," said Meeker in a mild voice. "No, that's all right."

"So. You bought a Hi-Standard Sentinel twenty-two revolver from George Lloyd, a customer at the store where you work, about the end of January. You—"

"How do you know that?" asked Meeker.

"Mr. Lloyd told us so," said D'Arcy.

"But—" Meeker's brow wrinkled.

"It was the gun, Mr. Meeker, that killed Mrs. Sylvia Brown. And ballistics told us that," said Maddox.

"Mrs.— Oh yes, I remember, it said in the papers that her real name— Sylvia Brown. But I don't understand," said Meeker. "How could you know—for quite certain—which gun did it?"

"The lab, Mr. Meeker. The ballistics tests told us."

"I don't know much about science. I didn't know—"

"Well, it was. And the gun seems to have been in your possession rather recently. Have you anything to tell us about that? Your wife was one of the regular attendants at the Community Circle of Light, wasn't she?"

Meeker's small mouth tightened and relaxed. "Now just a minute, just a minute here," he said fussily. "I don't see how anyone could possibly tell which gun did a thing. How?

Guns are guns. Oh, different sizes, and the size of bullet would tell the size of the gun, but I do not see how—"

They looked at him in surprise. A good many citizens did read the true-police magazines, and detective novels. Evidently Henry Meeker didn't. "Mr. Meeker," said Maddox, "the bullet from a gun is nearly as good as a fingerprint. Not quite, but very useful. In most cases the laboratory technicians can tell, by examining it microscopically, the kind of gun that fired it. And when they have both a gun and a bullet, they can always say yes, the bullet was fired by this gun, or no, it wasn't."

"*How?*" asked Meeker suspiciously.

"Most gun barrels are striated inside—they leave distinctive rifling marks on the bullets as they leave the gun. What are called lands and grooves. And one gun will put the same marks on every bullet it fires. So that's how we know, Mr. Meeker. The gun which was tossed away the other day, maybe because somebody knew it was the gun used on Sylvia Brown, fell into our hands, and it was the gun you bought from Mr. Lloyd in late January."

"How do you know *that?*" asked Meeker. And he didn't say it defiantly, or cunningly, but as if he really wanted to know. Maddox considered him. Mr. Henry Meeker, he decided, was one of those completely logical people who had to be shown a thing step by step.

"The gun was registered by its first owner," he told Meeker, "back in nineteen fifty."

"That's a long time ago. Registered? I'm not familiar with—"

"Registered with the police by its serial number. We started out with the original owner, and found out who had had the gun next, and so on. It had changed hands several times, but now we find that you acquired it last January, not very long ago, and also that you have a connection with

Mrs. Sylvia Brown. That's why you're here, Mr. Meeker."

"I was not connected with that—that faker," said Meeker emphatically. "I didn't know all that. How you could tell about the gun. I had no idea of that. I see. If I'd just kept the gun— Well." He drew a long breath. "I had certainly hoped no one would ever find out—but I still consider that I just destroyed evil. But it seems very, very strange to think that I have killed someone. Even her." His lip quivered; he took off his glasses and began to clean them with his handkerchief. "It was just, I'd taken all I could take. I was feeling *desperate*. You don't know. That idiotic Peebles woman had taken Mabel there first, and before I knew it she was obsessed with that woman. That faker. And it was blasphemous too. I've always been a churchgoer, and I tried to tell Mabel, but— We—you see, gentlemen, we lost our own little girl many years ago—she was only nine. And this—this woman had Mabel convinced she was calling up Annie from the dead—blasphemous! The dead are at rest, I do *not* believe that anyone— And aside from that, the money. Mabel was possessed—as if she were possessed of the devil, I swear. She wouldn't listen to a thing I said. I don't make a great deal of money—a modest living, no more, and these days with prices going up— She was spending money right and left on—on what she called private sittings—with this woman so she could imagine she was getting messages from Annie— Blasphemous! She had spent half of our entire savings before I discovered she was making withdrawals. I was *horrified*. I tried to talk to her, Mabel was always a sensible woman, but honestly, gentlemen, it was just as if—as if she'd got addicted to dope of some sort. All I got was this—this blasphemous and ridiculous *twaddle*," said Meeker in a suddenly loud voice, sounding unbearably frustrated. "Time and again—oh, Henry, if you'd only come and hear, have faith. And I had to give her money for the house, even after I had taken her name off the joint account—and time after time, she spent it on that woman and asked for more. I was at the end of my patience. The *end.*" Hs stopped, and then added hurriedly, "I—I really hadn't any such idea in my mind when I bought that gun. That was before I ever heard of the woman. And I do wish I had known all that—about the scientific examinations—or I'd never have thrown it away, and then you'd never have found out about it."

"You went to see Mrs. Brown last Sunday?" asked Maddox. "You understand what you're telling us, Mr. Meeker?"

"Yes, sir, I understand." Meeker looked gray and tired suddenly. "It doesn't seem to matter that you've found out. I'm nearly sixty years old, gentlemen, and at the rate the economy is going, all this inflation, I expect I'll be just as comfortable in prison as out. And I've quite lost patience or— really—any feeling for Mabel, when she could be so silly. Half of my life savings— I always tried to put by as I could, though I've never earned much. And then there were all the other people that woman was victimizing too, probably some who didn't have even as much as Mabel and I—to start with. Other silly women like Mabel, whose husbands— It was damnable, *damnable*, and I'm not a swearing man." His voice was shaking. "I'd never thought that I'd be capable of such a thing—a terrible thing, another person—but what she was doing, not only the blasphemy but—but bloodsucking the money out of all those silly sentimental fools— Yes, I went there. Mabel was out somewhere. I—we'd got out of the habit of talking much to each other, since— And I did. I meant to beg the woman—I was ready to do that!—to stop Mabel coming. Was I such a fool, to think she *would?* Any of the idiots she had her claws in—"

"And you took the gun with you," said D'Arcy.

"I did. So quite possibly I meant to kill her all the time," said Meeker. "Subconsciously, as they say. But I thought of

170

it—if I thought at all—like—like scotching a snake. Poisoning all those people—their minds—and robbing them too. Damnable. I didn't even know that she'd be alone, I could always come back—but she was. She let me in, and that room—with that silly crystal ball—the same idiotic sentimental talk I got from Mabel, if I could just have faith and believe—and the first thing I knew, I had done it. I brought the gun out and did it. And all I felt at the time was, Good riddance." Meeker sighed, leaning back in the chair. "That was really all. And I expect that's all you want to know. Oh, the reason I threw the gun away wasn't what you said. I never dreamed it could be scientifically connected with the—the death. No, I was afraid Mabel might come across it and suspect it had been me. I hadn't anywhere to hide it. I'd kept it at the back of my handkerchief drawer."

"Your wife didn't know you had it?"

"Indeed no. Women shouldn't have anything to do with guns. Of course I didn't know much about them myself, I got a book out of the library that showed me how to load it."

"Well," said Maddox, "we'd like you to sign a statement, Mr. Meeker."

"Yes. Anything. It doesn't matter." Meeker looked suddenly exhausted.

They were all nervous about voluntary confessions these days; they tied it up as tight as they could, with Eden as an additional witness and Daisy Hoffman taking it down, and they got Meeker to read it and initial each page and sign it. The application for the warrant had gone through, and about three thirty they took him downtown and booked him in.

"And in a way," said D'Arcy, "you can sympathize with the poor devil. These silly women."

"Yes," said Maddox. "Oh, yes. As you say. There is something there, D'Arcy—in the parapsychology, newest name for it. But the Sylvias are a detriment to the honest researchers. Even when the Sylvias are honest too—just wishful thinking."

D'Arcy was looking through his negative file at nine o'clock when the phone rang. "Is it Boniface?" asked Sheila. "I've got a copy of the Oxford Dictionary of English Christian Names."

"No, it's not. Why the hell you—"

"Gustavus?"

"No," said D'Arcy. "Look—"

"Um. Jedidiah?"

"*No*. And I'm not playing Rumpelstiltskin with you," said D'Arcy firmly. "I'll see you tomorrow night."

"I'll bet it's Marmaduke."

D'Arcy slammed down the phone. That damned persistent female—

Overnight, a squad car on tour had picked up a handful of juveniles climbing over the fence of the schoolyard at Bancroft Junior High, investigated, and discovered a king-sized job of vandalism in the school offices, a side window broken in. They had fetched the juveniles in and Brougham had subsequently sent them down to Juvenile Hall, having got names out of one of them but no addresses. He had left notes on it on Maddox's desk and Maddox was just glancing through them at eight ten on Sunday morning when he got an outside call.

"Sergeant Maddox?" The heavy male voice was abrupt and frightened. "Walsh here. Listen, we just found out Don never came home last night."

"He's safe enough, Mr. Walsh," said Maddox dryly. "Down at Juvenile Hall. Don, the Schultz boy, Rod Gorman, and a couple of other kids were picked up last night after committing some rather wholesale vandalism at a public school. A few cars left on the street outside had windows broken, et cetera, and we can assume they did that too. Also that it isn't the first time."

"*What?*" said Walsh. He sounded suddenly very angry. "*Don*—up to stuff like that? I swear to God— For God's sake, shut up, woman!"—off the phone. "So, all right, that's the best place for him. Can I come see you? I'd like to—"

"Any time," said Maddox. He felt sorry for Walsh: rough-hewn citizen, the honest man who'd tried what he thought was his best. How many more like him, getting the rude shocks from the younger generation? He thought about Jerry White's mother and felt tired.

But Mike Walsh had recovered from any shock and grief he had felt when he showed up at the station an hour later. Again he was dressed uncomfortably in suit and white shirt and tie, looking somehow too big for his clothes. "I went down there to see the kid," he said, sitting down. "They didn't want to let me in—Sunday—damn red tape. *My* kid, a place like that. Pulling senseless little-kid stuff like that. Breaking windows— His ma's soft on him, and I guess I took too much for granted. I dunno what you think, but me, I say it's just Satan finding work for idle hands. If the damn kids had chores to do, outside jobs keep 'em busy, they wouldn't be gettin' into trouble like they do. What'll they do to him?"

"Not much," said Maddox. "It's the first time any of them has been picked up on anything, and none of them is over seventeen. They'll be put on probation to their parents, a year. That's it."

Walsh looked astonished and then he said bluntly, "And that's a reason too, Sergeant. Coddling the kids. Just because they're kids. Kids! Listen, my dad went to work at twelve years old, full time, and by the time he was eighteen he was married and had a kid. *And* he never did any griping, on account he never had a chance to go to college either.

He worked hard and saved his money and he raised six kids and finally got his own farm. And none o' the kids ever got in any police trouble either. And goddamn it, I'd be back on that farm this minute, and a hell of a lot better for Don if I'd stayed there, but farming these days—unless you go in for the government subsidies, *which* I don't hold with— That's all they'll do to 'em? This probation?"

"That's about it."

Walsh got up, big and purposeful. "Then I got a little work to do."

"What?" asked Maddox.

"I'm goin' to find out whose cars got damaged, other private property. Don't suppose the school'd let me do nothing there. Schools just as bad, coddling 'em. But I'll find out about the cars, and by God that kid of mine's goin' to get what job he can, mowin' lawns or whatever, and he's goin' to earn the money to pay for the damage he done. And by God I'll see he sticks to it till he does. So maybe he'll think twice before doin' a damn-fool thing like that again."

"And more power to you," said Maddox. "A step in the right direction." But he wondered if it wasn't too late, with Don Walsh.

At any rate, now they knew what Don had had on his mind. Not Harry Arthur. Well, that had been a little far out; but now they had lost even that lead on Arthur. Don and his pals had, probably, been engaged on the vandalism last Saturday night too—not homicide.

Which left them nowhere to go on Arthur. Well, the GVL car. Yes? Look at all the plates on the cars owned by all Harry's friends and acquaintances—everybody in that contractor's crew he had worked with? It was conceivable that X had been one of them—that whatever quarrel had blown up had been just that day, so nobody had heard about it.

O'Neill rang him and said he had visitors. "Mrs. Meeker and Madame Cecilia. Very agitated and earnest."

"Oh, hell and damnation," said Maddox. "No. Not this soon after breakfast. Hang on." He went across the hall; Daisy was there. "If you want to save my sanity, go and administer a very little soothing syrup to these females. We really can't put up with them coming here. It's not her fault Henry Meeker came to the end of his patience—or is it—but—" Daisy laughed and said she'd get rid of them.

There had been a new call—a suicide in a motel over on Vine—and Rodriguez and Feinman were out on that. Maddox reflected that Thorsen would be coming up for arraignment tomorrow: the college boys sometime this week, which meant time out to appear in court. And probably by then they'd have a couple of new ones to work. Well, one down, two to go. And Sunday or no, he ought to do a little work: get the list of names from that contractor, and there'd be somebody at the D.M.V. office up in Sacramento.

He went out to the coffee machine in the hall and found Sue Carstairs emptying a paper tube of sugar into a paper cup of black coffee. "How anybody can drink sugar in coffee," she said. "But Johnny—"

Running errands for that damn— "You are not paid the reasonable salary," said Maddox, irritated, "for waiting on the desk sergeant. What the hell's got into you? Let him get his own damn coffee on his break."

"And just what has got into you," said Sue coldly, "I'd like to know. As a matter of *fact*, it just so happens—*which* I am aware you didn't know, and maybe you'll have the decent manners to apologize though I doubt it—as a matter of fact, they've only put him on a desk job for a while because he got very badly shot up last year by a bank robber and there are still a lot of bullet fragments in his left ankle and they're letting him take it easy until they find out if he'll be fit for active duty again. I know you didn't know. He doesn't like— Daisy only told me in c——"

"Well, I didn't know, damn it—all *right*," said Maddox, annoyed. "He goes around telling people in confidence, I suppose. Aunt Daisy—"

"Just *as* it happens," said Sue coldly, "he's called her that for a long time. He lived next door to them before her husband was killed, and as a matter of fact it was because he admired Sergeant Hoffman that he joined the force. And—"

"Well, for the love of God," said Maddox exasperatedly, "does he have to make a secret of it?"

"Nobody's making a secret of anything. You're simply impossible lately, Ivor," said Sue crossly, "and damn it, now this coffee's cold and I'll have to get another cup. Honestly, Ivor! . . . Daisy, have you got any more sugar?"

Maddox got his coffee and took it back to his desk. Females! he thought. And if it wasn't typical of that damn O'Neill to parade his wounds of honor and garner the womanly sympathy—while posing as a great martyr—

Hell. Do a little work, Sunday or not. He swallowed half of the coffee too hot, scalding his throat, and went out. It was only about eighty-eight today. Downstairs, O'Neill was sipping coffee, looking at the latest issue of *Guns and Ammo*, and softly whistling "The Croppy Boy" between his teeth.

Now Maddox thought, O'Neill did seem to favor his left leg a little. The damned martyr, basking in the feminine sympathy—

He found the contractor home, and got a list of the crew. He added to it the names of those of Harry's friends he'd talked to, and for good measure Rex Slaney and Harry's brother-in-law Bill Pollock. You never did know. He came back to the office and teletyped the list up to the D.M.V.

in Sacramento. What license plates were registered to these names, please? A little reverse twist for the D.M.V., usually asked to match names to license plates.

By then it was noon, and Rodriguez back typing a report on the suicide, which looked like a straightforward suicide. Maddox and Feinman went out to the Grotto for lunch, and Feinman talked about Scriptural prophecies. "I mean, Ivor, when you see all that's going on these days—and who's in a better place to see it than us, for God's sake?—the kids with no moral principles at all, and a lot of adults no better or even worse—the wife-swapping parties and the dope and all —look at that bunch in here the other day, that poor damn-fool kid that didn't know from nothing, on the acid and killing himself and the other people— Well, you read the seventh book of Daniel, all I can say is, it sounds very damn likely that we're right in the middle of what he predicted. Spiritual wickedness in high places and all. And—"

Maddox said he could be right, adding to the waitress that he'd have a Scotch and water and the steak sandwich.

"Right! I'll tell you, you can't get away from it," said Feinman. "The rabbi said to me—"

"Just the man I want to see," said Lieutenant Eden, pulling up the chair alongside Maddox. "Listen, Ivor—now I've got the damn Feds off my back, and those counterfeiters put away, I've had a chance to catch up on the reports. What, for God's sake, *about* this doctor? Grantby? Haven't you got anything on it at all?"

"Don't ride me," said Maddox. "What is there to get? We talked to everybody. We looked. We've got the fliers out, what else can we do? I *think* he was spirited away. I *think*. The stable, reliable man. Barring a genuine case of amnesia, which is very rare. But where does that take us? He hadn't had any trouble with anybody lately. Hadn't had any upsets in his personal life. Nothing shows—nothing. And if he's been murdered, where's the body and why hasn't it showed? We've been *on* it. Bricks without straw."

"And the Arthur—"

"Same thing there. I've got a query going—we got a little something new on that yesterday—but it's long odds it'll turn into a lead. Sometimes we get the tough ones, that's all."

"I didn't mean to ride you," said Eden, "exactly. I know we do. But the press has been sounding a little hostile—police admit no clue found yet—and that interview the other day with that awful woman, that daughter of Grantby's—in the *Times*—"

Maddox grinned without humor. "I think Mrs. Pierce has lost some of her civilian arrogance since, Lieutenant. I hope."

Eden glanced sideways at him. "I heard something about that from Johnny. And far be it from me to—um—say I didn't approve, Ivor, but that sort of business—we do have to be so damn careful—can backfire. The arrogant self-righteous cops."

"I tell you, Lieutenant," said Maddox, "that I know too, but—like Mr. Meeker—sometimes I come to the end of my patience."

"Don't we all," said Eden with a sigh.

The waitress for that table thought they all looked awfully serious. She liked the men from the Wilcox Street precinct coming in; it was interesting, to hear them talk and all. She worried about Lieutenant Eden when he looked dyspeptic, and she worried about D'Arcy because he looked underweight, and inevitably she was drawn to Maddox because of whatever mysterious attribute drew the females. Today, she thought they must have a bad case to worry about, and she made Maddox's drink and Eden's and put in an extra half jigger, when Eddy wasn't looking. Nobody would know.

Cops had a tough job, any way you looked at it, and any little thing she could do to help them—

She had waited on all of them here hundreds of times, noticing them, thinking about them, sympathizing with their tough job, and they had left her tips, seeing her vaguely, the pair of hands bringing them food and drink. None of them knew her name, which was Naomi Bishop, and very likely never would. But every night when she said her prayers, after she'd asked protection for her mother and sister and her boy in the army, she asked God to bless the cops at Wilcox Street, the good men doing the dirty thankless job.

At two forty a new call came in, and Maddox and Rodriguez went out on it.

"And I'd never have known until tomorrow if I hadn't come in to finish up that engraving job," raged the owner. "My God, even the safe. I had all Mrs. Osterdank's diamonds in for cleaning. My God, the insurance, but—"

Dabney and Rowan came with the mobile lab and looked around and scattered powder. And Maddox said to Rodriguez, "Are you thinking what I'm thinking?"

"*Tal vez,*" said Rodriguez. "A slick job. Yes. No prints. The safe blown nice and clean. Professional. Same like that other jewelry store on Sunset. When we come to make a list, probably only the most salable, valuable stuff gone. I'd lay odds."

"The same professional?" said Maddox. "Maybe?"

"Very possibly," agreed Rodriguez.

"And maybe hitting another jewelry store tomorrow night or next week?"

"I won't bet with you."

"Yes. How very nice," said Maddox. "We go look at m.o.'s. As on the first one."

"And that new shipment just in," moaned the owner. "The

eighteen-karat stuff from Italy and— My God, what the hell am I going to say to Mr. Osterdank?"

They left the lab men to do what they could on it, and Maddox typed the initial report. He had just rolled the last triplicate sheet out of the typewriter when a little disturbance broke out in the hall, and he and D'Arcy went out to see what it was. Rodriguez and Feinman were pawing through records downstairs, looking at the m.o.'s.

Two uniformed men were having a little wrestling match with a big young fellow out there. "You just calm down," panted Carmichael. "What the hell, you said you wanted to see a detective, lay a complaint—you just—"

"Beg pardon," said the civilian, suddenly standing up straight so Carmichael staggered back. "Thought you was double-talkin' me, gonna put me in the tank. These guys detectives? I ain't drunk."

He wasn't, really. He may have had a few beers, maybe a couple of shots; he wasn't drunk, but what he'd had had loosened his tongue a little. "What's this?" asked Maddox.

"Sorry, sir," said Carmichael. "It was just a brawl at a bar —out on Highland—that is, it started in the bar, what we got, but when we got there this guy and another one—an older fellow—were in the alley behind, this one had knocked the other one down—he got away, got up and ran—and we found a gun on this one, and he didn't seem very tight, he asked— Get in here, you!"

"Beg pardon," said the young man. "I'm not drunk. I'm mad. Good and. In spades. Nobody insults me and gets away with it, see? Name's O'Reilly—Pat O'Reilly. That's me. The goddamn fag propositioning *me*. Seen the guy hanging round there lately, Jimmy said so too, I asked him. Because he stood out, you know? Different from the guys drop in. Dressed to the nines, a fat old guy like that in Jimmy's

180

place, why? And he tries to proposition *me*—this dirty old fag!—and I say to him—well, never no mind what I say, but when the fuzz comes down, I tell 'em, they oughta drop on guys like that. It's against the law. Insultin' an honest working man." He leaned on Maddox's desk and looked at them earnestly.

"He had this on him," said Carmichael, putting it on the desk. It was a Colt .38.

"And I got a permit for it," said Pat O'Reilly. "All legal. I'm a trucker. I got it for protection, *and* the permit to carry it. All kosher. But that I happen to know is against the law —what they call solicit——solicitate—damn it, the goddamn fags go their own damn bars where all the same kind go, *let* 'em, but they come round the honest places like Jimmy's, ordinary guys, it's another thing. And I'm ready and willin' testify against him, you pick him up." O'Reilly banged one big fist on Maddox's desk. "Yes sir! Try to solicit——solicitate— me! And I can give you a good descrip——descrip—— I can tell you damn good what he looks like, the goddamn fag, too—reckanize him in a line-up—" It could be that O'Reilly had had a little more than a few beers, but he was rational enough: being, thought Maddox, an Irishman. "I can tell you—a fat guy about fifty, with real thick glasses, and a good tailored suit—and he's got the tip of a little finger gone, left hand—and when he ran, he got into a Buick—a maroon-colored Buick, about maybe four years old."

A faint bell rang in Maddox's mind. He thought, I saw a man like that—somewhere—just recently. Where?

twelve

All the while D'Arcy questioned O'Reilly, looked at his permit, and handed back the Colt with apologies, Maddox sat and ruminated; somebody matching that description, tip of left finger missing, heavy glasses, stout, middle-aged, good clothes—it was just on the edge of his mind, and at that it was a vague enough description. In a big city there might be—

At Bell's station that day. The customer. Bell said, a regular customer. Folson. Felton. Belton. *Bolton*. What Maddox remembered, the description fitted. But it couldn't say anything for him. Obviously not—had Bell said a stockbroker? Hanging around a cheap bar—

And there were upward of eight million people in L.A. County, and it was more than conceivable that two men could conform to the same vague description.

O'Reilly was gone. Maddox filed the report on the new burglary, went out—it was nearly the end of the day, twenty to six—and drove over to Bell's service station on Melrose. He answered Bell's questions, no, they hadn't made an arrest yet, hadn't placed that GVL plate. He said, "That customer of yours you introduced me to the other day— Bolton? You known him long?"

"What? Mr. Bolton? Oh yes, very nice feller. He's been a regular for a long time, it's on his way between his office and where he lives, he said once. Why?"

182

Maddox wondered what to ask. "You said, a broker?"

"Well, I guess he's what you'd call an adviser. At a place like that—brokerage. Knows about the stocks and bonds. It's a place out Beverly, I noticed it on account of knowing he works there, he gave me a card once. Stevens, MacDuff and Pfeiffer. Funny combination. Why?"

"Oh, I ran into somebody who knows him," said Maddox vaguely.

It added to nothing. And as to being any kind of a lead on Harry Arthur, less than nothing.

He told himself he was a fool, and grasping at straws (appropriate: bricks without) but he went back to Wilcox Street and added Bolton's name—William J.—to the list of names he'd sent the D.M.V.

Sometimes you took a chance on the longest shot.

On Monday morning D'Arcy had an appointment to do some more of the tedious routine.

Several schools had been hit by the vandals in the couple of weeks since schools had been closed, but Saturday night was the first time Bancroft Junior High had been hit. The police had called around and finally located the principal, just about to leave on his vacation. He'd have to put in a report of the extent and nature of the damage, and so of course would the police.

D'Arcy met him at nine o'clock at the entrance to the school on Willoughby Avenue. The school was locked up tight; the vandals had broken a window to get in.

"Mr. Evans? I'm D'Arcy, Wilcox Street."

"Dear me," said Evans, shaking hands, "this is deplorable. Deplorable. So much of this senseless destruction these days —no respect for property. I've just been waiting for Bancroft to get it. Every other school around— Well, well, I suppose we'd better go in and see the worst." He was a gangling thin man as tall as D'Arcy, with a shrewd face and unexpectedly humorous eyes. "In my small way, Mr. D'Arcy," he said as they went up the walk toward the wide double front doors, "I've been agitating for years for burglar alarms—proper ones—or night watchmen at public schools. With all this vandalism on the increase. Where do I get? What do I get? Silence. Bureaucracy—nobody wants to hear the still, small voice of common sense."

"I don't doubt," said D'Arcy. "Considering the cost to the taxpayers, property destroyed and so on, the cost would make up for—"

"Mr. D'Arcy," said Evans, producing a bunch of keys, "when you've lived a bit longer you'll realize one basic truth—for the taxpayers the bureaucrats don't give one tinker's dam. That's not a swear word, by the way, did you know that? I understand, a small tool formerly used by tinkers." The front door swung open and they went in to an atmosphere of dust, chalk, stale humanity and the mingled odors of an old building in long use. "It's usually the administrative offices they go for," he added, and started up to the right along the hall.

"Well, I know *that*," said D'Arcy. "About the taxpayers. Almighty God, look at the *mess*."

It was a mess all right. Satan finding work for idle hands. In the administration office, the long counter across the room had been deeply gouged with a chisel or ax, typewriters thrown on the floor, filing cases overturned, their contents strewn around and ink poured over them. In Evans' office next door, the leather of the desk chair was in shreds, white paint thrown on the carpet, more file cases ravaged, the Venetian blind torn down. The office of the girls' vice principal, next door, was even worse: there, the paint had been poured over the desk, chair, and carpet, and the carpet also slashed.

184

"Good God," said Evans plaintively, "and we're supposed to educate these savages. I know, only a few as bad as this, but—" He shook his head. "I suppose we'd better be thorough and see it all." They wandered in and out of classrooms, finding more or less damage in most—the vandals must have spent some time in here. A trail of white paint led to a door at the end of the hall, and Evans said, "Good God," again. "The basement too? Perhaps where they found the paint, though what Kowalsky would want with white paint— we'd better just see." He pulled open the unlocked door and revealed a flight of steps.

"Kowalsky?"

"Our chief maintenance supervisor here. He sees that the lawn out front is cut, and the cleaning jobs, windows and so on, and all that," said Evans vaguely. "Now the light switch is just here somewhere—ah." He pressed it, and the stairs and basement below were flooded with light. They started down. At the bottom of the stairs, the cemented basement stretched away barely: no more white paint. But Evans stood still and sniffed. "Good God, now what have they done *here?* What *is* that terrible odor? I can't tell where—"

But D'Arcy was looking, with all his nerves suddenly alert. He didn't have to ask what it was. He remembered the corpse they'd found last year in that apartment, and swallowed. There was something dead down here, and he only hoped it was an animal or a bird, but the smell—

The basement was enormous, and there were compartments and partitions: cleaning equipment, ladders, tools. D'Arcy prowled, sniffing, and presently came to another door. "What's in there?"

"The furnace. The central heating plant," said Evans. "It's off now, of course—a gas furnace. Kowalsky—"

D'Arcy opened the door. It was a big heating plant, an old installation, and in the side of the central unit was a panel about four by four feet, meant as an access to the big burners, for cleaning.

"What—" said Evans.

"You'd better not come too close, sir," said D'Arcy. "It might not be pretty." He didn't think he'd like it much himself. One thing, it was very unlikely that the rough-cast metal handle would hold prints. He took hold of it and yanked it open.

"*Oh, my God!*" said Evans. He retreated precipitately and began to retch.

And D'Arcy took one look and snapped, "Are the phones working?" Evans nodded faintly, handkerchief to his mouth, and stumbled up the stairs after him. D'Arcy got the station, told O'Neill to give him Maddox or whoever was in. "Ivor? Me. I think I've just found your missing doctor."

"Don't tell me—where?"

D'Arcy told him. "Whoever he is, he's been shut up in a metal box here, in this weather, for a little while, maybe about as long as the doctor's been gone, and you can guess— Yeah, but he's wearing a doctor's coat over gray pants, and as far as you can tell he matches the description—not very big, and— Well, we'll want the lab and so on."

"At this *school?*" said Maddox. "What the hell is he doing at a school? How did he— Yes. I'm on my way."

D'Arcy went out into the fresh air to wait. Evans had retired into the lavatory off his office.

It was, of course, a very messy thing. The ambulance that came was staffed with two interns who had known Dr. Grantby, and one of them, after one look, turned aside and was violently sick. He straightened, looking pale. "Sorry, I thought I was—all through medical, I never—"

Maddox and Rodriguez were there by then. "You recognize him?" said Maddox, and the intern shuddered.

186

"Not by his— But it's Grantby. *Grantby.* I—know—his hands," said the intern.

The lab took its photographs, and they got the body out with difficulty. It had been jammed in feet first. They laid it on a rubber sheet on the floor and the lab man took more photographs, and then they put it in the ambulance outside and took it away. Dabney and Rowan were going over the basement for surfaces that might take prints. Maddox looked around, but there were no nice obvious clues, so they went upstairs to talk to Evans.

The principal had recovered a little color, but still looked shaken. He was sitting in the ruined chair in his office, and D'Arcy and Rodriguez brought in some straight chairs from nearby classrooms. Maddox offered Evans a cigarette. "Oh dear, we're not supposed—school premises—but really I feel so— Thank you. We can use the soap dish for an ashtray."

"You understand, Mr. Evans, we have to ask you who has access to this building? Nobody brought the corpse in through a broken window. The school has been closed since when?"

"June the eleventh," said Evans. "Nobody would be setting foot here until—about the end of this week, perhaps. To prepare for summer school opening on July the fifth."

"All right. Who has keys to the school?"

"Well, I have of course. I hope you don't think I'm responsible for that." Evans managed a pale smile. "And Eric Kowalsky, and of course *he* wouldn't be responsible. We can try to reach him, by the way, he might be able to help. He's our maintenance supervisor."

"We'd like to talk to him," said Maddox.

"I've got his phone number—my address book—" D'Arcy took it and went into the next office to try to raise Kowalsky.

"Who else?"

187

"Miss Robertson—the girls' vice principal. And normally the boys' vice principal would too, but we lost Mr. Forcell just a couple of months ago—a great shock it was, dropped dead of a heart attack right in his office, only fifty-nine too. And the board hadn't—seeing there were only two months of the semester— But *that*," said Evans, "a woman wouldn't— Really this has been such a shock to me—" He puffed on his cigarette furiously.

They found Kowalsky more helpful. He came over in a hurry, upset and angry and surprised and defensive, a bulky dark man in the fifties, with a fringe of still black hair round an otherwise naked bald head, a forceful bass voice, and great suspicion of the cops.

"You saying somebody connected with the *school* did it?" he demanded. "It couldn't be so—the kids, my God, but kids wouldn't do nothing like that, bad as they are nowadays— nobody from the *school* would— My God, a corpse in my furnace! A corpse! I cleaned it all out right, I don't trust no man from the gas company, young punks they got now don't know from nothing—that is I seen Joe done it all right, when we turned it off middle of April. And now you saying—"

"We're not saying anything," said Maddox. "We don't know, Mr. Kowalsky, who brought the body in. But you can see for yourself—it is this Dr. Grantby, who was missing from the hospital a week ago last night. And the school's been locked since some time before that. And—"

"Damnedest thing I ever *heard*," said Kowalsky. "*Our* school." He had, he told them, been at Bancroft Junior High for nineteen years, worked up to his present job, and it was obvious he associated himself with the school, each clean window and offending dandelion in the lawn. "I can't figure how—"

188

"You have a set of the keys to the school?" said Rodriguez. "Now—"

"Sure I have. I—" Kowalsky turned purple. "You saying you think *I* brought the dead body in? Here? *Me?* You think—"

"We don't think anything," said Maddox hastily. "Of course not, Mr. Kowalsky. But somebody did, and not through a window, and so whoever did must have—"

"Well, nobody used my keys to do it with," said Kowalsky aggressively. "That I can tell you definite. June eleventh school closed, I went all round personal and saw that the windows was shut and the clocks turned off and all like that, we don't bother shut off the phones because it's only three, four weeks till summer session starts, see, but I saw to everything else and all the rest rooms cleaned up and the floors done. God, clean the halls every hour you could, the damn kids throwing stuff around like they do—and June twelfth, Friday, I lock up and go off. For two weeks. Before summer session. *And,* mister, I carry all my keys together, one chain, see, and I go off that Sunday up to my brother's cabin in the mountains, for a vacation with my brother and his wife. I'm not married, I lost my wife a matter o' four years back and I ain't made up my mind about this widow come chasing me. Up in the mountains, and my keys with me, and I just got back yesterday, so if you're goin' to say—"

"All right, I see," said Maddox. "Nobody used your keys. How many men do you have here as maintenance staff?"

"Four. Me and three under me. Joe Klein, Bill Cox, and Jim Selby."

"Do they have keys to the—"

"They do not, mister. I'm usually the guy comes first and unlocks everything."

"That's so," said Evans. "I said I've got keys, and Miss Robertson, but it's very seldom we use them."

"What happened to the other set?" asked Rodriguez suddenly. "The boys' vice principal who died?"

"Mr. Forcell—oh," said Evans, "his wife gave his keys back to me, after the funeral. As a matter of fact they should be here in my desk," and he opened the top drawer and rummaged. "Yes, here they are."

"Well, somebody—" Maddox wondered if somebody could have taken an impression of those keys. Evans would be out of his office sometimes. But what sense did that make? Had Grantby's murder been planned? And why the school, if there was no connection otherwise?

"All good guys," said Kowalsky. "Reliable. These guys. Not that I won't say I haven't had some— Oh. Oh." He looked suddenly angry.

"You think of something?" asked Maddox.

"Well, it ain't *anything*. But you talking about keys—" Kowalsky looked at Evans. "You remember that guy. The guy I caught sneaking back after hours, he stole a typewriter and an adding machine and all before we found out —I figured afterward how he'd stole my keys and had copies made. I was huntin' all one afternoon when I thought I misplaced 'em some place, and then he comes up nice as pie and says he found 'em on the front lawn, and I never gave a thought to it till the stuff started disappearing overnight."

"Who was this?" asked Maddox.

"Guy named Winkler—Carl Winkler. He only worked here part of one term, until that happened and I kicked him out. I mean, I figured out afterward about the keys, I didn't know for sure."

"If he did, you say. You didn't ask him at the time?"

Evans looked at Kowalsky. "Well," he said uneasily, "we talked about the possibility—we weren't absolutely sure the

190

man had— But he wasn't satisfactory otherwise, found drunk on the job once, and after we fired him we didn't have any more thefts. I had recommended to the board that the locks be changed, but—"

"Bureaucrats," said D'Arcy *sotto voce,* and Evans gave him a faint smile.

It was the only immediate lead they had, such as it was. They went back to the office after a sketchy lunch and Maddox called the hospital, asked for Dr. Edmunds. Edmunds sounded grumpy, and apologized; he was only just up; but he snapped to attention when Maddox gave him the news.

"*What?* At a *school?* In the— Oh my God. Yes. Yes, we'll get somebody here who knew him to make the formal identification, obviously not his daughter—my God. Grantby. And why on earth— What?"

"Did he ever have anything to do, professionally or otherwise, with a Carl Winkler? In the Emergency Room or anywhere? Do you keep records of emergency patients?"

"Oh, we have to keep *records.* Certainly. I can find out for you. You think you know who—?"

"No, we're just looking anywhere indicated," said Maddox. Of course the keys were the basic fact.

"Well, I'll have a look for you. My God— Does Prince know? I'll call him. What a hell of a thing. You didn't say how he was—?"

"The doctors'll tell us that. Looked as if his head was beaten in."

"Oh. My God. Thanks for letting me know, Sergeant. I'll have a look around in the records."

Maddox looked at the clock and ran: Thorsen was to be arraigned downtown at two thirty. That took up time; his name wasn't called until three fifteen. Then he got a five-hundred-buck fine and probation. He shook hands with Maddox cordially and said now everything was fine, Marian was out of the hospital and forgave him and all, and they were going back to K.C. together.

People, thought Maddox.

The school records had turned up an address for Carl Winkler, and Rodriguez and D'Arcy went to look for him.

"Though he's probably moved," said D'Arcy pessimistically. "Six months ago. It looked to me as if Grantby'd been beaten up. Head wounds did for him maybe."

"The doctors will say. He could have been stabbed or shot, the state he was in."

"Yeah. God, what a thing. And why, and who? This Winkler isn't what I'd call a *lead*. A good solid— Only, of course, whoever put the doctor there did have to have a key to the school. What a place to leave him."

"Well, Kowalsky or the principal don't look very likely for it either. Where the hell is this street?" Rodriguez peered at street signs.

Portia Street, downtown, it was. When they found the address, it was an old house with a sign in a front window, ROOM FOR RENT. "I'll bet he's moved," said D'Arcy. "He couldn't be anything to do with it anyway."

The woman who came to the door was fat and blonde and had a thick Swedish accent. She said, "Winkler? Yes, but not much more—I make him go. Bad, dirty, drunk. You are police? You like see his room? I have key—extra key. He is not here. When comes back, I tell, go." She smiled at them widely.

Since she had offered, they looked. It was a room added onto the old house; it had its own little bathroom. It told them this and that about Carl Winkler: it was dirty and very untidy and there were four empty bottles that had

192

held muscatel wine in the wastebasket. Odds and ends of old clothes, mostly dirty, strewn around: in the drawers of the old-fashioned bureau, on the bed and floor. An old foot locker under the bed was locked.

"I will just bet you," said Rodriguez, fastidiously inspecting an old tan work shirt with dark stiffened spots under the arms, "that that pro safe blower around is going to pull some more on our beat. And nothing, but nothing, on him, D'Arcy. Very cute, slick jobs."

"So you said." D'Arcy picked up a pair of old shoes and peered at them, dropped them. "Do you know what time this Winkler might come home, ma'am?" She shrugged and smiled. "There's nothing here, for— Well, look at this."

"What?" Rodriguez turned.

D'Arcy held up a blue sports shirt, which had been in a tangle of clothes heaped in one corner. He held it up mutely. Across one rolled-up sleeve was a broad light-brown smear. "Could be blood. My God, is there something to this after all?" He sorted out the heap and picked up a pair of gray pants.

"Even if it is blood, it doesn't have to be anything for us." Rodriguez looked at the shirt. "He could have had a nose-bleed."

"Please," said the woman. "Blood?"

D'Arcy inspected the trousers and pointed to another long dried smear on one leg. "It looks a little funny."

"Yes," said Rodriguez. "If it is blood, quite a lot of blood. For a nosebleed. Should we stake it out?"

"Listen," said D'Arcy, "I've got a date tonight and I'd just as soon take off in time for a shower and shave. The night shift doesn't come on till—"

"And he might not show before midnight anyway." Rodriguez tried to question the landlady about Winkler's habits, but she just shrugged some more.

"I find out, bad, dirty—not so when he first comes, a year, maybe sixteen month. Now, bad, drunk. I tell him go."

"I suppose we'd better stake it out," said D'Arcy gloomily. "If Ivor's turned up anything else on this guy—"

Rodriguez said to the woman, "Telephone? If I may use—"

"Why not?" She nodded.

"I'll call and find out," said Rodriguez.

Maddox wasn't in the office—still in court downtown—and O'Neill couldn't tell Rodriguez anything. "Feinman's here. If you want, I'll chase him down. If you want to stake it out—"

"I don't want to," said Rodriguez. "I don't think it's anything, for God's sake. A drunk who had a nosebleed, or cut himself by accident opening a bottle. But it is, probably, blood. And we're told that Winkler could have had keys to the building. If there now turns up any possible connection between him and Grantby—which I do *not* see happening—"

"Yes, I see that," said O'Neill. "As a once ranking detective, César, I think you'd better stake it out. Cover all bets."

"Oh, hell," said Rodriguez. "Well, tell Ivor to ring me here—" he read over the number—"and confirm it. When he does get in. When he does get this or that from the hospital."

"Will do," said O'Neill cheerfully. "Be nice if you cracked the case as soon as the body turned up."

"That optimistic I am not, Johnny," said Rodriguez.

Maddox got back to the office at three forty-five, and heard Rodriguez' message with a grunt. "Says nothing. A nosebleed. We don't even know for sure that Winkler had any keys. Talk about long shots."

"Do I tell César to keep staking it?" asked O'Neill.

Maddox hunched one shoulder. "Long shots," he said. "We do have to— I guess so. Yes." He went on upstairs and met Sue coming down with a paper cup of coffee. He gave her a look and went by, and Sue gave him a brilliant smile.

The office was empty. He called the hospital. "Oh, Sergeant," said Dr. Edmunds. "I tried to get you a while ago, but you were out. I've got a little something for you. What it might mean— This name you gave me. Carl Winkler. I can't imagine what it might mean, but he was through Emergency here just recently." He named the date. The Thursday before the Sunday night that Dr. Grantby had vanished away.

"What?" said Maddox, completely astonished. A slender little lead like that, not really a lead at all, and all of a sudden— "Through Emergency? An accident or what?"

"It was a traffic accident. A police case. The police came in with the ambulance—when I came across the record I hunted up the intern who was with Grantby on it, and he remembered. It was a county officer, he said. This Winkler was to be charged with something—after he'd been patched up, the officer took him away. Drunk driving, I think. The woman with him was killed. D.O.A. when she was brought in, nearly decapitated and bled to death. A Mrs. Jean Cantor."

"Well," said Maddox. "I'll be damned. Winkler wasn't badly hurt?"

"He's listed as having superficial cuts and bruises. Treated and released to police custody."

"I *will* be damned," said Maddox. "So maybe that's why he's not home. Thanks very much, Doctor. . . ." And what did that say? A connection to Grantby—if a very tenuous one. Winkler, the slender little possible lead all of a sudden—

Grantby stashed away at that school. Very funny.

Well, obviously call the sheriff's boys and find out more about Winkler. If they still had him. And so on. He reached for the phone, and Feinman came in and said there was a teletype in from Sacramento. "Not that it says anything, if you're pinning your faith to that GVL business. You can't know the guy remembered right. The citizens—"

Maddox looked at the teletype. Report from the D.M.V. on license plates: the contractor's crew, Harry's friends. About half the list covered, and nothing. Not one had a GVL prefix.

Well, he hadn't really expected much from that. He reached for the phone and told O'Neill to get him the sheriff's office.

Ken Donaldson showed up at six thirty and D'Arcy dashed home, took a shower, and donned a clean shirt— heat wave broken or not, it had still gone to eighty-seven today—and presented himself at the big old-fashioned house on Laurel Avenue at seven twenty.

"I'm not very late," he said to Sheila. His newest heartbeat beamed at him, her amber eyes teasing, her outrageous red hair only slightly tamed.

"I bet it's Gervase," she said. "Come in. Would you like bourbon or Scotch in a highball, or be ladylike like me with a Martini?"

"No, it's not," said D'Arcy. "You just cut it out, Sheila. It's my own business. Scotch."

Her father grinned at him, busy mixing drinks. "You don't want to start giving in to them, D'Arcy. It's just you've intrigued her. Female curiosity."

"Oh my God, I know. What's a man to do?"

"Hector?" said Sheila.

"No, for God's sake, let me enjoy my drink in peace and relax. After the day we've had—"

"Worse than usual? Sit down and relax," said Mr. Fitz-patrick. "Don't mind the girl."

"Micah," said Sheila meditatively. "Obadiah."

"Now you stop deviling the man," said Fitzpatrick.

"It couldn't possibly be worse than Obadiah," said Sheila. "Yes, Dad. Look, D'Arcy—tomorrow's your day off, isn't it? You like to come to the beach? I want to try some experiments with different filters, for cloud effects, and I thought—"

"Well, O.K.," said D'Arcy. "I've used that Kodak E-two yellow filter some, you get a good effect except for refraction, you've got to allow—but any of the red filters, the faster film—"

"But with Agfa—" Sheila put her drink down and leaned forward to argue. Her father regarded them amusedly. He liked D'Arcy. And with his tomboyish daughter all wrapped up in the photography, he was glad to see her take an interest in any male.

"With strobe—"

"Oh, don't be idiotic," said D'Arcy. "You get a kind of moonlight effect if you—"

Donaldson called Brougham at twelve fifty. "This Winkler just showed. He's drunk as a skunk—wonder he got here safe, driving. He's about to pass out. You want me to bring him in? What for?"

"Well, he showed just on the edge of this new body, Ken. He's drunk? Take him in to the tank overnight. Tell them to hold him for the boys in the morning. I'll leave a note for Maddox."

"O.K. Then can I go home?"

"Put him in the tank and go home," said Brougham.

thirteen

Tuesday morning, and D'Arcy was off. Maddox found Brougham's note on his desk, and a large manila envelope marked as from the Sheriff's Department. He picked that up with a grunt of satisfaction and, reading the note, went across the hall. "Oh, Sue, take this down to the lab for me, will you?"

"We're only here to run errands for you, of course," said Sue. "All right."

Maddox was on the phone when Rodriguez came in; putting it down a minute later, he said, "Well, Winkler showed up plastered and they shoved him in the tank overnight. They tell me down there he's still sleeping like a baby, and we can have him any time. You like to go bring him up for talking to?" Rodriguez said resignedly he supposed it had to be done. "We ought to get something definite from the lab, I just sent his prints down."

"Winkler's? Where'd you get them?"

"The sheriff's boys had him, remember? I got this and that yesterday and they said they'd send 'em over. They've got him charged with involuntary manslaughter—on the woman who was killed, passenger when he was driving—he was out on bail, supposed to appear last Thursday, he didn't, and they find he gave them a false address. They've been looking for him and were happy to know we've got him. So, let's talk to him, shall we?"

Rodriguez went out, grumbling about long shots, and Maddox called the lab. "Have you got anything on the Grantby thing yet? The stuff we sent you?"

"A bit," said Rowan. "Those clothes—it's blood all right—old blood. About a week. Type AB."

"Do tell," said Maddox thoughtfully. Grantby's type was AB, and it wasn't a common type. On Winkler's clothes? But such a tenuous connection. "I just sent you some prints."

"Yes. That hammer we picked up in the school basement —it's got some nice latents all over the handle. Along with more AB-type blood and some hairs. I was just going to get Dabney to start comparisons."

"Go and do so," said Maddox. He went down the hall to the coffee machine and ran into Daisy Hoffman.

"You sending Sue on errands now," she complained. "We've got another runaway, wouldn't you know. Stopped a priest on the street and asked for help—he just called. Oh, Sue, something new." They went into her office.

Maddox sipped coffee, wondering about Winkler, and started back to the office. At the door of the Communications room a uniformed man caught him. "Teletype from Sacramento, Sergeant."

Maddox took it. More plate numbers from the D.M.V. He went back to his desk, sipping coffee, and looked it over. More of the contractor's crew—Rex Slaney—Bill Pollock. No GVL prefixes.

And then he sat up and said aloud, "I'll be damned! I will be—" What was this?

William J. Bolton's license plate was GVL-790.

Now what the hell? thought Maddox. What could this say—if anything?

Bolton. Bell's regular customer—but Maddox seemed to recall, seldom stopping by at night. When Harry Arthur had been there.

Bolton. Who matched the description, if vaguely, of the man O'Reilly said had—

Talk about wishful thinking, thought Maddox. How many license plates would there be in the state with a GVL prefix? Even in L.A. County. And Bolton the utterly respectable stockbroker. Coincidence, that was all.

But he thought, all the same, that he'd like another look at Bolton; he hadn't really looked at him before, the once he'd seen the man. And César would be a while signing out Winkler downtown.

When he came past the desk, O'Neill was whistling "The Patriot Game" and doing a crossword. "If you're wondering where Feinman is, I sent him out on a new call just as he came in. Market out on Fairfax—they'd just discovered somebody broke in last night and stole all their liquor."

"Yes," said Maddox absently. Bolton. Ridiculous. Still, the plate number—but the long arm of coincidence—

Stevens, MacDuff and Pfeiffer, out on Beverly . . . It was a new building, a small and very elegant building, marble and black glass, with a chaste brass plate on the wall beside the door: their very own building, the classy brokerage. Inside, it was just as elegant, the hushed atmosphere, vaguely cathedral-like, of any place where Money was dealt with. Wall-to-wall carpeting, and svelte females, modest but smart, all over the place. Railings like those in a bank, shutting off the VIP's from *hoi polloi,* and a row of private offices at the back. Maddox approached a desk near the door labeled INQUIRIES and said to the modish female there, "Mr. Bolton. I'd like to see—"

"Would you like to make an appointment, sir? Mr. Bolton isn't in today, I'm afraid."

"Oh," said Maddox. "Er—vacation, or is he on sick leave?"

"I'm afraid I don't know, sir." She looked disapproving. "If you'd like to make an appointment—"

"No, thanks." Maddox went out, debating. Bolton not at work. If it had been Bolton who'd got knocked down by Pat O'Reilly, he might well—

Oh, the thing was ridiculous.

He went up to the drugstore on the corner and looked in the phone book, identifying the right William J. Bolton by the second number given, that of the brokerage. Crescent Heights Boulevard. He drove up there: it was an apartment house, of good class, and the row of mailboxes downstairs told him Bolton's apartment: Twelve. He climbed carpeted stairs and pushed the bell. He pushed it steadily for two minutes and got no answer.

Well. Wasting time. It was nothing—

But it stayed at the back of his mind.

He got back to Wilcox Street at nine thirty to find Rodriguez buried in the new *Saint Mystery Magazine*, alone in the office except for Carl Winkler, who was sound asleep with his head on D'Arcy's desk. "And where have you been?" demanded Rodriguez, putting down the magazine. "I get back here with this sleeping beauty, you've taken off somewhere."

"I've been chasing a wild goose," said Maddox, and told him about Bolton. Rodriguez uttered a disbelieving noise. "Coincidence, all right, it could be, but it's funny. I mean, a couple of coincidences. That the fag who approached O'Reilly should— And the GVL thing. I just—"

"The respectable stockbroker," said Rodriguez. "They do say coincidence has a long arm. Look, the fags have their own places and contacts. They—"

"Some of them still try to keep it covered up."

"All right, then they don't go wandering around public bars soliciting the customers at random. Or when they do they're not respectable stockbrokers," pointed out Rodriguez reasonably. "Do you want to talk to this bird or not?"

They looked at Winkler. Carl Winkler was not a prepossessing sight after his night in the drunk tank. He was a man about forty, a big man not yet running to fat, with thinning sandy hair and a big Roman nose. He was dressed in tan work pants and shirt, not very clean, and he slumbered peacefully, breathing heavily through his open mouth. "Maybe if we got a cup of coffee into him," said Rodriguez, "it'd help. They gave me his effects—what he had on him last night. On your desk."

Maddox looked at four crumpled dollar bills, a half-empty pack of Chesterfields, a book of matches, a ring of keys, a dirty handkerchief, sixty-eight cents in change, a cheap cigarette lighter. No billfold or I.D. That had been left in his room. The man had worked, but apparently not lately. He picked up the keys. "Yes, well, we can compare these with the school keys. There are a few more than you'd expect Winkler to keep on him, and this big Yale key—" The keys to the school building were still the main link. But the link—if you could call it that—to Grantby was just nothing at all. "Let's wake him up."

With some difficulty they got Winkler awake, brought him a cup of coffee. He sat sipping it, looking at them warily. "All right, Carl," said Maddox, "let's hear about how you happened to have the key to Bancroft Junior High."

"Huh?"

"You worked there for a little while. As a janitor. While you were there—" Maddox picked up the keys and dangled them before him—"you managed to get hold of a copy to a door key. Back or front. Didn't you? To get in at night and pick up the loot."

"Who says? I never—that Kowalsky, he fired me, a good job, and I never done nothing."

"Well, we'll be looking to see if one of these keys fits some door there."

Winkler thought about that, painfully, head down. He

finished his coffee and then he said, "You bring me up here about that? Listen, I explain to you about that. I never stole nothing there. Or anywhere, I mean. But I—well, I tell you, when I got that job—I mean while I was on that job, I—uh— I had a little bad luck with the ivories, and I got behind on my rent. I got thrown outta the room I had. And—uh—I didn't have no place to sleep, and that was how come I got myself a key for that school. So's I could come back, nice warm basement there, just a place to sleep. Till I got enough money, get another room. That's all."

"Oh," said Maddox. "But you kept the key when you got fired."

"Well, I sorta forgot I had it. When I got fired off that job—and I never done nothing—I just forgot about the key. I guess, I can give it back, and that'll be all right, won't it?" He made as if to get up, and Rodriguez pressed him down in the chair.

"That's not quite all, Carl. When were you inside that building the last time?"

"Oh gee, the day I got fired, I guess."

"Mmh," said Maddox. "Did you know the sheriff's looking for you, Carl? You were supposed to show up in court last week, and you didn't. Forfeited bail. You do know the charge on you, Carl?"

"No, I don't know nobody wants me for n—— I hadda accident, but I was drunk and I didn't hit nobody, just a telephone post."

"No, you didn't, but your girl friend got killed. Was she your girl friend? Jean Cantor."

All of a sudden tears filled Winkler's eyes. "Poor Jeanie," he said. "Poor Jeanie."

"Yes, poor Jeanie. The sheriff wants you for involuntary manslaughter. Which you knew, all right, or why did you give a wrong address?"

"Me? I never—it wasn't *me* hurt Jeanie—I'd never hurt Jeanie, she was the nicest girl I ever knew—nice to me."

"Who did hurt Jeanie?" asked Maddox. Winkler was silent; he wiped away the tears with the back of one hand. "How'd you get that blood on your clothes, Carl? Your blue shirt and gray pants? When? Was it a week ago Sunday night, maybe?"

"I dunno what you mean. Maybe I had a little accident."

"Cut yourself shaving?" asked Rodriguez.

"I don't remember."

"Quite a lot of blood, Carl," said Maddox. "You know, we found the doctor. Dr. Grantby. Did you think we wouldn't?"

"I dunno what you—" Winkler's response was automatic, dull.

"The doctor from the Emergency Ward—" What kind of connection was it? For a murder, and such a murder? The phone rang on Maddox's desk and he swore mentally; they should have taken Winkler to an interrogation room. "Maddox," he said in a low voice.

"I just thought you'd like to know as soon as we cinched it," said Rowan. "The prints you sent down from the sheriff's records—this Winkler—are all over that hammer from the school basement. On the handle. On the other end, a good deal of type AB blood. I told you that before—and some of Grantby's hair."

"Thank you *so* much," said Maddox. He looked at Winkler, and over his bent head nodded at Rodriguez, mouthed, "Prints checked out—his," and pointed at Winkler. Rodriguez' brows shot up. The tenuous connection—but now they knew. Maddox went round in front of Winkler and said hardly, "The doctor at the Hollywood Receiving Hospital, Carl—who treated you after the accident. The doctor you forced away with you somewhere a week ago last Sunday night, and killed with the hammer, and stuffed into that furnace in the basement of Bancroft Junior High. What the hell did you have against the doctor, Carl?"

Winkler raised his head slowly. His slate-gray eyes were dull. Not a bad-looking man once, before he started to go downhill on the *vino*. He didn't say anything for a while, and then he said, "Can I have a cigarette?" Maddox gave him one and lit it. "I—I never thought you'd find him at all. I sure never did. I mean, I knew that old furnace'd have been cleaned when they shut her off, so nobody'd go poking around before they turned her on again, maybe November. I just thought—"

"But why, Carl?" asked Maddox. Rodriguez was taking notes. Belatedly Maddox recited the little warning to Winkler, asked if he wanted a lawyer. Winkler just shook his head. "Why the doctor, Carl? The doctor never did you any harm —Dr. Grantby." And he thought, this lout, this good-for-nothing accomplishing nothing—and Charles Grantby, the capable man on the right side of things.

Winkler said loud and sudden, "He never *did* nothing— that's about right! He never did nothing atall! What kind of a doctor you call that, anyways? I remember rammin' into that pole—I was just a little tight, I wasn't really—and then the ambulance, and I ain't hurt much, so how could Jeanie've been?—and next I know I'm in that hospital, this guy inna white coat lookin' at me—and I hear him plain as day, he says, Don't bother with the woman, he says, this one isn't bad. Don't bother, he says! What kind o' doctor *is* he? Don't bother—he says it in plain English, and he means Jeanie! Don't bother."

For God's sake, thought Maddox. "But, Carl—"

"I heard him! A swell doctor he is! And the cops take and put me in jail, I'm there till the bail gets set, and I get out, I go ask about Jeanie—I wanta know how bad she's hurt, I

205

don't figure bad because I wasn't—and the landlady says she's dead! Jeanie! In that accident—how could she be? The nicest girl I ever—" Winkler began to cry a little, drearily. "Dead! And she wasn't hurt bad. It was that goddamn doctor, I heard him say it—Don't bother with her. And so she's dead. And what kind of doctor—"

"She was dead when they brought you in, Carl," said Maddox; but Winkler didn't hear him.

"All *right*, you found him, I never thought you would—thought he'd burn, and that was O.K. by me—but you found him, so I don't mind telling. I didn't believe it—Jeanie dead, because he said, Don't bother about her—and I got to thinking, What kind of a damn doctor—and I figured, beat him up good. Killing Jeanie. I had maybe a couple drinks, I went there that night—I remembered his name, one o' the young guys said it when I was there, Dr. Grantby—and I asked see him, outside that back door there, and when he comes there wasn't nobody else around and I just belt him one and haul him to my car. I ask him, when he comes to, what's he *mean* that time, say, Don't bother, don't bother about Jeanie —my Jeanie—and he gives me the double talk, I belt him ag——" Winkler hiccuped, swabbing at his eyes. "And I thought of the school before, place to work him over where nobody'll— And I got him there, he was a little guy, and I— he try to give me the double talk—but I heard him, Don't bother about Jeanie." He began to cry again.

Maddox looked at Rodriguez. That simple and that stupid. For no reason at all, the reliable Dr. Grantby cut off in his prime. Because he had looked at a dead woman and said don't waste time there, in effect.

"All right, Carl," he said heavily. "That's all right now." Take him back to jail; apply for the warrant; let the sheriff's boys know they had him on a heavier charge; and call Dr. Prince, Dr. Edmunds, tell them how, who, and why.

It was with very good reason that most cops got to feeling discouraged about the human race now and then. And very doubtful as to whether any real progress had been made since the days Neanderthal walked.

And Bolton stayed at the back of Maddox's mind. Coincidence? Two funny little coincidences . . . Prince made shocked noises at him and he said, "Yes, sir."

"For no reason—such a good man—and his poor daughter, I must—"

"Yes, sir . . ." Bolton? But what could it say, even if— One coincidence, he would accept, not two. But which could be the real coincidence? "Doctor, we'll want statements from some of the interns who were on duty the night Winkler and the woman were brought in. If I come over at, say, two o'clock, with a stenographer—" Always the paper work. Feinman was typing a report on the market job. "Yes, fine. Thanks."

"Such a very stupid little thing."

"Yes, sir," said Maddox.

"Amos," suggested Sheila lazily, stretched out on the sand beside D'Arcy, who was delicately screwing a filter onto the lens of the Medalist.

"No. Will you cut it out?"

"Claude? I've come across some lovely ones in this dictionary. Priceless. I've never heard of some of them. There was one I found— Well, a lot of the obsolete ones," said Sheila, "are just unusual, not funny. I don't think. Sounding terribly knightly and feudal and swords clashing, like that. I don't suppose it could possibly be Drogo?" Sheila rolled over and looked at him.

"Oh, my God!" said D'Arcy, and dropped the Medalist. Sheila shrieked, and they both scrambled for it and felt it tenderly all over. No harm done. D'Arcy breathed again; the Medalist belonged to Sheila.

She sat back on her heels and said, "Thank God. . . . D'Arcy, it *isn't?* Drogo? Not really? But how delicious. I *like* it. All the medieval banners and the Gaulish men and the chain mail. I *like* it."

D'Arcy stared at her.

They were busy on that most of Tuesday, all the paper work on Winkler. They got the statements from the interns, and one of them said, "My God, a thing like that—just a *mistake*. My God, I helped get that stretcher in, the woman was D.O.A. when the ambulance picked her up! She went straight through the windshield and cut her throat wide open. My God, and that stupid bastard—"

The warrant came through on Wednesday morning, and Maddox went down to the new facility on Alameda and saw Winkler booked in on it—first-degree homicide. And it would probably get changed to second, or even third. There'd be a psychiatric examination and ten to one the head doctors would say he hadn't known what he was doing —the jargon—and the charge would be reduced.

"So, all right," he said to Rodriguez when he came back, "nobody argues that an insane man deserves the same punishment as a man who really did know what he was doing. All I say is, it's unrealistic, César. Who's more dangerous, sane or insane? Reduce the charge because he's nuts? All I say is, all right, Winkler may not be all there—but he's shown he can kill, and pretty violently too, and I just do not like the idea of him being let out in about four years, maybe to get lit up the week after and get mad at another innocent respectable citizen."

"We're only paid to catch them," said Rodriguez.

"And speaking of innocent respectable citizens," said

Maddox, "that Bolton is still in my mind. Because two coincidences—"

"Reaching, reaching," said Rodriguez.

A new call came in just before lunch, an attempted hold-up at a liquor store on Vine. Sergeant Buck's nasal voice on the line reminded Maddox that it was again O'Neill's day off. And Sue's. He wondered suddenly if, possibly, they'd had another date. It wasn't ethical, that damned Irishman.

And what about Bolton? For a fact, it was the only GVL plate turned up. And however tenuous the link was—well, thinner than tenuous. But look at Winkler. The long shot sometimes—

He got William Bolton to answer his home phone at five o'clock on Wednesday. "Mr. Bolton. Sergeant Maddox, L.A.P.D. I met you the other day at Bell's service station."

"Oh, yes," said Bolton. He had a tenor voice. He sounded merely neutral.

"I was wondering if you wanted to reconsider anything you told me," said Maddox. "You said you hadn't been at the station that night—a week ago Saturday night. Possibly you forgot about being there—just a few minutes?"

"What? No, certainly not," said Bolton, sounding faintly indignant. "I wasn't there. I didn't go anywhere that day. What on earth do you mean?"

And of course, if he was indeed the perfectly respectable citizen, which he looked, they couldn't go obviously poking around, asking the insulting questions—by implication—with no solid reason.

He temporized with Bolton, put the phone down, and said, "D'Arcy." There was no reply, and he looked across at D'Arcy, who was sitting at his desk smiling dreamily into space. "Hey, D'Arcy. Oh Lord, I suppose you've fallen in love again. I thought you were still carrying the torch for that girl photographer."

"Carrying the—what a damned silly phrase," said D'Arcy with dignity. "What do you want?"

"That O'Reilly the other day. You typed the report, have you got his address?"

"Some place." D'Arcy looked and found it. Sierra Vista. Maddox looked in the book; no phone listed. And about then Sergeant Buck called up with a new one, the pure routine, man dropped dead probably of a heart attack at a drugstore on Vine.

It had turned out to be that kind of a day, and there was still some paper work to do on Winkler, and reporters hanging around on that too, and Ellis had picked up a bug somewhere, the weather notwithstanding, and was off sick, which didn't help.

Maddox left Wilcox Street at six twenty and went hunting for the Sierra Vista address. He found Pat O'Reilly just coming down the steps; it was an old house cut up into small apartments.

O'Reilly was cold sober this time, and he sat in the Maserati with Maddox and listened, and agreed. "Sure, I'll be glad to, Sergeant. Guys like that— Only thing is, before Friday, hah? I'm due take a rig out for Chi. on Friday. I been on a layover, you need four-five days off after a cross-country haul—and I never touch even a beer, driving. But when you're laying over, you got to relax." He gave Maddox a sheepish smile. "I guess I'd had a few, the other day. I mean, I was damned annoyed, who wouldn't be, guy propositioning me like that, but if I hadn't had a few I'd likely have told him to get lost and forgot it. And come to think, an older guy too, I shouldn't've hit him. But—"

"I'd just like you to take a look and say yes or no," said Maddox. "This is a far-out deal. I don't really think it's the same. He isn't at his office today either, but he'll have to go back sometime. I'll check tomorrow, and set it up with you if he's there—call you about ten, O.K.? I suppose he'll go to lunch, we can wait a little way down from the door and see."

"O.K.," said O'Reilly. "Guys like that— It's a charge, isn't it?"

"I'd have to look up the statute. Soliciting for immoral purposes. Well, I'll let you know."

The college boys were due to be arraigned on Thursday morning. Bergner came up about eight thirty and wanted to talk about Grantby—one of the doctors at the hospital had assisted him at the autopsy, and he had the report with him. Maddox cut him off. That was finished business, as offbeat as it had been. And as stupid. Of the offbeat cases, they still had Harry Arthur pending, and the other newer ones not involving homicide.

O'Neill rang him at nine o'clock. "We all have our crosses to bear, friend. Mrs. Pierce is here."

"Oh, hell," said Maddox, and went to send Sergeant Daisy to deputize.

"The worst little jobs always saved for us," said Sue, wrinkling her nose at him.

He called Stevens, MacDuff and Pfeiffer at nine thirty. "Is Mr. Bolton there?"

"Just one moment, sir, I'll connect you," fluted the female voice. Maddox put the phone down gently. This was, of course, woolgathering. The two coincidences—

The inside phone rang. "They do keep you busy here," said O'Neill. "Not like Central, of course. We now have an irate female citizen complaining that her bag was snatched just now over on Santa Monica. She demands a detective."

"Call Aunt Daisy," said Maddox rudely.

"Shirking your duty, Sergeant."

Maddox dialed the number O'Reilly had given him. "Sorry

to be early—I've got to be in court at ten thirty. This fellow's in his office today. Can you meet me there at noon?" He read out the address. "We'll wait it out. He might not go to lunch until one, but—"

"Sure thing," said O'Reilly. "I'll be there. Glad to oblige."

Footsteps down the hall beyond the open door, and a slow plaintive female voice. "Are you a *detective?* I didn't know they had girl detectives." Sue's voice in a quiet murmur. "What I mean is, there's never a cop around when you want one, of all the impudence, I'm walking down Santa Monica Boulevard minding my own business, looking in windows but just walking along, I'm on my way to work, I'm an honest working woman, I work at the Sears store up there, and I'm just walking along and this kid—just a kid, a great big kid maybe seventeen but just a kid, he runs by and grabs my purse, and I yelled, sure, I'm surprised, but does anybody *do* anything? A couple of men standing around on the sidewalk, they just look at me—and the kid runs down the side street, a big kid, my God, kids these days— and there was nine dollars and some in my change purse and all my papers—Social Security card and all—and my God, I look for a cop, of course they're never around when you *want* them."

Maddox looked at the clock and ran. That arraignment. No. Cops never around. In court on the routine, or, of course, out committing their quota of police brutality for the day.

Downstairs, O'Neill gave him a sunny smile. Feinman and Rodriguez were just bringing in the liquor-store manager, for a session with the Identi-Kit.

He met O'Reilly half a block away from the classy new building belonging to Stevens, MacDuff and Pfeiffer, at twelve o'clock. "This is probably going to be n.g.," he said. "I just want you to take a look."

"Sure," said O'Reilly amiably. They sat in the Maserati, parked a hundred feet from the front door of the building, and waited. There was a new-looking coffee shop down this way, and it was a little gamble that people from businesses along here might choose it for lunch rather than the drugstore up the other way. "This is a nice job," said O'Reilly. "Italian, hah? Handles nice, I bet. The rigs I get to handle—boy, I'm happy climb in my Corvair. You don't think this is the guy in Jimmy's place the other day?"

"Let's say it's a long shot."

"Oh. Well, you said it's a charge. Legal. I thought about it," said O'Reilly, "and I guess what made me mad—aside from the couple I'd had—well, maybe four-five beers—was, he says to me, this guy, you like to make some good money, handsome? Calling me— Good money. I'm not handsome, Sergeant, and I guess—well, it was like he was saying I'd do anything for the money, see? That sort of riled me."

"Oh, yes," said Maddox thoughtfully. "I see that." And he was wondering if he would recognize William Bolton when and if he came out of the building: he'd only seen him casually, in a car, once before.

In, he remembered suddenly, a maroon Buick about three years old. Lombardi saying, medium-sized car, an Olds, a Buick.

And the GVL plate. You would notice your own initials, wouldn't you?

Suddenly O'Reilly clamped a hand on Maddox's arm. "There he *is!*" he said. "That's *him.* I'd swear it on a stack of Bibles."

Maddox looked. The man had come out of the building up there and was walking this way. A man about fifty, a good dark suit, white shirt and dark tie, a man about five ten, solid-looking, stout but not flabby, thinning dark hair— an ordinary looking man, the respectable stockbroker with the respectable firm.

"That's *him*," whispered O'Reilly again as the man passed the Maserati. "Look at what's left of the nice black eye I gave him—he's got pancake make-up over it."

fourteen

Maddox sat on in the Maserati after O'Reilly left him, thinking. So there was now this queer little fact, plus the GVL plate, and what did it say, specifically?

Something funny, thought Maddox. The fags—they had their own places, the known hangouts, where gaiety was joined and the contacts made. A middle-aged man like Bolton hadn't suddenly turned into a queer; that was sure. So, Bolton keeping his extracurricular activities under cover. That was a very high-class business outfit, and it could be guessed that if Bolton's little tendency was found out, he'd be out the door the next minute. He wasn't one of the partners, after all.

But. But. So what the hell had Bolton been thinking of, risking his reputation by accosting a stranger at a public bar?

But Maddox was beginning to think that Bolton added up in other ways. About Bolton he could bear to know a lot more. . . . And that wasn't a brand-new apartment house on Crescent Heights; he might have lived there some while. Maddox lit a thoughtful cigarette and started the engine.

At Apartment Eleven, a rangy middle-aged woman in a dirty apron interrupted his introduction of himself as a representative of the thus-and-so insurance company. "Sorry, I'm just the help and they're both out, I wouldn't know a thing." At Apartment Ten (he got no answer at Fourteen, again noting that even in this supposedly sophisticated century the hotels and apartments tended to shy away from Thirteen) he found Mrs. Constance Withycombe, who was home alone and delighted to have someone to talk to, on whatever subject. It was no wonder, thought Maddox, that the con games were so rife; cops met a lot of Mrs. Withycombe's type. It never occurred to her to ask him for credentials; she took him at face value. A fluffy little old lady dressed prettily in gray silk, she welcomed him in with little exclamations, she hadn't got round to dusting, he mustn't mind the curtain being down, she was mending—She gave him a chair, and gossiped happily.

Yes, they knew Mr. Bolton, just as a neighbor, not really well of course, her son—she lived with her son, her unmarried son, the other one lived in La Crescenta—was out all day, and Mr. Bolton not very social, but of course living here so long they knew all about him. "A very successful man, I'd say he is, and awfully dignified. Just a little bit aware of his own importance, Mr. Um, which is naughty of me to say, but I'm sure a very fine man. He always contributed to the Red Cross when I was up to collecting—my arthritis these days—we've lived here nearly twelve years, and he's been here longer, ever since the place was built, I believe." No, she didn't think he entertained much, he was a very quiet neighbor. She understood he'd never been married, he must be a lonely man. "But a fine neighbor—he offered to advise my son if he ever wanted to invest." Servants? Well, people didn't really have servants now, did they? No, he hadn't, not now, and that had been quite a little upset for the poor man, Mrs. Withycombe was afraid. Most people here, if they had any domestic help at all, it was a maid twice a week, like that, but Mr. Bolton had had a houseman—living in—maybe an old family retainer as they used to be called, because he'd been about Mr. Bolton's own age—Dexter, his name was, Dexter Drake. Mr. Bolton had told her afterward that Dexter had been with him for nearly thirty years. "It was a terrible shock to him, you could see. He turned the most awful color and really I thought he was going to faint. The poor man dropped dead right out there in the hall, bringing home a bag of groceries—the Dexter man, I mean—my son found him, and we had the police up, and then Mr. Bolton came home and he *was* upset, you could tell. He seems to live such a quiet life— and this man with him so long, used to do everything for him, meals and all. I expect it's made a change in his life. What? No, I don't think Mr. Bolton's tried to replace him. Well, you couldn't, could you? One like that? What? Oh, that was about six months ago—yes, all of six months." But Mr. Bolton was a very fine man, and her son had remarked once that that office where he worked was certainly first-class, a fine firm probably. "I think he's been there for years, and I'm sure they'd give him a good—er—recommendation. Is he taking out insurance with you? Well, he always looks very healthy, I must say—a fine-looking man, and seems very well for his age."

She'd have gone on happily, but Maddox thought he'd heard all he wanted, and probably she hadn't anything else new to say to him. He escaped with profuse thanks, and sat in the Maserati and thought about that.

That really said something interesting. If you read be-tween the lines. Bolton a fag, but keeping it very cannily covered up. The ultra-respectable front. Contrary to popular fiction, you really couldn't tell them by appearances. That brokerage would heave him straight out on his ear if they suspected.

How had he kept it covered? By all that, you could read it. The houseman. Dexter Drake. Living in. Together thirty years. Oh, yes? Could even be that it was Dexter who seduced him first. Dexter the dominant partner? But at any rate, Maddox had heard of such affairs before. The long-term affairs—and you got it with the lesbians too, occasionally. Both partners thinking of it, often, as a kind of marriage.

And so Bolton had never had to make the contacts. He had Dexter—or vice versa, could be. And then Dexter dropped dead. A heart attack.

How would Bolton react to that? The confirmed queer, not remotely suspected of being one by anyone but the dead man—no contacts among his own kind—not knowing any of the local homos around—and left without a partner?

Maddox started back to the office, wondering. Would the craving, the need, drive Bolton eventually to the random approach? Well, apparently it had. And if he'd done it once, he could have done it twice. And there was also the fact that Harry Arthur— Yes. And Harry had once built some bookcases for— And even, of course, Mr. Bell's safe—

But how the hell to get any evidence? There wasn't any solid evidence.

He was still thinking as he came into the station; but almost at once he stopped. O'Neill was on the phone; he gestured savagely at Maddox, shoved buttons to transfer the call upstairs, and said, "Holdup going on at the Security-First National on Hollywood—I'll contact the Feds." Maddox turned and ran for the lot.

That one occupied the rest of Thursday. By the time they got there, and the Feds a little later, the holdup men were gone, along with something like twelve thousand dollars of the bank's money; nobody was hurt, no shot had been fired, but they had to question about forty people who had witnessed it, and try to get descriptions out of those who'd seen the men closest, and it all took time. Maddox hadn't a chance to discuss Bolton with anybody, and when he went home at seven o'clock he suddenly remembered that he'd never had any lunch at all.

But he went on thinking about Bolton; and on Friday morning he laid it out for discussion, Eden sitting in. "It's a thing," said Eden when he'd heard it all, "but you'd never find any evidence. Not even very good circumstantial evidence. Not enough for a warrant."

"I wonder," said Maddox. "I wonder. We've got a charge. O'Reilly's willing to press charges. Not a statute often used against adults, but the law's still on the books. That would scare him. Like hell. His nice front—the reputation he's so careful of. Because I swear to you, that's the answer to that part of it. The deceased houseman."

"Sure," said Rodriguez, "but on Arthur you've got damn all."

"I wonder," said Maddox again. He thought he'd like to sound Bolton out a little; at nine thirty he took time out and drove up Beverly Boulevard. They were still taking statements from witnesses to the holdup.

He thought Bolton would have liked to refuse to see him; but he couldn't very well show, in the office, as hostile to the police, and Maddox had announced himself clearly.

"I'm afraid I don't understand how I can help you, sir," he said stiffly. Maddox sat down without invitation and studied him. Bolton had a private office, carpeted, with a violently surrealistic painting on the wall behind his desk.

"Where'd you get the black eye, Mr. Bolton?" asked Maddox conversationally, taking out a cigarette.

"I—a stupid accident, I ran into an open cupboard door." The discoloration was only faintly noticeable now. Bolton had remained standing; he didn't like Maddox coming here. "I'm sorry, sir, I haven't much time to give you—a client—" He looked at his watch.

"You're quite sure you weren't at Bell's service station that Saturday night?" asked Maddox.

"I've said I wasn't." Bolton's voice sharpened. "Surely my word—a man of my position—when I have nothing whatsoever to— This sordid murder, and it's quite unwarranted of the police to come here and ask me silly questions all over again. Now, really, I am expecting a client."

Maddox didn't move. "Have you been getting into any more brawls in bars, Mr. Bolton?" he asked genially.

Bolton turned gray, snatched at control, and said with a little gasp, "What— I cannot imagine what you mean, sir— insulting me. I'll ask you to get out of my office!"

"The fellow I heard about it from," said Maddox, "seemed to feel it was you who'd insulted him. How about it, Mr. Bolton? You've been feeling lonesome for Dexter Drake, haven't you?"

Bolton took the double shock without revealing obviously how deep a shock it must have been; but Maddox saw the naked fear in his eyes, the split second before he dropped his head. "I would rather not guess what you mean to imply," said Bolton in an icy tone, "but I am *not* going to be harassed and insulted in my own office by stupid police. I—" He pressed a hand to his chest. "I am not feeling well, if you don't leave I shall—"

"Call up some more cops?" asked Maddox. He got up. "I'll be talking to you again, Mr. Bolton."

As he went out, he had a glimpse of Bolton, still dirty white, collapsing into his desk chair. A little shock for Bolton, that anyone even suspected: but he wouldn't know about Pat O'Reilly, the honest and indignant man, complaining to the police. Bolton would think—he was no fool—

220

and he would come to the conclusion that they wouldn't have any evidence at all, on that. He would assume, on the affair in the bar, that the squad-car men had given a sketchy description of him and Maddox had leaped to conclusions, having seen Bolton recently. Would he? That wasn't evidence. He could assume that Maddox had heard about Dexter Drake from one of his neighbors, but that wasn't evidence either. No. Bolton, on thinking it over, and now prepared, would put up a much better show if they tackled him again. Maddox could hear him: very much upstage, obviously a case of mistaken identity, and a man of my reputation can hardly be suspected—

The building had its own parking lot; Maddox went and looked at Bolton's car. The maroon Buick, two-door sedan. The trunk would be locked; and why not?

He started the Maserati, and he was thinking about the autopsy report on Harry Arthur. Bolton was a sedentary man, and a man probably (he had hired Harry to build bookcases for him) unaccustomed to tools. Yes.

And he wondered if he was wasting time here. Never be any evidence, said the lieutenant. Those cases came along too, the ones where you were pretty sure who, and how, and why, but hadn't a chance in hell of proving it in court. Like the cute Mr. Halliday and his death trap, thought Maddox. Yes. But the proverb did say, Actions speak louder than words. And the psychological effect—

He sought that Chrysler agency where Rex Slaney worked, and talked to him again in the manager's office. "Don't tell me you're still working on it!" said Slaney bitterly. "I thought you'd forgotten Harry last week."

"Now, Mr. Slaney. Sometimes these things drag out. Tell me something. Just suppose, like with the fairy tales. If somebody had approached Harry and offered him, say, substantial payment to—um—partner a queer, possibly as the

221

dominant partner—what would his reaction have been?"

Slaney stared at him. "Goddamn it, are you saying Harry—"

"No. We know he wasn't. But suppose somebody had thought—knowing him very casually, the ambitious young man—that he might be willing to do anything for the nice extra money, and approached him?"

"Well, my God, he'd have told him to go to hell," said Slaney. "Like any guy would. *Did* somebody? Was that it? For God's sake—"

"Early to say," said Maddox. "And it's very, very long odds we'll ever get any evidence. Don't talk about it, Mr. Slaney. You could get yourself charged with slander. I'm mentioning no names."

Slaney looked very angry: he went dead white. "It was *that*—a thing like that," he said. "Somebody just afraid—for God's sake. Some goddamned little queer—and a good straight guy like Harry, the rightest guy I ever knew—"

Yes, Maddox would rather like to avenge Harry. But rules of evidence cops had to know something about.

"If you're not seeing ghosts," said Rodriguez, "Eden's still right. Absolutely no evidence. And never will be."

"I just don't see a fellow like that taking the risk," said D'Arcy. "Could O'Reilly be sure, just one look?"

"Reckoning without psychology," said Maddox. "It's him, D'Arcy, that we know. And once we know that about him, he's the only answer. . . . The ones like that, unstable—whatever they look like outside. Compare him to a secret drinker, D'Arcy. For years he's had his supply on tap, right at home—no necessity to go out and buy it, to show to anybody as what he is. In fact, passing all dignified as the—mmh—total abstainer. Then all of a sudden the supplier

222

drops dead. He's used to it, he's got to have it, but he's never had to go find it for himself. Don't you think eventually he's going to get starved enough that he'll go looking, and all too likely in the wrong places? Forget the metaphor. I mean—"

"I see what you mean," said D'Arcy, "and all right, I'll buy that. If O'Reilly's sure, of course we know he did. But you're reading the hell of a lot between the lines. And I also see—we've got to be realistic—what you said about his being no fool. He'll see there's no real evidence. On the fag bit— He won't be thinking you've had any wild ideas on the other. There's nothing, really—just your Celtic imagination. All he has to do is say, Sir, you are slandering my good name. And with his reputation— No judge would look at an application for a warrant."

Maddox finished his drink as the waitress brought their plates. It had cooled off nicely the last two days and barely reached eighty today. "You'd like some extra butter, Sergeant Maddox," said the waitress. "And Mr. Rodriguez wants whole wheat instead of white, I'll bring it right away."

They thanked her absently. "Psychology," said Maddox, picking up knife and fork. "Yes. Pat O'Reilly is on his way to Chi., but Mr. Bolton doesn't know that. And that statute isn't often used any more, and Mr. Bolton doesn't know that either."

"The soliciting for immoral purposes bit? But even if we could make it stick—and I'll grant you that O'Reilly would probably impress a judge—what good would it do?" asked D'Arcy.

"I'm betting on psychology," said Maddox. "That we won't actually be making that charge. If we tell him it's going to be made, it'll scare him like hell. That high-class place would have him O-U-T out the minute there was a hint of such a thing. However many years he's been there."

"But what possible use would it be on Arthur?" asked Rodriguez.

Maddox looked at the poised forkful of steak sandwich. He said, "Psychology, César. Or, in plain English, people. It's people we've got to deal with. I'm thinking about that autopsy report on Harry. Did either of you notice, by the way, that Pat O'Reilly is vaguely the same physical type as Harry? Bigger, but the strong-arm stocky muscle man? I wonder what Dexter Drake looked like."

"So all right, be mysterious," said D'Arcy. "You and your imagination. All I'd advise you is, clear it with the lieutenant before you do anything."

But Rodriguez cocked his head at Maddox and said, "Así, así. I see what you're driving at, but it's a hell of a long chance, Ivor."

"I never said it wasn't."

At two thirty Maddox and Rodriguez descended together on the brokerage and asked for Bolton. Maddox half expected to hear that he'd gone home; he'd had a little shock, after all. And that too was a gamble, that he wouldn't have leaped to the ultimate conclusion and scurried home to— But he was there: his logic would have been working, telling him the police had nothing, sit tight, it was all bluff.

They would be giving him another shock.

"You needn't announce us," said Maddox to the female at the Inquiries desk.

"Oh, but I'm supposed—"

"Never mind." They went past the railing and to the door at the back of the room labeled in gold, WILLIAM J. BOLTON, and walked in.

Bolton started up from his desk, face red with anger. "I will not have my time wasted by—"

"Mr. Bolton," said Maddox, "I have some information to give you. No questions. Or at least only one. Does the name Patrick O'Reilly mean anything to you?"

"No," said Bolton coldly.

"Mr. Patrick O'Reilly is the gentleman you accosted in the bar the other day, and he has instructed us to charge you formally with soliciting in public for an immoral purpose. The warrant has been applied for, and also a search-warrant for your premises and your automobile. Both will undoubtedly be signed by tomorrow morning, and you will be taken into custody. There will be bail set, that's up to the judge, but meanwhile—"

"I—what do you *mean?* You can't—" Bolton gaped at them.

"Oh, but we can, Mr. Bolton," said Rodriguez. "The charge has been signed and the warrants are in the works. Tomorrow. I don't suppose," and he looked around the office, "the firm will like it much, your name in the papers—on that charge."

"You can't—" Bolton's color drained away. "You—" He tried for his usual pompous manner, his self-confidence. "This is absolutely ridiculous—obviously a case of mistaken identity, my reputation certainly should prove—"

"Tomorrow, Mr. Bolton," said Maddox. "If you should wish to consult an attorney, that of course is your privilege."

They left him white and motionless.

"The old one-two," said Rodriguez on the sidewalk outside. "And as I said before, let us just hope it was a sufficient shock that it doesn't occur to him that the police don't as a rule announce their intention of arresting people twenty-four hours in advance. It is a hell of a gamble, Ivor."

"My God, don't I know it. All he's got to do is sit tight, and he's safe. All right, we wait for O'Reilly to get back and really sign the charge—and meanwhile, unless—"

"Well, I think it's a waste of time," said Rodriguez frankly, "but I'll play along. Now I sit on him the rest of the day. O.K."

"And for God's sake don't let him see he's got a tail."

"I made rank some time ago," said Rodriguez.

"I'll brief Ken to take over from you. Call in when the night shift's on and say where he's led you."

"Yes, yes. I have done this before, you know."

"If he spots you, there goes any chance at all."

"I know. I'm on it." Rodriguez got into his car at the curb and unfolded a morning paper in front of him. Mentally crossing his fingers, Maddox went back to the Maserati.

He was, he frankly admitted, no use at all the rest of the day. He fidgeted around the office, telling himself that he just had too vivid an imagination; this was a complete waste of time, there was nothing to find at all.

But he knew. The sudden cold hunch up his spine, the split second he had seen the naked fear in Bolton's eyes. Whether anything ever showed up or not, he knew.

They were still finishing up the paper work on the bank job, and distributing the fliers the Feds handed out. A couple of new calls had come in—routine and the endless paper work, nothing spectacular.

He went home, having briefed Donaldson at six thirty, had a meal he couldn't remember after he'd eaten it, fidgeted around, restless, over an old Agatha Christie, and went to bed at ten thirty.

Half an hour later the phone rang. He leaped to answer it. By God, had the long shot paid off—or had it?

"Ivor?" Donaldson sounded worried. "I've stuck my neck out on this, and let's hope to God we're not both wrong. The guy looks very kosher."

"What's up?"

"You know that apartment's only got open car ports?

Well, César shepherded this Bolton home and I took over there. Nothing happened at all till about half an hour ago, I see him come out and go to the car port where he left his car. You said the car might be the important thing to watch, and there's no back entrance there anyway. It's damn dark, and I got out of my car and eased up along the hedge there, to try to see what he's up to. He had a flashlight. He opens the trunk, and takes something out, I can't see what."

"Oh, my God," said Maddox. "You didn't let him—"

"Wait for it. He took me by surprise, turned around, and came straight down the drive, and his flashlight on— I guess I made a noise, and he spotted me. He came at me, Who's there and What do you want, and tried to hit me. I had to tangle with him, and he dropped this—Look," said Donaldson, "I saw it, I heard what you said, I took the chance and brought him in. And he looks absolutely kosher, a real gent, and he's sitting here yelling for a lawyer and talking about false arrest and saying he naturally thought I was a burglar and had a right to defend himself, and, by God, if you're wrong about him—you said it was a hell of a long—"

"What was it? *What did he take out of the trunk?*" demanded Maddox.

"A wrench," said Donaldson. "The business end of it's got stains all over it."

Maddox let out a long, long breath. It had been the longest chance he had ever played. Or maybe ever would.

And it was supposed to be his day off, but he came in, to finish up the case. He could only hope that the lab was going to give them the real solid evidence.

"So now we know, Mr. Bolton," he said. "I had worked it out for myself, but it's always nice to be sure. You'd been feeling, mmh, lonely since Dexter Drake died, hadn't you? And you didn't know how to contact any of that kind. The local hangouts you didn't know. Maybe you got to feeling a little desperate? And you had your fine reputation to think of—your job—but I think you felt enough desperate that you just went hunting. At random. After your first little idea," said Maddox gently, "failed to pan out. Or did you maybe reason, after that, that in a public bar you'd find men so far outside your ordinary social contacts, there'd be no risk? You like to tell us, Mr. Bolton?"

Bolton sat tight-lipped. The ascetic-looking man beside him said distastefully, "I have advised my client to remain mute."

"Which is his privilege," said Maddox. "Yes. But we can build it, can't we, César?" Rodriguez refolded his arms the opposite way and looked cynical. "Something else entered in too. You deal with money. Wealth. Somewhere along the line you acquired the notion that money will buy anything. You've learned better the hard way, haven't you?

"Well, you missed Dexter, and you thought—feeling desperate—that you could buy the substitute. Not knowing where to look for the willing substitute. Harry Arthur had done a little work for you once—those bookcases. Had you, maybe, admired his muscles then? And you'd heard from Bell what an ambitious, hard-working young man he was, anxious to get ahead, to pile up the money, and you jumped to the conclusion—he'd do anything for the nice money. You decided to make the pitch, and you showed up at the service station that night, late. Just before closing time. So you could argue with him, if he raised any little objection, in private.

"And I think Harry must have thought, naturally enough, that you had some other little job for him, like the bookcases. He may have been a little surprised that you dropped by that late, but he was only on duty there at night, after all. And he never gave a thought to your being there when he closed the station—opened the safe to put the money away—

because you were the respectable regular customer. Up to then.

"But when you made him the proposition, he let you see just how he felt, didn't he? Maybe he said a few things you resented?" Bolton just sat, gray and shrunken, head down. The lawyer regarded his fingernails. "We can guess what Harry said to you. At any rate, he turned you down—emphatically, shall we say? And very probably said other things that set your temper off. Or very possibly something that made you think he'd tell Bell—other people—and your well-kept secret would be out? He'd just turned away from you, hadn't he, toward his car, when you hit out at him, and he slipped in the grease there and fell face down—knocked out. Just by a fluke. I think you thought he was dead—and you were afraid that late customer had noticed you waiting there—you hadn't expected a customer to come by that late. And so you thought of hiding the body, of covering up somehow. Or did you think first about making it look like a holdup? But the safe was locked, you couldn't do that. You had the brainwave about the park. But when you got up there, and rolled him out of the car, you found he wasn't dead. And by that time you wanted him dead. So you looked for the nearest tool handy—"

Bolton said suddenly, in a petulant voice, "It isn't *fair*. We can't all be alike."

"Mr. Bolton," said the lawyer.

"It was such a very long shot," said Maddox mildly, "that you'd been so shaken and upset by the whole thing that you just pushed it to the back of your mind, tried to forget it— and so you just left that wrench in the trunk of your car, still stained with Harry's blood, when you finished him off with it."

Maybe still stained with Harry's blood. Would the lab come through?

There was still a lot of work to do on it. But the wrench ought to clinch it, if the lab—

Maddox came back to Wilcox Street, after a very belated lunch, at three that afternoon. A new homicide had broken, a body as yet unidentified found in a parked car along Gramercy Place. Rodriguez and D'Arcy were out trying to trace the woman whose name appeared on the car's registration.

Johnny O'Neill was leaning back in his chair scanning *The American Rifleman* and softly whistling "The Tri-Colored Ribbon." "Ah, Sherlock," he said. "The lab just sent up a report to you. Rowan was feeling pleased with himself. The right type blood all over that wrench, and some hair. The same color as Arthur's—if you want to be dead sure you'll have to dig him up."

"Which we might just do. How very nice."

"And they're vacuuming Bolton's car, may get something there too."

"Very, very nice," said Maddox, and started up the stairs.

"Oh—Maddox," said O'Neill. "One thing." Maddox turned around. O'Neill was grinning at him: his crooked disarming grin. "You don't really have to be so jealous of me, boy. I'm not the settling-down type maybe. She's a nice kind girl—being nice to me—that's all. What the hell's the poor girl to do, you about the only unattached male in the place —César being another one like me—and you blind as a bat just because she's a member of the force? But all the same, I kind of do think your subconscious mind must have noticed our Sue—the way you've been walking stiff-legged around me, all the hackles up. Down, boy. You've got the edge— you've been here longer." He sounded merely amused.

"Why, you— *Jealous?* What the hell—" Maddox was suddenly, reasonlessly furious; he turned and pounded up the stairs. That damned—what the hell, of all the ridiculous—

And across the hall from the communal detectives' office, there was Policewoman Sue Carstairs, the office door open, industriously typing a report, neat dark head bent over her notes. Maddox came to a sudden halt, there in the hall, and looked at her. Sue. *Jealous*—of all the— That damned—

And belatedly it hit him. Policewoman Carstairs, and he wasn't quite such a fool as not to see she was a good-looking, a damned good-looking female: only a fellow officer, and maybe first the fellow officer—reliable Carstairs —and so anything else, anything more, he'd shoved it down below the conscious level. But all of a sudden a little window opened in his mind, and he acknowledged it. Maddox —who, for some unaccountable reason only had to look at the females and they came flocking round—and so he'd never looked at the honest ones. The nice ones. Sue.

The little window open, light on the subconscious—or whatever—it just dawned on him. At the back of the mind it had been, dormant. Carstairs, pretty sensible honest Policewoman Carstairs—private property. To be called for.

And then, maybe not.

Only Johnny O'Neill—

Maddox began to laugh, and Sue jumped and looked up from her typewriter.

"What's funny?" she asked coldly.

"Me," said Maddox. "People. Such a stupid senseless thing. Human nature."

"Oh?" said Sue.

He pointed a finger at her. "You go home and get all dressed up and I'll pick you up for dinner. A real date. And listen—you stop flirting with the desk sergeant."

"I do *not*— What?" said Sue.

Maddox grinned at her. "You heard me." But of course Johnny O'Neill was really a very nice fellow, when you knew he wasn't, after all, after your best girl. Your best girl—

a funny, and kind of nice, thought. After all the tiresome females chasing you.

"What?" said Sue.

"I'll pick you up at seven. In your best dress," said Maddox, and went into the office across the hall.

Sue stared after him, her mouth still open.